TISHOMINGO BLUES

ELMORE LEONARD

VIKING
an imprint of
PENGUIN BOOKS

VIKING

Published by the Penguin Group
Penguin Books Ltd, 80 Strand, London WC2R 0RL, England
Penguin Putnam Inc., 375 Hudson Street, New York, New York 10014, USA
Penguin Books Australia Ltd, 250 Camberwell Road, Camberwell, Victoria 3124, Australia
Penguin Books Canada Ltd, 10 Alcorn Avenue, Toronto, Ontario, Canada M4V 3B2
Penguin Books India (P) Ltd, 11 Community Centre,
Panchsheel Park, New Delhi - 110 017, India
Penguin Books (NZ) Ltd, Cnr Rosedale and Airborne Roads,
Albany, Auckland, New Zealand
Penguin Books (South Africa) (Pty) Ltd, 24 Sturdee Avenue,
Rosebank 2196, South Africa

Penguin Books Ltd, Registered Offices: 80 Strand, London WC2R 0RL, England

www.penguin.com

First published in the United States of America by HarperCollins 2002
First published in Great Britain by Viking 2002
1

Printed in Great Britain by Clays Ltd, St Ives plc

A CIP catalogue record for this book is available from the British Library

HARDBACK ISBN 0-670-91295-6
TRADE PAPERBACK ISBN 0-670-91296-4

For Christine

I'm going to Tishomingo to have my ham bone boiled,
I'm going to Tishomingo to have my ham bone boiled,
These Atlanta women done let my ham bone spoil.

Performed by Peg Leg Howell
Atlanta, Georgia, November 8, 1926

DENNIS LENAHAN THE HIGH DIVER would tell people that if you put a fifty-cent piece on the floor and looked down at it, that's what the tank looked like from the top of that eighty-foot steel ladder. The tank itself was twenty-two feet across and the water in it never more than nine feet deep. Dennis said from that high up you want to come out of your dive to enter the water feet first, your hands at the last moment protecting your privates and your butt squeezed tight, or it was like getting a 40,000-gallon enema.

When he told this to girls who hung out at amusement parks they'd put a cute look of pain on their faces and say what he did was awesome. But wasn't it like really dangerous? Dennis would tell them you could break your back if you didn't kill yourself, but the rush you got was worth it. These summertime girls loved daredevils, even ones twice their age. It kept Dennis going off that perch eighty feet in the air and going out for beers after to tell stories. Once in a while he'd fall in love for the summer, or part of it.

The past few years Dennis had been putting on one-man shows during the week. Then for Saturday and Sunday he'd bring in a couple of young divers when he could to join him in a repertoire of comedy dives they called "dillies," the three of them acting nutty as they went off from different levels and hit the water at the same time. It meant dirt-cheap motel rooms during the summer and sleeping in the setup truck between gigs, a way of life Dennis the high diver had to accept if he wanted to perform. What he couldn't take anymore, finally, were the amusement parks, the tiresome pizzazz, the smells, the colored lights, rides going round and round to that calliope sound forever.

What he did as a plan of escape was call resort hotels in South Florida and tell whoever would listen he was Dennis Lenahan, a professional exhibition diver who had performed in major diving shows all over the world, including the cliffs of Acapulco. What he proposed, he'd dive into their swimming pool from the top of the hotel or off his eighty-foot ladder twice a day as a special attraction.

They'd say, "Leave your number," and never call back.

They'd say, "Yeah, right," and hang up.

One of them told him, "The pool's only five feet deep," and Dennis said no problem, he knew a guy in New Orleans went off from twenty-nine feet into twelve inches of water. A pool five feet deep? Dennis was sure they could work something out.

No they couldn't.

He happened to see a brochure that advertised Tunica, Mississippi, as "The Casino Capital of the South" with photos of the hotels located along the Mississippi River. One of them caught his eye, the Tishomingo Lodge & Casino. Dennis recognized the manager's name, Billy Darwin, and made the call.

"Mr. Darwin, this is Dennis Lenahan, world champion high diver. We met one time in Atlantic City."

Billy Darwin said, "We did?"

"I remember I thought at first you were Robert Redford, only you're a lot younger. You were running the sports book at Spade's." Dennis waited. When there was no response he said, "How high is your hotel?"

This Billy Darwin was quick. He said, "You want to dive off the roof?"

"Into your swimming pool," Dennis said, "twice a day as a special attraction."

"We go up seven floors."

"That sounds just right."

"But the pool's about a hundred feet away. You'd have to take a good running start, wouldn't you?"

Right there, Dennis knew he could work something out with this Billy Darwin. "I could set my tank right next to the hotel, dive from the roof into nine feet of water. Do a matinee performance and one at night with spotlights on me, seven days a week."

"How much you want?"

Dennis spoke right up, talking to a man who dealt with high rollers. "Five hundred a day."

"How long a run?"

"The rest of the season. Say eight weeks."

"You're worth twenty-eight grand?"

That quick, off the top of his head.

"I have setup expenses—hire a rigger and put in a system to filter the water in the tank. It stands more than a few days it gets scummy."

"You don't perform all year?"

"If I can work six months I'm doing good."

"Then what?"

"I've been a ski instructor, a bartender . . ."

Billy Darwin's quiet voice asked him, "Where are you?"

In a room at the Fiesta Motel, Panama City, Florida, Dennis told
him, performing every evening at the Miracle Strip amusement
park. "My contract'll keep me here till the end of the month," Dennis said, "but that's it. I've reached the point . . . Actually I don't
think I can do another amusement park all summer."

There was a silence on the line, Billy Darwin maybe wondering
why but not curious enough to ask.

"Mr. Darwin?"

He said, "Can you get away before you finish up there?"

"If I can get back the same night, before showtime."

Something the man would like to hear.

He said, "Fly into Memphis. Take 61 due south and in thirty minutes you're in Tunica, Mississippi."

Dennis said, "Is it a nice town?"

But got no answer. The man had hung up.

This trip Dennis never did see Tunica or even the Mighty Mississippi. He came south through farmland until he began to spot hotels
in the distance rising out of fields of soybeans. He came to signs at
crossroads pointing off to Harrah's, Bally's, Sam's Town, the Isle of
Capri. A serious-looking Indian on a billboard aimed his bow and
arrow down a road that took Dennis to the Tishomingo Lodge &
Casino. It featured a tepeelike structure rising a good three stories
above the entrance, a precast concrete tepee with neon tubes running up and around it. Or was it a wigwam?

The place wasn't open yet. They were still landscaping the
grounds, putting in shrubs, laying sod on both sides of a stream that

ran to a mound of boulders and became a waterfall. Dennis parked his rental among trucks loaded with plants and young trees, got out and spotted Billy Darwin right away talking to a contractor, Dennis recognizing the Robert Redford hair that made him appear younger than his forty or so years, about the same age as Dennis, the same slight build, tan and trim, a couple of cool guys in their sunglasses. One difference, Dennis' hair was dark and longer, almost to his shoulders. Darwin was turning, starting this way, as Dennis said, "Mr. Darwin?"

He paused, but only a moment. "You're the diver."

"Yes sir, Dennis Lenahan."

Darwin said, "You've been at it a while, uh?" with sort of a smile, Dennis wasn't sure.

"I turned pro in '79," Dennis said. "The next year I won the world cliff-diving championship in Switzerland, a place called Ticino? You go off from eighty-five feet into the river."

The man didn't seem impressed or in any hurry.

"You ever get hurt?"

"You can crash, enter the water just a speck out of line it can hurt like hell. The audience thinks it was a rip, perfect."

"You carry insurance?"

"I sign a release. I break my neck it won't cost you anything. I've only been injured, I mean where I needed attention, was my first time at Acapulco. I broke my nose."

Dennis felt Billy Darwin studying him, showing just a faint smile as he said, "You like to live on the edge, huh?"

"Some of the teams I've performed with I was always the edge guy," Dennis said, feeling he could talk to this man. "I've got eighty dives from different heights and most of 'em I can do hungover, like a flying reverse somersault, your standard high dive. But I don't know what I'm gonna do till I'm up there. It depends on the crowd, how the show's going. But I'll tell you something, you stand on the perch looking down eighty feet to the water, you know you're alive."

Darwin was nodding. "The girls watching you . . ."

"That's part of it. The crowd holding its breath."

"Come out of the water with your hair slicked back . . ."

Where was he going with this?

"I can see why you do it. But for how long? What will you do after to show off?"

Billy Darwin the man here, confident, saying anything he wanted.

Dennis said, "You think I worry about it?"

"You're not desperate," Darwin said, "but I'll bet you're looking around." He turned, saying, "Come on."

Dennis followed him into the hotel, through the lobby where they were laying carpet and into the casino, gaming tables on one side of the main aisle, a couple of thousand slot machines on the other, like every casino Dennis had ever been in. He said to Darwin's back, "I went to dealers' school in Atlantic City. Got a job at Spade's the same time you were there." It didn't draw a comment. "I didn't like how I had to dress," Dennis said, "so I quit."

Darwin paused, turning enough to look at Dennis.

"But you like to gamble."

"Now and then."

"There's a fella works here as a host," Darwin said. "Charlie Hoke. Chickasaw Charlie, he claims to be part Indian. Spent eighteen years in organized baseball, pitched for Detroit in the '84 World Series. I told Charlie about your call and he said, 'Sign him up.' He said a man that likes high risk is gonna leave his paycheck on one of these tables."

Dennis said, "Chickasaw Charlie, huh? Never heard of him."

They came out back of the hotel to the patio bar and swimming pool landscaped to look like a pond sitting there among big leafy plants and boulders. Dennis looked up at the hotel, balconies on every floor to the top, saying as his gaze came to the sky, "You're right, I'd have to get shot out of a cannon." He looked at the pool again. "It's not deep enough anyway. What I can do, place the tank fairly close to the building and dive straight down."

Now Darwin looked up at the hotel. "You'd want to miss the balconies."

"I'd go off there at the corner."

"What's the tank look like?"

"The Fourth of July, it's white with red and blue stars. What I could do," Dennis said, deadpan, "paint the tank to look like birchbark and hang animal skins around the rim."

Darwin gave him a look and swung his gaze out across the sweep of lawn that reached to the Mississippi, the river out of sight beyond a low rise. He didn't say anything staring out there, so Dennis prompted him.

"That's the spot for an eighty-foot ladder. Plenty of room for the guy wires. You rig four to every ten-foot section of ladder. It still sways a little when you're up there." He waited for Darwin.

"Thirty-two wires?"

"Nobody's looking at the wires. They're a twelve-gauge soft wire. You barely notice them."

"You bring everything yourself, the tank, the ladder?"

"Everything. I got a Chevy truck with a big van body and a hundred and twenty thousand miles on it."

"How long's it take you to set up?"

"Three days or so, if I can find a rigger."

Dennis told him how you put the tank together first, steel rods connecting the sections, Dennis said the way you hang a door. Once the tank's put together you wrap a cable around it, tight. Next you spread ten or so bales of hay on the ground inside for a soft floor, then tape your plastic liner to the walls and add water. The water holds the liner in place. Dennis said he'd pump it out of the river. "May as well, it's right there."

Darwin asked him where he was from.

"New Orleans, originally. Some family and my ex-wife's still there. Virginia. We got married too young and I was away most of the time." It was how he always told it. "We're still friends though . . . sorta."

Dennis waited. No more questions, so he continued explaining how you set up. How you put up your ladder, fit the ten-foot sections onto one another and tie each one off with the guy wires as you go up. You use what's called a gin pole you hook on, it's rigged with a pulley and that's how you haul up the sections one after another. Fit them onto each other and tie off with the guy wires before you do the next one.

"What do you call what you dive off from?"

"You mean the perch."

"It's at the top of the highest ladder?"

"It hooks on the fifth rung of the ladder, so you have something to hang on to."

"Then you're actually going off from seventy-five feet," Darwin said, "not eighty."

"But when you're standing on the perch," Dennis said, "your head's above eighty feet, and that's where you are, believe me, in your head. You're no longer thinking about the girl in the thong bikini you were talking to, you're thinking of nothing but the dive. You want to see it in your head before you go off, so you don't have to think and make adjustments when you're dropping thirty-two feet per second per second."

A breeze came up and Darwin turned to face it, running his hand through his thick hair. Dennis let his blow.

"Do you hit the bottom?"

"Your entry," Dennis said, "is the critical point of the dive. You want your body in the correct attitude, what we call a scoop position, like you're sitting down with your legs extended and it levels you off. Do it clean, that's a rip entry." Dennis was going to add color but saw Darwin about to speak.

"I'll give you two hundred a day for two weeks guaranteed and we'll see how it goes. I'll pay your rigger and the cost of setting up. How's that sound?"

Dennis dug into the pocket of his jeans for the Kennedy half dollar he kept there and dropped it on the polished brick surface of the patio. Darwin looked down at it and Dennis said, "That's what the tank looks like from the top of an eighty-foot ladder." He told the rest of it, up to what you did to avoid the 40,000-gallon enema, and said, "How about three hundred a day for the two weeks' trial?"

Billy Darwin, finally raising his gaze from the half dollar shining in the sun, gave Dennis a nod and said, "Why not."

Nearly two months went by before Dennis got back and had his show set up.

He had to finish the gig in Florida. He had to take the ladder and tank apart, load all the equipment just right to fit in the truck. He had to stop off in Birmingham, Alabama, to pick up another eighteen hundred feet of soft wire. And when the goddamn truck broke down as he was getting on the Interstate, Dennis had to wait there over a week while they special-ordered parts and finally did the job. He said to Billy Darwin the last time he called him from the road,

"You know it's major work when they have to pull the head off the engine."

Darwin didn't ask what was wrong with it. All he said was, "So the life of a daredevil isn't all cute girls and getting laid."

Sounding like a nice guy while putting you in your place, looking down at what you did for a living.

Dennis had never said anything about getting laid. What he should do, ask Billy Darwin if he'd like to climb the ladder. See if he had the nerve to look down from up there.

THE TANK, PAINTED A LIGHT blue with curvy white lines on it to look like waves—Billy Darwin's idea but okay with Dennis—was in place out on the sweep of lawn. Dennis changed his mind about using that river water full of silt. He spoke to Darwin about it and Darwin got the Tunica Fire Department to fill the tank from a hydrant by the hotel, giving each of the firefighters a hundred-dollar chip they could play with or cash in. Dennis would bet they played and hoped they won.

It was the Tishomingo Lodge & Casino's celebrity host, Charlie Hoke, the ex-ballplayer, who got Dennis a place to stay, a room in a private home for a hundred a week. No meals, but he could cook if he cleaned up after.

"Vernice," Charlie said, "is on a diet and hardly cooks anymore, goddamn it." Vernice, a nice-looking redhead if a bit plump— which was okay with Dennis, he liked redheads—owned the house, a three-bedroom bungalow with a screened porch on School Street in Tunica, the school at one end, two bail bond offices at the other. Vernice was a waitress at Isle of Capri. Charlie Hoke was supposed to be her live-in boyfriend, but had his own room so Dennis couldn't tell how much time he spent with Vernice. They acted like they'd been married twenty-five years. After Dennis looked at his room and agreed to take it, Vernice said, "I never met a high diver before. Is it scary?" Dennis believed he could get next to Vernice without breaking Charlie's heart.

It was Charlie, also, who got Dennis a rigger.

This was a man by the name of Floyd Showers from Biloxi, a skinny guy in his fifties with a sunken mouth and skidrow ways about him. He always had a pint of Maker's Mark and cigarette butts in the pockets of the threadbare suitcoat he wore with his overalls, wore it even during the heat of day. Floyd had worked county fairs on the Gulf Coast and showed he knew how to stake down and tie off guy wires, adjusting the block and tackle to pull forty to sixty pounds of pressure. Charlie mentioned Floyd had done time on a burglary conviction, but said don't worry about it, Floyd wasn't apt to get in any trouble.

This final day of setting up they were working late to finish. Dennis in red trunks stood on the top perch—there was another perch below at forty feet—looking down at Floyd tying off the last of the wires. Dennis pressed down on his end and felt it taut.

It was early evening, the sun going down over Arkansas across the river. No one sitting by the pool, the patio in shade now. About an hour ago Dennis had spotted Vernice in her pink Isle of Capri waitress uniform with Charlie out on the lawn talking. It surprised Dennis to see her here at Tishomingo. She had looked this way to give him a wave as she walked back to the hotel. Charlie had returned to the weird attraction he worked and was still there: a wire-fence enclosure that looked like half a tennis court and a sign on it that read:

CHICKASAW CHARLIE'S PITCHING CAGE
LET'S SEE YOUR ARM!

What Charlie had there, inside the enclosure, was a pitching rubber at one end and a tarp with a strike zone painted on it hanging sixty feet six inches away. You made your throw and a radar gun timed the speed of the baseball getting to the tarp and flashed it on a screen mounted in there on the fence. Five bucks a throw. Get three in a row in the strike zone, you got three more chances free. Hum one in ninety-nine miles an hour or better, you won ten thousand dollars. Or you could challenge Chickasaw Charlie. If this big ex-ballplayer with the beer gut, fifty-six years of age, failed to beat your throw, you won a hundred bucks.

It looked easy.

The first time Dennis left his work and wandered over there to see what was going on, Charlie said to him, "Watch 'em. These young hotshots and farm boys come here thinking they have an arm. Watch this kid with the shoulders." Wearing his John Deere cap backwards. "He throws harder'n sixty mile an hour I'll kiss him on the mouth." The kid went into his stretch, brought the ball up to his chest with both hands and threw it, Dennis believed, as hard as he could. The radar screen flashed 54. Charlie said, "See?" and to the kid, "Boy, my older sister can throw harder'n that. You ever see a knuckleball? I'm gonna show you a knuckler. Look here, how you hold it with the tips of your fingers." Charlie stepped on the rubber, went into his stretch and threw a ball that seemed to float toward the tarp before it dipped into the dirt and the radar screen registered 66. Charlie said to Dennis, "They throw with their arm, you notice? 'Stead of using their whole body. You play any ball?"

"Not once I climbed up on a diving board. I follow the American League," Dennis said. "Now and then I'll bet the Yankees, except if they're playing Detroit."

"You're smart, you know it? How 'bout the '84 Series?"

"Who was in it?"

"De-troit won it off the Padres. You remember it?" No, but it didn't matter, Charlie kept talking. "I was up with the Tigers and pitched in what became the final game. Went in in the fifth and struck out the side. I got Brown and Salazar on called third strikes. I hit Wiggins by mistake, put him on, and got the mighty Tony Gwynn to go down swinging at sixty-mile-an-hour knucklers. I went two and a third innings, threw twenty-six pitches and only five of 'em were balls. I hit Wiggins on a nothing-and-two count, so you know I wasn't throwing at him. I come inside on him a speck too close. See, I was never afraid to come inside. I've struck out Al Oliver, Gorman Thomas and Jim Rice. Darrell Evans, Mike Schmidt, Bill Madlock, Willie McGee, Don Mattingly, and I fanned Wade Boggs twice in the same game—if those names mean anything to you."

Later on that day Billy Darwin had come out to see how Dennis was doing. By then he and Floyd Showers had put up four sections of ladder and the metal scaffolding that supported a diving board three meters above the rear side of the tank. Dennis told the boss they'd finish tomorrow and then started talking about Charlie Hoke, amazed that a man his age was still able to throw as hard as he did.

Darwin said, "He tell you about all the big hitters he's struck out, and what he threw them?"

"I can't believe I've never heard of him," Dennis said, and saw that hint of a superior grin Darwin used.

"He tell you where he struck them out?"

"*Where?* I don't know what you mean."

"Ask him," Darwin said.

Dennis thought of it now looking down from his perch. Have a beer with Charlie and listen to baseball stories. He believed Charlie was still over at his pitching cage across the lawn. He hadn't seen him leave, though it was hard to tell, the wire fence dark green against a stand of trees over there. He could yell for Charlie to come out and when he appeared show him a flying reverse somersault.

Dennis' gaze lifted from the pitching cage and the trees to a view of empty farmland reaching to hotels that seemed to have no business being there. The hotel next door invited its patrons to enjoy "Caribbean Splendor" but was called Isle of Capri. Like the Tishomingo's patio bar looked more South Seas than Indian.

Two guys in shirtsleeves, one wearing a hat, were by the bar. Dennis hadn't noticed them before. It looked like a cowboy hat.

When the hotel did try for Indian atmosphere—like the mural in the office reception area: Plains Indians in war bonnets hunting buffalo—they got it wrong. Charlie said Chief Tishomingo and his Chickasaws might've seen buffalo in Oklahoma, after they got shipped there, but they sure never saw any in Mississippi. Tishomingo himself never even got to Oklahoma. Charlie said he was a direct descendant of the old chief, born in Corinth over east of here, fifteen miles from the Tishomingo County line.

The two guys were out at the edge of the patio now, this side of the swimming pool. Yeah, it was a cowboy hat, light-colored.

Dennis was wearing sneakers, no shirt or socks with his red trunks. He looked down to see Floyd Showers hunched over lighting one of his cigarette butts. A couple of times Dennis had found him under the scaffolding behind the tank smoking a joint. Dennis didn't say anything and neither did Floyd, didn't even offer a hit. Which didn't bother Dennis, not sure he'd toke after it'd touched Floyd's mouth. Floyd hardly ever spoke unless asked a question; he'd answer and that would be it. Dennis looked down at his sneakers, stepped to the edge of the perch and was looking at the lower perch halfway down, the diving board below that and the tank you aimed for, the tiny circle of water so still the tank could be empty. For the night dive he'd light the water. He'd need a dive caller, a cute girl in a bathing suit, one with the nerve to stand on the narrow walk that rested on the rim of the tank. Announce the dives and splash the water if he had trouble telling the surface from the bottom. He was thinking it would be good if you could dive wearing sneakers, and raised his eyes.

The two guys were out on the lawn now, coming by the tank.

The cowboy hat was that shade between white and tan, the brim rolled where he'd take hold of it. This one walked tall in what looked like cowboy boots, long legs in slim-cut black jeans, his starched-looking white shirt buttoned up and tucked in tight. His bearing, along with the sunglasses under the hat brim, gave him a straight-up military look. Or a state trooper on his day off. The other one had a smaller frame, wore his clothes loose, his shirt hanging out and what hair he had slicked back hard.

Dennis kept waiting for them to look up; he'd give them a wave. They didn't though, they walked past the tank toward Floyd Showers, Floyd pinching his cigarette butt, looking up as the one with his hair slicked back called to him, "Floyd . . . ?" and Dennis heard it the way he might hear a voice, a word, when he was at the top of his dive, bringing his legs up to go into a reverse pike . . .

"Floyd . . . ?"

And Floyd had that look as if caught in headlights and turned to stone, the poor guy hunched inside that suitcoat too big for him, now reaching up to hang on to a guy wire.

It was never in Dennis' mind these guys were friends. If anything he thought the straight-shooter in the cowboy hat might produce a pair of handcuffs. It was the other one doing the talking, words Dennis couldn't make out. He watched Floyd seem to stand taller as he shook his head back and forth in denial. Now the slick-haired one drew a pistol from under his sportshirt hanging out. A long thin barrel—it looked to Dennis like a .22 target pistol called the Sportsman, or something like that. The one in the cowboy hat and trooper shades stood looking out at the grounds like this was none of his business. But then he followed once the slick-haired one took Floyd by the coat collar and brought him around back of the tank, out of view from the hotel.

Now they were under the scaffolding, eighty feet directly below Dennis.

He turned on the perch to face the ladder and was looking at the Mississippi River and Arkansas and a wash of color way off at the bottom of the sky losing its light. He wanted to look down but didn't want to stick his head over the top rung of the ladder and see them looking up at him. He wanted to believe they'd come all the way across the lawn from the hotel without noticing him. He wanted to dive, enter the water ten feet from them in a rip so perfect it wouldn't make a sound and then slip out of the tank and run, run like hell. He heard Floyd's voice. He heard the words "Swear to God," and heard a sound like *pop* from down there, a gunshot or somebody driving a nail with one blow of the hammer, a hard sound that reached him and was gone. Dennis waited, looking at Arkansas. He heard three more *pop*s then, one after another in quick succession. There was a silence, Dennis thinking it was done, and the sound reached him again, that hard *pop*. A minute or so passed. He saw them come around to the side of the tank, moving away from it.

Now they were looking up at him.

Dennis turned enough to watch them, the two talking to each other, having a conversation Dennis couldn't make out until their words began to reach him, talking as they held their gaze on him.

"You think I cain't hit him?"

"You fire enough rounds maybe."

This coming from the hat and sunglasses looking up at him in the gloom.

"Shit, I bet I can hit him on the fly."

"How much?"

"Ten dollars. Hey, boy"—the one with his hair slicked back raising his voice—"let's see you dive."

"Would you dive offa there?"

Talking to each other again.

"I'd jump."

"Like hell."

"I was a kid we'd jump off a bridge on the Coosa River."

"How high was it, twenty feet?"

"It wasn't high as this'n, but we'd jump off 'er." He called out again, "Hey, boy, come on, dive."

"Tell him do a somersault."

The same thing Dennis was telling himself, a triple in a tuck, as small a target as he could make himself, hit the water and stay there. It was his only move and he had to go right now, before the one started shooting. Dennis turned to face the tank, raised his arms . . . and the lights came on in the pitching cage across the way.

First the lights and now he saw Charlie Hoke coming out on the lawn, Charlie in his white T-shirt that said LET'S SEE YOUR ARM across the front, Charlie yelling at the two guys, "The hell you bums doing here?"

Sounding like he was calling to a couple of friends.

They saw him. They'd turned and were walking toward him, Charlie saying, "Goddamn it—you trying to mess up my deal?"

That was all Dennis heard.

The three were walking toward the pitching cage now, Charlie paying attention to the one in the cowboy hat who seemed to be doing the talking. While Dennis, watching—wound tight and rooted to the perch—tried to make sense of two guys Charlie knew shooting the guy Charlie had brought to work here. They stood talking by the cage a couple more minutes. Now the two walked off toward the hotel and Charlie was coming out on the lawn again.

About halfway to the tank he called out to Dennis, "You gonna dive or what?"

HE DOVE, DYING TO GET off that perch, showed Charlie a flying reverse pike and ripped his entry without seeing the water, came up with his face raised to smooth his hair back and could hear Charlie out there clapping his hands. Dennis pulled himself up to the walk that circled the rim of the tank, rolled his body over it, hung and dropped to the ground.

Charlie stood waiting for him in the early dark.

"That was pretty, what I could see of it. We got to get you a spotlight."

"Charlie, they shot Floyd." Dennis saying it and wiping his hands over his face. "They took him back there and shot him five times. The little guy. He had what looked like a twenty-two, like a target pistol." All Charlie did was nod his head and Dennis said, "Maybe he's still alive."

That got him shaking his head. "They want him dead, that's what he is."

"Charlie, you know those guys? Who are they?"

Now he looked busy thinking and didn't answer.

"The one in the cowboy hat," Dennis said, "I thought at first he was a sheriff's deputy or a state trooper."

Charlie said, "You ought to see him with his sword. When they dress up as Confederates and refight the Civil War. But listen to me. You don't know nothing about this."

"I don't even know what you're talking about."

"Floyd. What you saw. You weren't here, so you didn't see nothing. I'm the one found the body."

"You want to protect those guys?"

"I'm keeping it simple, so neither one of us sticks our neck out."

"What if somebody was looking out the window? They see me up on the ladder, and the two guys?" Dennis glanced toward the hotel saying it.

"People come here to gamble," Charlie said, "not look out the window. Anybody happened to, what would they see? Nothing. It was dark."

"It wasn't that dark."

Charlie put his hand on Dennis' shoulder. "Come on, let's move away from here." They walked toward the hotel, Charlie saying, "You ever see anybody in the swimming pool? Hell no, they're inside there trying to get rich. I mean it, you got nothing to worry about."

Not sounding worried himself, talking Southern in his way. It didn't help Dennis. "But you know those guys. They kill Floyd and you say to them, 'You trying to mess up my deal?' "

"I meant their hanging around here. I know 'em as the kind you don't want to be associated with. Understand, I did *not* know they shot Floyd till they told me. I come out, I thought they mighta stopped by to scare him, remind Floyd to keep his mouth shut is all."

"About what?"

"Anything. Hell, I don't know." Charlie let his breath out sounding tired of this.

Dennis kept after him. "You said Floyd had been to prison but don't worry about it."

They stopped at the edge of the patio.

"I was talking about the kind of person Floyd is, or was. I told you he went to Parchman on a burglary charge. Floyd sucked up to some cons there, but they had no use for him, beat him up when they felt like it. I thought, well, since you didn't know anything about that, the kind of people he tried to associate with, there's nothing to worry about."

"Charlie, the police, the sheriff, they're gonna ask me questions, you know that. The man worked for me."

"He ever talk about his life? Tell you the kind of snake he was, ready to give up people to get his sentence reduced?"

"Why would you get me a guy like that?"

"You wanted a rigger—you think you find riggers walking down the goddamn street? Did he talk about himself or not?"

"He hardly opened his mouth."

"So you won't have nothing to tell, will you?"

"Except what I saw. They start asking questions—what if I slip up, say the wrong thing?" He could tell Charlie wanted this over with and was losing his patience.

Charlie saying, "Listen to me. I'm gonna go inside and call nine-eleven. They'll send out sheriff's people and I'll show 'em Floyd. I say I was out there looking for you and tripped over him. A homicide, the sheriff himself's likely to come, get his picture in the

Tunica Times making a statement. Floyd won't be worth too much press. Before you know it it's blown over."

"They would've shot me, too," Dennis said, not letting Charlie off the hook, "and you know it. But I'm suppose to act dumb."

"What I heard, it sounded like they were playing with you, having some fun."

"You weren't up there, no place to hide. Charlie, I saw 'em kill a man. I can pick 'em both out of a crowd and they know it."

Charlie was shaking his head, the best he could do.

"Look, I told 'em you're okay, you work for me. I told 'em you and I'll have a talk and there won't be nothing to worry about. Listen," Charlie said, "you go on home. I'll give you my keys and get a ride from somebody after."

"What'd they say?"

"They know I'm good for my word."

"But what'd they say?"

"That you better keep your mouth shut."

"Or what?"

"You want their exact words?" Charlie showing his irritation now. "Or they'd shoot you in the goddamn head. You know that. What're you asking me for?"

"But I'm not suppose to worry about it. Jesus Christ, Charlie."

Now Dennis was looking at the T-shirt in front of him, LET'S SEE YOUR ARM, and got a whiff of cigarette breath as Charlie turned to him, saying in a calmer tone of voice, "I told 'em take it easy, I'd handle it. See, I go way back with the sheriff's people." Charlie glanced toward the hotel and went on in a quieter tone. "There was a time after I lost my ninety-nine-mile-an-hour zinger and left organized ball—this was a while ago—I ran liquor down from Tennessee to dry counties around here. Some moonshine too. There's people can get all the bonded whiskey they want legally still prefer shine. Some take the jars and put peaches in 'em to set. This stuff I ran was top of the line, hardly any burn, 'cept you better drink it holding on to something or you're liable to fall and hit your head. I was pulled over now and then but never brought up, as I got to know the deputies on my routes. See, these boys aren't paid much to fight crime and have to look for ways to supplement their income. There's only so much house-painting they can do. All right, they get here they're gonna recognize Floyd right away. They got sheets on him that tell of way more funny business'n I was ever in. What I'm saying is, they'll have a good idea who did it. If they want to pursue it, that'll be up to them."

Dennis said, "This is all about running whiskey?"

"I won't say all, no."

"Who are those guys?"

"I'll tell you in two words," Charlie said, "why I'm not gonna tell you any more about it."

"Two words—"

"Yeah. Dixie Mafia."

Charlie said come on, he was going to tell Billy Darwin and then make the call. Dennis said he had to get his clothes. Charlie didn't like the idea of his going back out there. Dennis didn't either, but said he wouldn't have finished work and left his clothes there, would he? Charlie said okay, he'd give him time to get away from here before he told Billy Darwin and made the call. He said go on home, but don't tell Vernice. Get her to make you one of her toddies.

Dennis walked out across the lawn, his wet sneakers no longer squishing, to the tank with wavy lines and the ladder standing against the night sky.

His clothes, his jeans, T-shirt and undershorts, hung from a bar of

the scaffolding head high, but not in the way of seeing Floyd Showers lying face up in his suitcoat, a dirty brown wool herringbone, Jesus, the poor guy. Dennis took time to look at him, the third dead
man he'd seen up close. No, the fourth. The one in Acapulco who hit
the rocks, the two amusement park workers cut down by broken ca-
bles . . . He saw a lame horse shot in the head, brains draining like red
Cream of Wheat. Floyd was the first one he'd seen killed by gunshot
and even the ones who did it. He had spent the weekend in a holding
cell with a guy who'd shot and killed a man in a bar fight, but that
didn't count. It was the time in Panama City, Florida, they went
through his setup truck looking for weed or whatever, and the guy in
the holding cell who'd killed somebody still wanted to fight. That
mean ugly kind of drunk. Dennis had to punch him out—no help
from the deputies—and bang the guy's head against the cinder-
block wall to settle him down. It wasn't bad enough getting hit a few
times, the guy a wildman, the guy threw up on him and Dennis had
to wash off his shirt and pants in the toilet bowl. He remembered being a sight Monday morning, but nothing the court hadn't seen before. When they let him go he said to a deputy, "I have to put up with
all this shit and I didn't even do anything." The deputy said he'd put
him back in the cell he didn't shut his mouth.

That's why he had trouble talking to cops, they always had the
advantage.

Getting dressed he turned away from Floyd lying dead but kept
seeing the two guys looking up at him on the perch. Then seeing the
one holding a sword as he remembered what Charlie had said, Charlie's tone, just for a second there, making fun of the guy. *You oughta
see him with his sword.* And something about them dressing up as
Confederates and refighting the Civil War. It reminded Dennis now
of a poster he saw in Tunica, something about a Civil War battle
reenactment.

The lights were still on in the pitching cage.

Dennis walked back to the hotel thinking he'd better not waste time. Duck through the back work area to the employee's entrance. His setup truck was over at the far side of the parking lot. Go home and spend a quiet evening with Vernice. Work on what he'd say and how he'd act surprised when the deputies stopped by for him.

There was a guy standing on the patio.

A black guy. But not one of the help. No, a cool-looking young guy in pleated slacks, a dark silky shirt open to his chest, a chain, the guy slim, about Dennis' size, the guy starting to smile. Dennis got ready to nod, say how you doing and walk past.

The guy said, "I saw you dive," and Dennis stopped.

"You did? Where was it, Florida?"

"No, man, right here. Just a while ago. I gave you a ten."

With the smile and Dennis turned enough to look out at the ladder. "You could see okay? It was pretty dark."

"Yes, it was."

"Tomorrow night it'll be lit up."

"The way I'd have to be, go off that thing, lit with some kind of substance." He said it nice and easy, his tone pleasant. "I've been noticing the signs in there, 'Dennis Lenahan, World Champion, From the Cliffs of Acapulco to Tunica, Mississippi' . . . Doing your thing, huh?" He offered his hand. "Dennis, I'm Robert Taylor. It's a pleasure meeting you, a man with no small amount of cool, do what you do."

"I've been at it a while."

"Well, I hope you stay with it."

Dennis began to feel the guy was somebody, and said, "You were out here?"

"Mean when you dove? No, I was in my suite."

Dennis said, "Looking out the window?" and knew it sounded

stupid, the guy, Robert Taylor, staring at him, then beginning to smile a little.

"Yeah, as I'm getting dressed I happen to look out, see you up on the ladder, the two redneck dudes out there watching, I thought, Hey, maybe we gonna see a show."

Dennis said, "The two guys standing there."

"Yeah, looking up like they talking to you."

Dennis said, "Yeah, they were watching," and right away said, "They wanted to see a triple somersault." Dennis shrugged, telling himself, Jesus, relax, will you, as Robert Taylor kept looking at him with his pleasant expression.

"You waited till they left. Man, I don't blame you. Dangerous occupation, you don't do it for free."

The guy wasn't exactly smiling—it was in his tone of voice, mild, sociable, giving Dennis the feeling the guy was somebody and he knew something. "I'm paid by the week or the season," Dennis said, "but you're right, you can't put on a show for anybody happens to come by." He paused and said, "Like those two guys. I never saw 'em before in my life."

He waited for Robert to pick up on it, mention he saw them around or coming out of the hotel. No, what he said was, "You did perform for Chickasaw Charlie."

And the two guys, Dennis hoped, were left behind.

He said, "Yeah, well, Charlie's a good guy. You try your arm over there?"

"I threw some," Robert said. "But I think that radar machine the man has favors him. You know what I'm saying? Except I don't see how he'd work it. You know, set the speed up for when he throws. So I give him the benefit, say fine, this old man can still hum it in— till I study what he might be doing."

"You're staying here a while?"

"Haven't decided how long. Came down from Detroit."

"Try your luck, huh?"

"We got casinos in Detroit. No, you have to have a good reason to come to Mississippi, and losing my money ain't one of 'em."

He let that hang, but Dennis wasn't going to touch it—as much as he wanted to know what the guy was up to. He didn't like the feeling he had. He said, "You know Charlie pitched for Detroit in a World Series?"

"Uh-huh, he told me. Went in and struck out the side."

"Well, listen," Dennis said, "I gotta get going. It was nice meeting you."

They shook hands and he walked off, reached the door to go inside and heard Robert behind him, Robert saying, "I meant to ask you, you don't stay at the hotel, do you?"

Dennis held the door for him. "I'm at a private home, in Tunica. I rent a room."

Robert said, "I thought you might be staying in town. You ever run into a man name Kirkbride?"

"I've only been here a week."

"Walter Kirkbride. Man has a business over in Corinth, makes these mobile homes aren't mobile. They called manufactured homes, come in pieces and you put 'em together on your lot, where you want. There's one called the Vicksburg has like slave quarters in back, where you keep your lawn mower and shit. There's one, a log cabin—I know it ain't called the Lincoln Log, this man Kirkbride's all the way Southron." Robert telling this to Dennis following him along a back hall.

Dennis said, "If he lives in Corinth—"

"I forgot to mention, he's putting up like a trailer park of these homes near Tunica he calls Southern Living Village. For people work at the casinos. Kirkbride stays in one he uses for his office."

"You want to see him about work?"

Robert said, "I look like I drive nails, do manual fuckin labor?"

With a different tone, sounding like a touchy black guy who believes he's been disrespected, and it rubbed Dennis hard the wrong way. Shit, all he was doing was making conversation. He didn't look at Robert as they came to the employees' entrance; Dennis pushed through the glass door and let Robert catch it, coming behind him.

Outside on the curb Dennis turned to him in the overhead light. He said, "I'll believe whatever you tell me, Robert, 'cause it doesn't make one fuckin bit of difference to me why you're here. Okay?"

He got a good look at the guy now in his pale-yellow slacks and silky shirt that was dark brown and had a design in it that looked Chinese, the shirt open to his chest, the gold chain . . . the guy giving him kind of a sly look now saying, "So you come alive, the real Dennis Lenahan, huh?" Robert's mild tone back in place.

"We out there talking I feel you hanging back. I'm thinking, a man that puts his ass on the line every time he goes off, why's he worried about me, what I saw? Ask was it from my window. Did I get a good look at the ones watching you."

"I never asked you that."

"It's what you meant, what you wanted to know. How much did I see of what was going on. One thing I did wonder about—the man that was working for you all day? I see him finish up. I go in the bathroom, take a quick shower, I come out he's gone. Now those redneck dudes by the tank are talking to you. I'm thinking, what happened to your helper? He didn't want to see you dive?"

Dennis said, "You know who he is?" feeling his way, but ready to give up the two guys if he had to.

Robert shook his head. "Never saw him before."

"Then why're you asking about him?"

"I thought it was funny he seem to disappear."

"You don't do manual labor," Dennis said. "You want to tell me what you do?"

It brought Robert's smile back, Robert taking his time before saying, "You think I'm the man, huh? Not some local deputy dog, you think I might be a fed, like some narc sniffing around. Hey, come on, I'm not looking into your business. I saw you dive, man, I respect you." He said, "Listen, I bet I've been in your shoes a few times. You know what I'm saying? I think we both had our nerves rubbed a little. You ask me am I looking for work and I jump on it, 'cause I don't seek employment. Any given time I got my own agenda. Like I ask if you know this man Kirkbride."

Dennis said, "You're talking, man, I'm through."

"You want to get a drink?"

"I'm going home," Dennis said, felt the pocket of his jeans and said, "Shit."

"What's wrong?"

"I'm suppose to take Charlie's car. He forgot to give me the keys."

"You going home, I'll drive you."

"My truck's over there," Dennis said, looking across this section of the lot where the help parked, rows of cars and pickup trucks shining under the lights, "but I can't leave it where I'm staying, Vernice has a fit."

"I don't blame her," Robert said, "that's a big ugly truck. Come on, I said I'd drive you."

Dennis hesitated. He needed to get away from here but didn't want to walk around to the front and run into Charlie, and maybe sheriff's people arriving. He said, "I'd appreciate it. But could you get the car and meet me by my truck? I have to get something out of it."

No problem.

He couldn't tell the year of Robert's car, new or almost, a black Jaguar sedan, spotless, shining in the lights, rolling up to Dennis still wondering what the guy did.

They kept to themselves driving away from the hotel, leaving behind the neon Dennis didn't think was as tiring as amusement park neon; this was quiet neon. He began to relax in the dark comfort of leather and the expensive glow of the instrument panel. He closed his eyes. Then opened them as Robert said, "Old 61. *Yes*." And turned right onto the highway to head south.

He said, "Down there's the famous crossroads." He said, "You like blues?"

"Some," Dennis said, starting to think of names.

"What's that mean? *Some*."

"I like John Lee Hooker. I like B. B. King. Lemme think, I like Stevie Ray Vaughan . . ."

"You know what B. B. King said the first time he heard T-Bone Walker? He said he thought Jesus himself had returned to earth playing electric guitar. They cool, John Lee and B.B., and Stevie Ray's fine. But you know where they came from? What they were influenced by? The Delta. The blues, man, born right here. Charley Patton from Lula, lived on a cotton plantation. Son House, lived in Clarksdale, down this road." Robert's hand reached to the instrument panel and pushed a button. "You don't get off on this you don't know blues."

The sound came on scratchy, a guitar setting the beat.

Dennis said, "Jesus, how old is it?"

"Recorded seventy years ago. Check it out, that's Charley Patton, the first blues superstar. Listen to him. Rough and tough, man. Hits you with it. He's doing 'High Water Everywhere,' about the flood of 1927, changed the geography of the Delta around here. Listen to him. 'Would go to the hilly country but they got me barred.' Turned away by the law, the high country for whites only. They made songs out of what was going on, their life, how they were getting fucked by the law or by women, women leaving 'em. All about man and woman, about living on plantations, on work farms, chain gangs . . . This man, Charley Patton, his style begat Son House and Son House begat the greatest bluesman ever lived, Robert Johnson. Robert Johnson begat Howlin' Wolf and all the Chicago boys and they put their mark on everybody since, including the Stones, Led Zeppelin, Eric Clapton . . . Eric Clapton use to say, you don't know Robert Johnson he won't even talk to you."

Dennis had to think, trying to recall if he'd heard of the man Robert Johnson.

Robert Taylor still talking, telling him, "Thirty-seven miles down this highway past Tunica you come to the famous crossroads . . ." He paused and said, "Shit."

Dennis saw high beams coming at them, headlights and the wailing sound of law enforcement on a dark country road and a pair of sheriff's cars blew past, going toward the hotels.

Robert looked at his rearview mirror. "I know they not after me. How about you?"

Dennis let it go, turning to watch the taillights until they disappeared.

"I expect sooner or later I'll be pulled over," Robert said, "driving around in an S-Type Jag-u-ar 'stead of out in the field choppin' cotton." He glanced at the mirror again, then touched the button to turn off the blues.

"Where they going could be something big. Security man I talk to at the hotel? A brother use to be with the Memphis Police, he say the Isle of Capri's been held up twice. Two dudes come in the front wearing ski masks in Mississippi, scoop up three hundred thousand from the cage, security cameras getting the whole scene. They take off, run into a roadblock and one of 'em's shot dead. The second heist, the newspaper makes a point of saying was *un*professional. Three dudes walk out with a hundred thousand and disappear into the night. It makes you think you don't need to be a pro, do you? A dude robs both Harrah'ses, the old casino on Sunday, the new one on Wednesday, gets away with sixty thou. Witness say the man's front teeth are gold. You bet they gold, the man's a success. Yeah, Tunica County, Mississippi," Robert said, "use to be the poorest county in the U.S. Jesse Jackson called it our Ethiopia. There still people farm. . . . Look on the backseat, all the pamphlets and shit I've picked up. The one calls Tunica a place where, I think it says, small-town friendliness is still a way of life. That's long as you don't get mugged, your car jacked or nobody passes off any funny money on you. Counterfeiters, man, love casinos."

Dennis had questions, but kept quiet, listening.

"The sheriff they use to have? Went down for extortion, getting payoffs from drug dealers and bail bondsmen. Drew thirty years. A deputy was brought up, but he made a plea deal, testified against the sheriff and only drew two to five. A man running for sheriff, to take the one's place went down? They find him lying in a ditch, shot in the head. They elected a brother as sheriff and now it's cool, least the bad dudes aren't wearing badges."

Dennis was becoming at ease with this Robert Taylor from De-troit, a guy with style and what he called his own agenda. Robert was giving him leads and Dennis felt he could say anything he wanted and Robert would play it back in his own way, showing off, and they'd talk the talk with each other.

"You learned all that from the hotel security guy?"

"Some. Some I had looked up for me."

"Planning your trip."

"That's right."

"See what there is to offer."

"Check it out."

"What to look out for, like the crime situation."

"You can't be too careful."

"Historical points of interest?"

Robert turned his head to look at Dennis. "You being funny, but history can work for you, you know how to use it."

It stopped Dennis for a moment.

"You look into business opportunities?"

"You could say that."

"Like mobile homes that aren't mobile?"

Robert said, "Hey, shit," grinning at him in the dark. "You quicker than I thought."

4

"I STARTED TELLING YOU ABOUT this man name Kirk-bride," Robert said. "He started his business from what he made owning trailer parks. But you go back a couple of generations the Kirkbrides are farmers. Was Mr. Kirkbride's grandpa, the first Walter Kirkbride, owned land over in Tippah County and had sharecroppers working it for him—one of 'em being my great-granddaddy. Worked forty acres of cotton, what he did his whole life. He's the one I'm named for, the first Robert Taylor. Lived with his wife and children in a shack, five little girls and two little boys, my granddaddy being number seven, Douglas Taylor."

Dennis said, "This is a true story?"

"Why would I make it up?"

They turned off the highway to approach Tunica, leaving open country and the night sky for trees lining the road and the lights that showed Main Street.

"That's the police station," Dennis said, "coming up on the left. The squad cars we saw were county, they didn't come from here."

Robert said, "Like you been checking up on crime yourself."

"Go up past the drugstore and turn left, over to School Street and turn left again."

"You want to hear my story or not?"

"I want to get home."

"You gonna listen?"

"You're dying to tell it. Go ahead."

"See if you can keep quiet a few minutes."

Dennis said, "I'm listening." But then said, "Is this how the Taylors came to Detroit and your granddad went to work at Ford?"

"Was Fisher Body, but that isn't the story. I'm holding on to my patience," Robert said. "You understand what the consequence could be, you keep talking?"

Dennis was starting to like Robert Taylor. He said, "Tell the story."

"Was my granddaddy brought his family later on to Detroit. He's the one told me this story when he was living with us. About how my great-granddaddy had a disagreement with Kirkbride's grandpa—a black man accusing the white man of cheating him on his shares—and the white man saying, 'You don't like it, take your pickaninnies and get off my land.' "

"This is School Street."

Robert said, making the turn, "I can *see* it's School Street."

"The house is on the right-hand side, end of the block."

"You through talking?"

"Yeah, go on. No, wait. There's a car up there," Dennis said, "in front of the house."

"Man, what's your problem?"

"I don't know whose it is."

"Your landlady's."

"She drives a white Honda."

"Well, it ain't a cop car."

"How do you know?"

"It doesn't have all that shit on top."

"Stop a couple of houses this side."

Robert crept the Jaguar down this street of tall oaks and old one-story homes set back among evergreens, drifted to the curb and killed the engine. The headlights showed the rear end of a black car. Robert said, "'96 Dodge Stratus, worth maybe five," turned the lights off and said, "You happy now?"

"Your grandfather," Dennis said, "got in an argument with Kirkbride's grandfather, and?"

"Was my *great*-grandfather. They have a disagreement over shares and the man tells my great-granddaddy to get off the property."

"With his pickaninnies," Dennis said.

"That's right. Only he didn't feel he should take this shit off the man. Where they suppose to go? He's got his wife and seven children to feed. What he does, he takes a drink of corn and goes up to the house, see if he can reason with the man. Goes to the back door. The man ain't home, but his woman is and maybe Robert Taylor gets ugly with her. You know what I'm saying? Ugly meaning disrespectful, like he raises his voice. The woman becomes hysterical a nigga would talk to her like that. Keeps screaming at him till Robert Taylor says fuck it and walks away. Goes home. He believes that's the end of it, they may as well pack up the few things they own and go on down the road. Except that night men come with torches and set his house on fire, his shack, with his family inside."

Dennis said, "Jesus." No longer looking at the black Dodge or Vernice's house.

"He gets his wife and the kids out, the little children screaming scared to death. Can you see it?"

Dennis said, "That kind of thing happened, didn't it?"

Robert said, "Few thousand times is all. They told my great-granddaddy this is what you get for molesting a white woman. That's the word they used, molesting. Like he'd want any of that grandma. They stripped him naked, tied him to a tree and whipped him, cut him up, cut his dick off and left him tied there through the night. In the morning they lynched him."

Dennis said, "Jesus—Kirkbride did it?"

"Kirkbride, men that worked for him, people from town, any-body wanted to see a lynching. But you know why they waited till morning? See, they didn't lynch him right there." Robert stopped. His gaze moved, inched away, and Dennis turned his head to look toward the house, Robert saying, "I believe that's the cowboy."

It was, coming down the walk from the house, Vernice by the front door holding it open.

"One of the dudes," Robert said, "wanted a free show."

Dennis said, "It could be, but I don't know him."

"He knows your landlady, if that's her."

"Vernice," Dennis said.

The one in the cowboy hat looked back at the house and waved as he reached his car and Vernice went inside, Dennis noticing she didn't wave back. The one in the cowboy hat glanced this way as he opened the door of his car, stared a moment, got in and drove away.

"Man would like to know who the fuck around here owns a Jag-u-ar."

Dennis watched the taillights going away.

"I don't have any idea who it is."

"You keep reminding me of that," Robert said, "in case I forget."

"It doesn't matter," Dennis said. "I know he didn't come by to see *me*."

Robert said, "Dennis?"

"Yeah?"

"Look over here at me."

Dennis turned his head.

"What?"

"That man gives you any shit, tell me."

Dennis almost said it again, insisting he did *not* know the man. But he saw Robert's expression, Robert's cool showing, his confidence, Robert knowing things he didn't have to be told, and it was strange, the feeling it gave him, that he could rely on this guy, the guy maybe drawing him into something, using him, but so what; he liked the feeling of not being on his own—standing exposed on the perch, the two rednecks looking up at him. Dennis said, "They waited till morning to lynch your great-granddaddy."

"You know why?"

Dennis shook his head saying no.

"So a man from the newspaper could take pictures. Get all these white trash people standing there, some with grins on their ignorant faces, alongside Robert Taylor hanging from a tree, the way it's mostly done. Can you see it?"

Dennis nodded.

"But then the photographer had an idea—the way photographers to this day fuck with you taking your picture, put you in poses that don't make any sense. What they did, they took Robert Taylor down to a bridge over the Hatchie, the river east of here some, tied one end of the rope around his neck, the other end to the iron rail, and lifted him over the side. He's hanging there in the picture naked, his neck broken, a bunch of people lining the rail."

Dennis said, "You have the picture?"

"The one took it had postcards made and sold 'em for a penny apiece. Yeah, I have one."

"You brought it with you?"

"Yes, I did."

"You're gonna show it to Mr. Kirkbride?"

There was Robert's smile again, in the dark.

"Yes, I am."

5

DENNIS ASKED IF CHARLIE HAD called and Vernice said, "He hardly ever does. I don't have to worry about meals for him, so he comes and goes when he wants." She said, "You're hungry, aren't you? There some Uncle Ben rice bowls in the fridge. There's Teriyaki Chicken and some Lean Cuisines, different ones. The Chicken l'Orange's my favorite."

They were in the kitchen, Dennis at the table where she told him to sit down after working on his ladder all day. Vernice's Georgia accent was slow-paced, but the words full and rich the way she rolled them out. Dennis at the table and Vernice with her back to him making toddies—Early Times over crushed ice and a sprinkle of sugar on top—in her Isle of Capri uniform, its short skirt tight around her rear end, which Dennis was staring at no more than three feet in front of him.

He wanted to know if Charlie had called Vernice and told her what happened. He wanted to know who the cowboy was and why he was here. And he wanted to know if Vernice and Charlie were old friends or if they were getting it on.

"He calls if he wants me to do something for him. Throw his T-shirts in the washer. He'll wear ten'r twelve of those let's-see-your-arm T-shirts before he thinks to wash 'em. I don't ordinarily bother with him."

"I thought you two were close."

"Two months in a trailer, that was close encounters with a man never shuts up. Three months in this house I bought with my own money. I get tired of hearing him talk's the thing. Couldn't stand it in that little trailer, so I told him he had to go. It was at one of those Kirkbride Trailer Havens. Mr. Kirkbride's making prefabs now, or whatever they are."

"Manufactured homes," Dennis said.

"You see 'em on the highway," Vernice said, "they have that sign, 'Extra Wide Load,' on the back end? He's putting up a mess of 'em right over here, calls it Southern Living Village. They're not too bad. Dishwasher and microwave in the kitchen."

"You know Kirkbride?"

"I've met him. He has an office at the Village, but he's mostly in Corinth. I gave Charlie the end of the month to move out. He was broke, had no job or place to live, and I didn't care."

"Couldn't stand him talking all the time."

"Telling baseball stories if he didn't have nothing else. What a star he was. All the big-name hitters he'd struck out. I said, 'Honey, who gives a shit.'" Vernice turned from the counter with a drink in each hand. "Here, sweetheart, sip it, do you good. Let the bourbon work its way down your tired young body."

Dennis took a sip and made a sound, *Mmmmm,* to show he liked it. He said, "I bet I'm older'n you are."

Vernice said, "Well, of course you are," sitting down at the table. "I tell Charlie he has to leave? This is when we're living in the trailer. He says there's a job waiting he knows he's gonna get. Celebrity host at the Tishomingo. Oh? I said, 'What qualifies you, being a relative of Big Chief Tishomingo, or a onetime famous ballplayer no one's ever heard of?' Charlie says he can go either way, talk the talk. I said, 'Charlie, you ever get hired as a celebrity host, I'll lose twenty pounds and get a job as a keno runner.' You know what he said? 'Better make it forty pounds.' " Vernice got up and went over to the counter to get her cigarettes. "I've always been full-figured, it runs in my family." She came back to the table patting her tummy, holding it in. "Since then I've lost almost thirty pounds. I started out on what they call the Jenny Crank diet? If you know what I mean."

"You're on speed?"

"I said I started *out* on it. One weekend I painted every room in the house without stopping, day and night till it was done. I knew you could get hooked, so I quit."

"Don't lose any more," Dennis said. "You look great."

She said, "I do?"

He watched her sit at the table sideways to face him and cross her legs, showing him the whitest thighs he had ever seen. Just about any time he looked at Vernice he'd try to picture her naked.

"So Charlie talked his way into the job?"

"He goes to see Mr. Darwin and starts bragging how he can still pitch. Mr. Darwin says, 'Okay, if you can strike me out you got the job.' Charlie says he'll do it on three pitches. Mr. Darwin says he'll give him four. They get a kid to bring a ball and bat, meet at a field . . ." Vernice paused to light a cigarette.

"Charlie struck him out?"

"He threw one at him, trying to come inside? And Mr. Darwin had to hit the dirt to save his life."

"He got the job anyway?"

"That's what I asked him. 'He hired you even though you knocked him down?' You know what Charlie said? 'Honey, it's part of the game.' He let Mr. Darwin hit one and got hired."

Dennis said, "He's a character."

Vernice said, "He's a pain in the butt. He comes in my bedroom asking can he use the treadmill you might've noticed in there? Before I know it he's sitting on the side of my bed with his beer gut. You're lucky, you have a nice trim body from swimming."

"Divers don't have to swim much."

"You still have a nice physique." She said, "Oh. I'll be there to see you—I forgot to tell you, I start working at Tishomingo next week. Charlie put in a good word with the human resources guy. Don't you hate that, calling personnel human resources?"

"I think of bodies laid out in a stockroom," Dennis said.

Vernice drew on her cigarette and blew out a stream of smoke. "I start as a cocktail waitress. The outfit's real skimpy—you've seen it—it looks like buckskin only it's polyester with fringe. And you wear the headband with the feather sticking up? It's cute."

Dennis said, "If you're gonna be there every day . . . I was thinking, how'd you like to be in my show?"

"You don't mean dive."

"Call the dives. You have a mike and you tell the audience what dive I'm gonna do next."

"I'd have them, like on a sheet of paper?"

"Yeah, and things you can say to the crowd. Like, 'You have to clap real hard if you want Dennis to hear you, way up there eighty feet in the air.' "

"What do I wear?"

"Whatever you want."

"When would I start?"

"Tomorrow night. They're gonna televise it."

"Really?"

"It's in the local paper and there're posters around town."

"I know, 'From the Cliffs of Acapulco to Tunica . . .' But tomorrow night, you're not giving me much time."

"Charlie said he'd do it if I don't find a good-looking girl. You want to think about it?"

Vernice sipped her drink and smoked.

"I have to let Charlie know," Dennis said. "Give him time to look at the script. Shouldn't he be back pretty soon?"

"He sees any new faces in the bar, he'll hang around to tell baseball stories."

"I got a ride," Dennis said. "We pulled up, I saw a car drive away. I thought Charlie might've come and gone."

"No, it was that shitbird Arlen Novis stopped by to see Charlie."

"A friend of Charlie's?"

"Maybe at one time. Arlen was a sheriff's deputy till he went to prison for extortion. He'd make bail bondsmen give him a cut of their fee or he wouldn't okay the bond. They also had him for accepting payoffs from drug dealers. I don't know, either they couldn't make a case or it was part of a deal he made. Plead guilty to the extortion and testify against the sheriff, he'd only do a couple years. The sheriff's doing thirty years on those same charges."

"What's Alvin do now?"

"Arlen. Walks around in his cowboy hat like he's a country-music star, Dwight Yoakam or somebody. Ask him what he does, he's head of security at Southern Living Village they're putting up over here. Mr. Kirkbride hires a criminal to see none of his building supplies get stolen."

Dennis said, "Yeah . . . ?" knowing there was more.

"But what he really is, Arlen's a gangster. He got into disorganized crime with the Dixie Mafia and pretty soon he's in charge. Some call it the Cornbread Cosa Nostra, making it sound cute, but they're all dirty dogs."

"You get this from Charlie?"

"The talker."

"What's Arlen's name?"

"Arlen Novis. There was another Tunica deputy at Parchman the same time as Arlen. Jim Rein, he was in there for assaulting prisoners. He'd beat 'em with a nightstick for no reason other'n they were colored. You'd never think Jim Rein to look at him would do that. He's a good-looking young man with quite a nice physique on him. They call him Big Fish or just Fish, but I don't know why."

"He's in the Dixie Mafia, too?"

"Works for Arlen. They took over from the ones had the drug business. Charlie says just like in the regular Mafia. Arlen had Jim Rein shoot some of 'em and the rest they run off."

"That's where you get your speed?"

"Crystal meth—I told you, it was just for a while. They sell it to the casino crowd, people that stay up all night trying to win their money back. There's a honky-tonk called Junebug's? Down by Dubbs, just south of here. Arlen took it over along with the drug business. You go to Junebug's you can get all the uppers or downers you want. Speed, crack cocaine, marijuana. They have illegal gambling there, prostitutes, girls in trailers out back of the place."

"Why hasn't it been shut down?"

"Well, you know they're paying off somebody. There's a raid, Arlen gets word of it and they close for alterations. Honey, people come to Tunica for fun, all kinds of it, and spend their money. Like

I read a billion dollars a year right in this county. That's what it's all about, money. Drugs are sold, casinos are robbed, people are shot . . . Last year a waitress from Harrah's was stabbed to death in her trailer, up in Robinsonville. I've thought seriously of moving back to Atlanta, but you know what? I love it here, something always going on."

Vernice took time to smoke. Dennis sipped his drink seeing Arlen Novis by the tank, looking up at him on the perch. He wondered who the other guy was.

"Has a nice taste, doesn't it?"

Dennis said yeah, looked at the glass and took another sip.

"I don't put sugar in mine no more, it's still a treat."

"Vernice, why would Kirkbride hire a guy for security who's a known criminal?"

"Arlen told Mr. Kirkbride it takes one to know one. Says he can spot anybody hanging around the property who's up to no good."

"According to Charlie?"

"Who else. He has the ear for all the dirty stuff that's going on. He talks and people talk to him. He says Arlen told Mr. Kirkbride he had been cleansed of his sins by his conscience beating on him and time served."

"He talks like that?"

"Arlen's a bullshitter."

"And Kirkbride believes him?"

"Not 'cause of anything Arlen has to offer, like drugs. The reason they're close, they both love to dress up and take part in those Civil War battle reenactments. They been doing it for years. I mean you wouldn't believe how serious they are. Mr. Kirkbride's always the general. Arlen's under him and brings along his boys, Jim Rein, Junebug, all these gangsters in Confederate uniforms."

It reminded Dennis of the posters he had seen in the hotel and around town, big ones in color that announced the TUNICA CIVIL WAR MUSTER, the dates and the name of a battle they'd reenact.

He mentioned it to Vernice and she said, "Yeah, they're thinking of making it an annual affair. This year they're doing the Battle of Brice's Cross Roads. Not on the site, but just east of here a few miles. The actual site's way over by Tishomingo County. Charlie says Mr. Kirkbride's grown a beard so he can be Nathan Bedford Forrest. He's the general won the battle."

"Charlie's not into dressing up, is he?"

"You betcha he is. It's why Arlen was here to see him. He said he heard Charlie's gonna be a Yankee this time. Arlen comes by to threaten him out of it. Charlie says he's tired of that Confederate gray. It reminds him too much of the road uniforms he wore playing baseball. Charlie says they always look dirty."

He came home right as Dennis finished his shower and was in his bedroom getting dressed, putting on a fresh T-shirt and jeans from the clothes Vernice had laundered for him and laid folded on the chenille bedspread—Vernice doing for him what she didn't do for Charlie, which Dennis liked to think told him something. By the time he had dressed and walked across the hall to the kitchen he could see Charlie had told Vernice what happened. They both sat at the table with their drinks, not talking, Vernice looking up with worry on her face. She said, "Dennis . . . ?" And Charlie said, "I'll tell him." So now he had to get ready to act surprised and then say . . .

What he said was, "Why would anyone want to shoot Floyd? . . . Jesus, the poor guy," and felt it, he did, seeing that pathetic figure in that mangy suitcoat too big for him.

"You called the cops?"

This was the part he wanted to hear, what happened after.

Charlie said he called nine-eleven. Sheriff's deputies came in about twenty minutes. Then a couple of detectives, also from the Sheriff's Department. Then the crime-scene people arrived and the medics. They took pictures, fooled around. The medics were ready to haul Floyd away, but were told to wait. One of the detectives was chewing out a deputy for calling the state police on his own. A new guy, Charlie said, one he hadn't seen around before. They waited over an hour for the guy from the CIB—that's the Criminal Investigation Bureau of the Mississippi Department of Public Safety— to come from Batesville, the closest district office, fifty-two miles away.

"The investigator arrives," Charlie said. "He tells me he's John Rau and starts asking the same questions the local guys asked me. How it was I found the body, all that. What Floyd was doing here. He looks over the crime scene and asks if they lifted Floyd's prints. One of the sheriff's detectives says, 'We *know* who he is. Jesus Christ, don't you? It's Floyd Showers. He ratted somebody out and got fuckin popped for it.' This John Rau has a suit and tie on, a nice way of handling himself. He's reserved, never raised his voice once. He said he wanted the prints sent to Jackson. Meaning the Criminal Information Center. John Rau told me later they have a method of handling prints now—like you put 'em in a machine and the guy's sheet comes out."

Vernice said, "How do you remember all that?"

Charlie said, "You remember what you want to remember," turning his head to look at Dennis. "One of the local dicks says, 'We can tell you anything you want to know about this piece of dog shit.' John Rau looks at him and says, 'I want him printed.' What I'm getting at," Charlie said to Dennis, "John Rau wasn't taking the word

of the Tunica sheriff's people for what happened. He didn't act superior to them. As I said, he never raised his voice or even said
much. But you knew he was taking over the investigation and they
better do what they were told. He's a low-key type of person and
smart, the kind you better watch."

Vernice said, "What're you telling him that for?"

Charlie was wearing a sportshirt hanging open over his T-shirt.
He took a business card from the pocket and handed it to Dennis.
"This is the guy. He wanted to come out and talk to you this
evening. I said why not wait till tomorrow? I told him you were beat
from working twelve hours getting ready for your show, and you
didn't know anything anyway. I told him I was the one hired Floyd
Showers for you." He turned to Vernice. "Man's name was Showers
and looked like he never took one in his life. Floyd was a miserable
sight, years beyond saving."

Dennis looked up from the business card. "Where do I meet
him?"

"At the hotel. He'll come by some time in the morning. I said
come in the afternoon and see the show."

"What'd he say?"

"It'll most likely be around eleven." Charlie squinted then. "I ran
into this colored guy staying at the hotel? Robert Taylor, doesn't
have a bad arm. He's in seven-twenty. Wants you to call him tomorrow. You know this guy?"

"He saw me dive," Dennis said, his eyes holding on to Charlie.
"He was looking out his window and saw me dive."

Vernice subscribed to the *National Enquirer,* preferring it over
other supermarket tabloids because "they get deeper into the stories

and're better written." She kept back issues she hadn't had time to read on the screened porch, saying, "They come every week, but it seems like near every day."

Dennis had a couple of microwaved Lean Cuisines for supper, both chicken but different, and came out on the porch to look through a few *Enquirer*s. He sat by a lamp reading, not sure if the sound he heard was the hissing in his ears from diving—a constant sound when he thought about it—or insects out in the yard. Sometimes he thought it sounded like steam from a radiator. He had read a few stories, finished "Jennifer Lopez Warned: Leave My Puff Daddy Alone," and was starting on "Jane Fonda Finds God" when Charlie came out to the porch.

"This Robert Taylor saw you dive, huh? What else?"

"He saw Arlen Novis and the other guy . . . What's his name?"

Charlie hesitated but then told him, "Junior Owens. They call him Junebug."

Dennis said, "The guy that runs the honky-tonk, but it's really Arlen's?"

"Jesus Christ—she tell you everything's going on? That woman sure likes the sound of her own voice."

"Charlie, all Robert saw were two guys talking to me up on the perch. He wasn't watching when Floyd was shot."

"But he was in the crowd come out to the crime scene." Charlie sounding hoarse keeping his voice down. "He knows what happened now and he can put you there."

"He won't," Dennis said.

"How do you know?"

"Robert's got his own agenda."

"The hell does that mean?"

"Take my word," Dennis said, not wanting to get into Kirkbride and the granddaddies. "Robert isn't the kind's gonna volunteer in-formation. We're talking, I must've seemed nervous. You know, after what I saw. He said, 'Come on, I'm not looking into your business.' "

Charlie seemed to give it some thought before he said, "You saw Arlen. You sure he didn't see you, in Robert's car?"

"He couldn't have."

"But you recognized him?"

"I see the Lone Ranger coming out of the house—shit yeah, I recognized him. Vernice told you, didn't she? He wanted to talk to you about uniforms? Doesn't like you going Yankee on him."

"That's what he told *her*."

"You dress up and play war with those guys? Pretend to shoot each other? It's hard for me to imagine."

" 'Cause you don't know anything about it."

"I remember you saying—I told you I thought the one looked like a deputy or a state trooper? And you said, 'You oughta see him with his sword'? I didn't know what you were talking about. Then Vernice tells me Arlen and his gang all get into it, playing war." He could tell Charlie didn't like the way he was talking, but didn't care. He said, "You gonna let him talk you out of being a Yankee?"

Charlie said, "You're sure a lot spunkier'n the last time I saw you."

"I'm trying to forget what happened. Since I wasn't there."

"That's good, 'cause Arlen just phoned."

"About the uniform?"

"Will you forget the goddamn uniform?" Charlie's voice rising now, irritated. "He wanted me to know they killed Floyd because he *might* talk, not 'cause he did. Arlen says we ever put him at that scene we'd end up in a ditch."

"What did you say?"

"I told him to stay away from us. And had another drink."

"What're you gonna do?"

"Watch my goddamn back. What you think I'm gonna do?"

Dennis thought of Robert Taylor, Robert's voice in the dark saying, "That man gives you any shit, tell me." Dennis hesitated but kept looking at Charlie before he said, "I think of what happened . . . I'm up on the ladder . . . Could they have walked out from the hotel and not seen me?"

"They couldn't miss seeing you."

"So they don't care I'm a witness. It wasn't gonna stop 'em from shooting Floyd."

Charlie said, "You're just some squirt stuck up there on the ladder. They might've wished they brought a rifle."

Dennis said, "They were having fun talking about it—making a bet whether the one could hit me or not, Junebug, with the slicked-back hair. He said, 'Shit, I'll hit him on the fly.'"

"I heard 'em," Charlie said, "but couldn't tell what they were saying."

"I think about it now," Dennis said, "it pisses me off. They didn't see me as any kind of problem. Who's the guy in the red trunks? Where? Up on the ladder. That's nobody—fuck him. You know what I mean? When Arlen threatened you, on the phone, didn't it piss you off?"

"Sure it did."

Dennis watched Charlie looking down at his big hands, the left one that years ago could throw a baseball ninety-nine miles an hour.

"You bet I was pissed."

Dennis said, "You're bigger than he is."

"Yes, I am," Charlie said, looking up. "I use to buy him cheap when he was a two-bit deputy and I was running liquor."

Dennis sat in the lawn chair, *National Enquirer*s on his lap. "Did you know Tom and Nicole fell out of love way before Tom pulled the plug?"

"I suspected it," Charlie said, "but wasn't ever sure. You want a beer?"

6

ROBERT OPENED THE DOOR IN a hotel terry-cloth robe smoking weed, knowing who it was and what happened, curious to see how Dennis was handling himself this morning. One to ten— ten being all the way cool—Dennis was about a seven, up from the five he was last night; though before he got out of the car at Vernice's he might've inched up to a six. It surprised Robert Dennis wasn't tighter strung, Dennis looking around the suite now. Robert offered the joint and Dennis took it saying, "One hit, I have to dive." Robert watched him take it in deep and let it work inside him before blowing it out. He took another quick one saying, "I have to see a state cop from the CIB in about ten minutes. You know what CIB stands for?"

"What it means every place they have it," Robert said, watching Dennis again looking around the suite, still holding on to the joint, pinching it, looking at the balcony open to blue sky and around to the table by the sofa, looking at Robert's stack of CDs now and the jam box, where John Lee Hooker was coming from.

Dennis said it. "John Lee Hooker."

Robert said, "You got the ear." Dennis told him he used to have the CD, "King of Boogie," and Robert said, "I'll try another one on you. See how good you are."

He watched Dennis take his third hit. This time he handed back the joint saying, "That's good stuff."

"It's all right. I scored it last night."

"After you dropped me off?"

"Way after, with my friend the security brother use to be a Memphis policeman? He took me to a place called Junebug's, a white man's idea of a juke joint, full of ugly people giving us dirty looks, except some young ladies and the management. The young ladies wanted to show us their trailers and the management wanted to sell us uppers. I said I go the other way, chief, and scored a bag, three bills the local rate for a half. We leave, some of the uglies come outside, their intention I'm feeling to kick our heads in. But they see the gleaming black Jag-u-ar and their minds go, shit, who is this nigga owns a car like that? We drive off I give 'em a toot."

He could see Dennis was anxious to tell him something and there were things Robert would like to know, but wanted Dennis sitting down first, at ease—on the sofa, good—and a cool drink? Uh-unh.

Dennis said, "The two guys, the ones looking up at me on the ladder . . . ?"

"The ones shot your man Floyd."

"They own Junebug's."

"Hey, shit, you don't mean to tell me." It brought a grin. "The one being Junebug himself and the other one was Arlen . . . Novis?"

"The one we thought was the Lone Ranger," Dennis said, looser than when he walked in, up from a seven to eight, grinning back, Dennis saying, "But how do you know that?"

"I told you, I do my homework. And Junebug and Mr. Novis musta done Floyd before I started watching, huh?" Dennis looked toward the balcony and Robert said, "Not out there, the bedroom window. I was getting dressed."

He offered Dennis the joint but he shook his head.

"Don't want to go off the perch baked."

"I have. It's not a good idea."

"So they saw you and they know you saw them."

"I have to meet the CIB guy," Dennis said, looking at his watch. "You were me, what would you tell him?"

"Tell him I wasn't there. Tell him I'm just a dumb white boy dives offa eighty-foot ladders. Why didn't they shoot you?"

"Charlie came out."

"That's right. Why didn't they shoot him, too?"

"He knows those guys. Charlie use to run whiskey."

"They friends of his?"

"He knows 'em, that's all."

"Tells 'em you won't say nothing, but you not sure they believe it. They know if you point 'em out they gone."

"That's where I am," Dennis said.

"Saying to yourself, what the fuck am I doing here? Thinking it might be best to take off."

He watched Dennis frown and shake his head saying he wasn't going anywhere, he had his show set up.

Good. He was cool, gonna face whatever, ride it out.

"Let's me and you," Robert said, "stay close. You know what I'm saying? Help each other out. Like I wouldn't mind you coming with me to see Mr. Kirkbride." It got Dennis frowning again. "For fun. Watch the man's face when I show him the picture. Watch how I play him."

"You want an audience," Dennis said, getting up from the sofa. "I have to go."

"I watch you perform, you watch me. Listen, I phoned, the man's over at his Southern Living place today."

"And you know who works there?" Dennis said, wandering over to the balcony. "The Lone Ranger."

"I heard that," Robert said. "Understand he did some time, too. See, the security brother still has friends on the Memphis Police. They look up sheets, tell him, and he tells me what I need to know."

"You pay him, huh?"

"Way more than he earns making people feel secure." Robert watched Dennis step out to the balcony and remembered he wanted to play a CD for him. He heard Dennis say Billy Darwin was down there. Talking to the hotel electrician.

"What's he doing? I told him I'd set the spots tonight."

Robert was up now shuffling through his stack of CDs, telling Dennis, "I arrive, check in, I give the cashier ten thousand in cash, so they know I'm here."

"You said you don't gamble."

"I put on a show, play some baccarat like James Bond. I'm using the cashier as a bank for my tip money I don't have to carry around. Understand? I get the suite comped, I get tickets to the shows in the Tom Tom Room, and I get to meet Mr. Billy Darwin, shake his hand. Mr. Billy Darwin is cool. He looks you in the eye and you know he's reading you. Mr. Billy Darwin can tell in five seconds if you for real or you hy ciditty. You know what I'm saying?"

Dennis turned from the balcony. "I don't have any idea."

"From that Shemekia Copeland song 'Miss Hy Ciditty'? Means a person puts on airs, fakes it." He found the CD he wanted and re-placed John Lee Hooker with it.

Dennis said, "So how'd you come out with Darwin?"

But the CD came on, a dirge beat, and Robert said, "Listen, see if you can name who this is."

Dennis heard a baritone male voice half singing half speaking the words:

> *I got a bone for you.*
> *I got a bone for you.*
> *I got a little bone for you.*
> *I got a bone for you 'cause I'm a doggy*
> *And I'm naked almost all the time.*

"The harmonica could be Little Walter," Dennis said, "but I don't know."

"Little Walter, shit. Man, that's Marvin Pontiac and his hit song 'I'm a Doggy.' "

"I never heard of him."

"Shame on you. Marvin's my man. Marvin Pontiac, part of him came out of Muddy Waters. Another part was stolen *from* him by Iggy Pop. You know Iggy?"

"Yeah, I see what you mean. Iggy's 'I Want to Be Your Dog' must've come from . . . yeah, 'I'm a Doggy.' "

Marvin Pontiac's voice saying, singing:

> *I'm a doggy.*
> *I stink when I'm wet 'cause I'm a doggy.*

"Some of his music," Robert said, "he calls Afro-Judaic blues. Marvin always wore white robes and a turban like Erykah Badu's before she went baldheaded. Had his own ways. Lived by him-self. . . . Listen to this. A producer begged him to cut a record? Marvin Pontiac said yeah, all right, he'd do it—if the producer would cut his grass."

"His lawn?"

"Yeah, his grass, his lawn, the man did it to get Marvin in the stu-dio. That's what you listening to, *The Legendary Marvin Pontiac Greatest Hits*. 'Pancakes' is on there. 'Bring Me Rocks' is on there. It's the one has the line 'My penis has a face and it likes to bark at Germans.' That's funny 'cause Marvin Pontiac's face was never photographed. There shots of him taken from far away, you see him in his white robes and the turban? But there's not any up close."

"He still around?"

"Died in '77 in Detroit. Got run over by a bus and they picked his bones, Iggy and some others, David Bowie. But listen, you better get ready, do your dive. You know what one you gonna do?"

"Not till I'm up on the perch. This afternoon's a warm-up."

"Look over the house. Big crowd, give 'em the triple somersault with some twists and shit. Small crowd—"

"Flying reverse pike. I gotta go," Dennis said, "meet the CIB guy."

Robert said, "Wait," and edged toward the balcony. "Remember I was telling you about the famous crossroads?"

He saw Dennis shake his head.

"Last night in the car, driving you to Tunica." Robert paused but didn't get a reaction. "I'm telling you about the great Robert John-son the bluesman and the cop cars go flying past?"

"Yeah, I remember."

Robert pointed out at the sky. "That way thirty miles down the road, where Highway 49 crosses Old 61."

"Yeah?"

"That's the famous crossroads. Where the great Robert Johnson sold his soul to the devil. You understand what I'm saying to you?"

No, he didn't.

He didn't understand half of what Robert said to him.

Was Robert here because this was where some serious blues got started? The way tourists visit Elvis' house in Tupelo with the bed in the living room? Robert was too cool to be a tourist. Robert wouldn't visit a site, Robert *was* the site. Was he here looking for talent? Some forgotten bluesman missing link, another Marvin Pontiac, and take him back to Motown?

Or was that a side deal while he set up Mr. Kirkbride?

Why would he show Kirkbride the photograph of a man hanging from a bridge unless he expected to get something out of it? Restitution. Play on Kirkbride's sympathy. Hope the man is a rich bleeding heart. Willing to contribute to . . . what? Some kind of appeal, the Robert Taylor scholarship fund for the heirs of a man who was lynched. Robert drives up in his cool S-Type Jaguar looking legit, Robert soft-spoken . . . and the man hanging from the bridge isn't even his great-granddaddy.

This is what Dennis was thinking in the elevator, cutting across the lobby and down the hallway past the rest rooms, the beauty shop, the workout room and sauna toward the patio bar.

Robert had the confidence to be a confidence man. You believed him. He said in the car last night, "That man gives you any shit, tell me." Dennis believed him as he said it and still believed he was the guy he could go to. Robert knew what was going on here. He knew Arlen Novis had been to prison and worked for Mr. Kirkbride, because Robert had looked into Mr. Kirkbride, he must have, to see if the man was worth going after.

Dennis pushed through the glass door to the patio.

"Mr. Lenahan?"

It was the CIB man, John Rau, it had to be, getting up from a table, his hand extended. Dennis walked over and they shook hands. John Rau, in his shirtsleeves but wearing a tie, his navy-blue suitcoat on the back of his chair, gave Dennis his card and asked in a pleasant voice if he'd like a cold beverage. Dennis said no thanks, feeling the grass laying him back now just enough. Good stuff.

John Rau had a Coca-Cola and a dish of mixed nuts on the table. They sat down and Dennis let him explain who he was and what he was investigating, John Rau saying it shouldn't take too long, he understood Dennis was getting ready to do a show.

Dennis was staring at John Rau's tie, blue, with an American flag in the center of it. He said, "It's more of a warm-up than a show. I haven't gone off the top in more than a month." He looked at the mixed nuts now and wanted some. "Of course anybody who'd like to watch is more than welcome." He said, "Do you mind?" reaching for the nuts.

"Help yourself." John Rau gestured and looked out at Dennis' setup. "I was telling Mr. Darwin the investigation could help your show."

Now Dennis turned enough to look over his shoulder. Billy Darwin was still out there with the electrician.

"He seemed to agree. He sees the local people as your main audience." He waited for Dennis to turn to the table again. "What time was it you left here last night?"

"Going on seven."

"Showers was still working."

"Checking the pressure on the guy wires."

"You trusted him to do that? Wasn't Showers a rummy?"

"He knew what he was doing," Dennis said, looking at the American flag on John Rau's necktie. There was something wrong with it.

"He tell you he was a confidential informant?"

"No, he didn't. He barely spoke to me."

Dennis reached for the mixed nuts and John Rau pushed the dish closer. He looked in it to see cashews, peanuts, almonds, one pecan . . . Dennis came away with a fistful of nuts.

John Rau saying, "You know about his background?"

"I know he was in prison. And from what I've heard, talking to people, Floyd was in the Dixie Mafia and they didn't trust him."

"Who were you talking to?"

"Charlie Hoke and our landlady."

"They said he was in the Dixie Mafia?"

Dennis watched John Rau pick out a single nut, the pecan, and put it in his mouth. "I guess I just assumed it."

"What do you know about this Dixie Mafia?"

"Nothing. The first time I heard of them was in Panama City, Florida. Maybe a couple years ago."

John Rau took a little round hazelnut. "They're not like the organized crime families. There's a bunch right here that deals drugs. There's a bunch that hijack trucks and commit armed robberies. A bunch in prison who extort money from homosexuals on the outside. There're moonshiners, bootleggers, methamphetamine manufacturers . . . they're not associated with each other. The only thing they have in common, they're all violent criminals."

"Was Floyd one of them?"

"You saw the type of person he was. Can you see him pulling any kind of rough stuff? Showers said if we'd reduce his sentence to time served he'd work for us, keep us informed."

Dennis said, "I wouldn't think he was that smart."

"He wasn't. I had him down as an idiot. It turned out he wasn't even close to what was going on. He'd tell us things were already common knowledge, in the newspaper, or he'd make something up. I don't know why they shot him. Five times, as a matter of fact. The medical examiner said, 'This man was harder to kill than a cockroach.' "

Dennis was staring at John Rau's tie again. He said, "I think there's something wrong with your flag but I don't know what it is."

John Rau smiled. "You count the stars?"

"I tried, they're too small."

John Rau picked up the wide part of the tie and looked down at it. "There are only thirty-five stars, the number of states in the Union by 1863. Even though we were now at war with the states that seceded, Lincoln would not allow the stars representing those states to be removed."

There was something wrong with that, too.

Dennis scooped another handful of nuts, craving them, but held off stuffing them in his mouth. "You said the states *we* were at war with, sounding like a Yankee."

John Rau said, "You know what it is? Whenever a reenactment's coming up I begin to assume the attitude of the side I'll be on. This first Tunica Muster won't be a major one, Yankees'll be in short supply. Since I can go either way, I'll wear Federal blue this time. Probably represent the Second New Jersey Mounted Infantry. They were at Brice's."

"Brice's Cross Roads," Dennis said.

And John Rau's eyebrows raised. "You're taking part?"

"No, but Charlie Hoke is, and I hear Mr. Kirkbride's gonna be Nathan Bedford Forrest."

John Rau was smiling again. "Walter loves old Bedford. Yeah, it was Walter and I put this one together. I happened to mention there's terrain east of here reminds me of Brice's, full of that scrub oak they call blackjack. I'd see it driving up from Batesville. Walter jumped on it. He said, 'You want to do Brice's?' I hesitated because we have the Battle of Corinth coming up in September, one we do over there. Usually we feature the assault of Battery Robinett, which most every Southerner knows about. You've heard of it?"

Dennis said, "Battery Robinett?"

"It was a Confederate assault on a Federal gun position. One of the heroes was a colonel of the Second Texas, William Rogers, KIA, shot seven times as he stormed the redan."

"Who won?"

"The Federals pushed them back. I reminded Walter of Corinth. Also the fact that Brice's Cross Roads was two years *after* Shiloh and Corinth. Not that it matters, but I felt I should mention it. Well, then Billy Darwin heard about it. Right away he saw it as a promotion, a minor reenactment but a major annual tourist attraction. The crowd gets tired of standing in the hot sun and comes in the casinos to play the slots."

John Rau stopped, his gaze raising, squinting as he said, "Is that Darwin up there?"

Dennis looked around and the next moment was on his feet because it *was*, Billy Darwin standing on the top perch of the ladder. Dennis watched the way he was holding on with both hands looking up at the sky. "I think he froze," Dennis said. "I'll have to bring him down."

"That fella by the tank," John Rau said, "he's shining the spotlight on him, but you can't see it."

"I gotta go," Dennis said.

"Mr. Lenahan, one more question."

Dennis stopped and looked back. "Yeah?"

"If you were to think of Floyd Showers as an animal, what kind would he be?"

Was he serious? Dennis said, "I don't know," and took off across the lawn, a picture popping into his mind now, too late to tell the CIB man: some kind of roadkill out on a highway, brown fur that looked like Floyd's suitcoat.

He kept his gaze on Billy Darwin up there in shorts and a T-shirt, holding on to the ladder with one hand now, looking down, waving. Dennis reached the hotel electrician hunched over a spotlight mounted on the ground, aiming it toward Billy Darwin.

"The hell you doing?"

The electrician, bib overalls and a hunk of snuff behind his lower lip, said, "You tell me and I'll know."

"I told you I set the spots."

"You the boss or him?"

"You think he's gonna place the ones up on the ladder, forty feet and at the top?"

"What do you want 'em up there for?"

"To light the pool. So I can see the goddamn water. I told him, I light the show. And I do it when it's dark, not in bright sunlight."

Dennis stood looking up at the top perch again.

"You think he can get down?"

"He went up there like a monkey."

"Coming down," Dennis said, "isn't the same as going up."

Not more than a few minutes later Dennis was watching Billy Darwin start down: careful at first, both feet on the same rung before taking the next step, descending a whole section of the ladder this way. But then he seemed to have the feel of it and the goddamn wavy-haired show-off was coming down one rung after another, his hands sliding down the outer sides of the ladder. Dennis waited for him to come over.

"You made it."

"I had to see what it was like," Billy Darwin said. "A great view of the river, all the bends in it. But you know, I think the tank looks bigger than a half dollar. More like a teacup."

"You have to see it at night," Dennis said, "after somebody climbs up there one-handed carrying spotlights."

The son of a bitch said, "Oh? I thought you'd use a hoist. What do you call it? That thing you hauled up the ladder sections with— a gin pole?"

By two o'clock Dennis had counted thirty-eight people gathered on the lawn, some with plastic chairs they'd brought from home. These would be local residents, Dennis believed, though they didn't look much different from the hotel guests who wandered out. He spotted Robert Taylor and Billy Darwin standing together, a couple of dudes in sporty summer apparel.

Vernice was supposed to be here—see for the first time what high diving was all about—but she was home studying the script for tonight. Charlie Hoke would call the dives. He'd stand on the plywood deck below the three-meter board, no mike, he'd announce through a bullhorn he used to attract contestants to his pitching cage. Dennis said that each time he came out of the water he'd tell him what the next dive would be and Charlie would announce it. "Be sure to tell them," Dennis said, "this will be my first performance in over a month and it's only a warm-up for the show at nine-fifteen tonight. You'll have to ad-lib, too, use some of the information that's on the poster. 'From the Cliffs of Acapulco,'

ABC Wide World of Sports world champion, I'm good to my mother . . . Tell them not to applaud until I'm out of the water or I won't hear it. Also, not to get within ten feet of the tank. That's the splash zone."

Charlie introduced Dennis and he opened with a flying one and a half somersault from the forty-foot perch to get the crowd's attention.

"Remember," Charlie told all the faces looking up at him, "Dennis is only warming up, keeping his best stuff for the big show tonight."

Dennis did a triple somersault from the three-meter board, and Charlie said, "I can tell you personally, having pitched eighteen years in organized baseball, that you better take enough time to warm up before you go in there to face some of the sluggers I've pitched to. Wasn't that a beauty? A triple somersault. Come on, let Dennis hear it."

Dennis did a back one and a half pike from the forty-foot perch. "That was a back dive with a flip," Charlie said. "I knew I was in shape the times I faced legendary hitters like Don Mattingly, Mike Schmidt, and was fortunate enough on occasion to put 'em down swinging. Let's hear it, folks, for world champion Dennis Lenahan."

Dennis came up to him pushing his hair back. "Whose show is this, yours or fuckin mine? I'm going off the top."

Charlie said, "And now world champion Dennis Lenahan, a man with a lot of character, folks, is going for the fence with a flying backward reverse pike from the top of that eighty-foot ladder. Ladies and gentlemen, boys and girls, you want, you could say a little prayer for Dennis, going off from a perch that's higher'n the cliffs of Acapulco, where he dove one time and broke his nose. And please hold your applause till we see Dennis come out of the tank in one piece."

Charlie said, after, "How was I?"

Robert said, "They love you, man."

Billy Darwin said, "That's the show?"

Dennis said, "You might've caught from the commentary it was a warm-up."

Billy Darwin had his assistant, Carla, with him, Carla a knockout, tan, dark hair, Carla in a slim brown sundress. He said to her, "What do you think?"

Carla said, "It was cool," looking at Dennis.

Billy Darwin said, "Okay," and they left.

Robert said, "Time to go see Massa Kirkbride."

7

THE BLACK MAN IN THE photograph was hanging naked less than ten feet above the river. Lining the rail of the bridge above him were fifty-six people. Dennis counted them—more than he got for his diving exhibition—women in sun hats, children, men in overalls and felt hats, one man in a dark suit of clothes with his arm raised, holding on to a support strut, his other hand in his pocket. The banks of the river were thick with old trees and scrub, the water motionless. The tone of the photograph had turned sepia and there were a few cracks. Hand-printed across the bottom were the words HE MOLESTED A WHITE WOMAN—TIPPAH COUNTY, MISS.—1915.

It was lying on the seat when Dennis got in the car and he studied the eight-by-ten all the way to Old 61, where Robert made the turn south toward Tunica. Blues came out of the speakers turned low, "Background music for the picture," Robert said. "Robert Johnson doing 'I Believe I'll Dust My Broom' first, and now Elmore James dusting his broom, a heavier beat working, electrified, Elmore riding on Robert Johnson's back, plugs in the Broom and has a hit. Then you gonna hear Jimmy Reed riding on Elmore's back to get where he got. It's how you do it. Later on we'll catch Sonny Boy Williamson II, and the poet of the blues, Willie Dixon."

"There little children in the picture," Dennis said.

"A bunch of 'em. Couple of dogs, too, wondering what the fuck everybody's doing out on the bridge."

Dennis held up the photo. "Where should I put it?"

"In my case, on the backseat."

Dennis reached around for it, laid the dark-brown attaché case on his lap and snapped it open. The black checkered butt of a pistol showed beneath a file folder.

"You're not gonna shoot him, are you?"

Robert glanced over. "Nooo, we gonna talk is all."

"What is it?"

"Walther PPK, the kind James Bond packs. No, it's just—you know, in case. Like I find myself in the kind of situation you find yourself in."

They turned into Southern Living Village to Sonny Boy doing "Don't Start Me Talking" past a billboard that showed what the village would look like finished: one-story homes with peaked roofs on winding streets lined with trees, that didn't look much at all like the models they came to on bare plots of ground. Dennis said, "They're like regular houses."

"Sonny Boy's gonna tell everything he knows. Yeah, once they get the garages and shit added on. Bring 'em here in big pieces and nail 'em together. See up ahead, the transit mixer? Pouring a slab, what the houses sit on."

Signs in front of the models they passed identified the VICKS-BURG, the BILOXI, the GREENVILLE. "The Yazoo," Robert said. "That's my dream, live in a house called the Yazoo."

The big manufactured log cabin with no name turned out to be the office of American Dream, Inc., Kirkbride's manufacturing company. They angle-parked in front.

Walter Kirkbride stood by his desk wearing a Confederate offi-cer's coat, gold buttons, gold braid on the collar, over a pair of khakis. They took him by surprise coming in unannounced—no one in the front display room—but within a moment the man was in charge.

"I hope you boys have come to sign up." A Confederate battle flag filled the wall behind him. "You want a job, you got it. You want to buy a house, take your pick. Ah, but if you came in here to join Kirk-bride's Brigade your timing couldn't be better, as I'm looking for a few good men. I'll commission you a lieutenant," he said to Dennis, and to Robert, after a pause, "I'll find something special for you, too."

"Something special, huh?"

That was all Robert said. Dennis gave Kirkbride their names. They shook hands and Dennis said, "If I didn't know he was deceased, I'd swear, Mr. Kirkbride, you were Nathan Bedford Forrest."

"I've been the general many times," Kirkbride said. "And it's kind of you to say that. But my wife has refused to kiss me if I dye my beard again. I have a lot of nerve posing as Ole Bedford anyway. There he is," Kirkbride said, turning to a wall of paintings, "in his prime."

Robert said, "The man that started the KKK?"

"It wasn't as racially oriented as it is now. Oh my, no." He turned to the wall again. "Left to right you have Forrest, Jackson, Jeb Stuart and Robert E. Lee, the most loved by his men of any general who ever lived. Outside of Ole Stonewall and maybe Napoleon."

"Got their love," Robert said, "and then got 'em killed."

A flush came over Kirkbride's face. "They fought and died," he said, "out of a sense of honor."

"Six thousand killed and wounded," Robert said, "three days before the war ended. That make sense, die knowing the war's good as over?"

"You're certain of your facts?"

"Battle of Sayler's Creek. Had to be April '65."

Dennis looked at Robert. Sayler's *Creek*? Did he pull that out of the air or . . . Now Robert was saying, "Mr. Kirkbride, I have something I'd like to show you, if I may."

The man was still flushed, but saw Robert raising his attaché case and said, "Here, use the desk." He looked at Dennis as he moved aside. "You probably wonder what I'm doing in uniform, or half in and half out, but I swear to you I am not a farb. I'm as hardcore as John Rau, if you happen to know him from reenactments. John's a Yankee at heart, even though he got his law degree from Ole Miss. I think he's originally from somewhere in Kentucky. No—what I'm doing, the reenactment coming up, I'm getting used to wearing wool on a summer day. It's not bad in here with the AC on, but I go outside—man. Do it right, I should also be wearing my longjohns."

Robert had the photo out of his case. He said, "Mr. Kirkbride?" Handed him the eight-by-ten and waited until he was looking at it. "That's my great-grandfather hanging from the Hatchie Bridge, August 30th, 1915."

Walter Kirkbride said, "Oh my God."

"And that's your grampa up there," Robert said, "in the dark suit, his arm raised?"

Kirkbride stared at the photo. He took it around to his desk, brought a magnifying glass out of the middle drawer and studied the picture now through the glass.

He said, "How do you know it's my grandfather?"

"I have what you'd call circumstantial evidence," Robert said, "that my great-granddaddy sharecropped on your family's plantation in Tippah County and the dates. I have the newspaper account of his murder. I expect you know they didn't call it that. They said lynching was sometimes necessary when the authorities failed to maintain law and order. I have birth records, including your grampa's, his age at the time."

Kirkbride said, "That doesn't prove anything to me."

"And I have the eyewitness account of my own grandfather, Douglas Taylor," Robert said, "who was there."

He let that settle on Walter Kirkbride, giving Dennis a deadpan look, before he said, "You might've heard of my old grampa. He was a famous Delta bluesman, went by the name of Broom, Broom Taylor. Played in juke joints all around here and down to Greenville. Moved to Detroit and cut his big record, 'Tishomingo Blues.' Was at the same time John Lee Hooker moved there."

Dennis listened. He saw Robert pulling Broom Taylor out of the same hat where he had Sayler's Creek and all kinds of unexpected things stored. If he didn't make them up on the spot.

"Mr. Kirkbride," Robert was saying, "my grandfather was in the shack they called their home when your people came and burned it down—just a little boy then, the youngest of seven children. He was present when they beat his daddy with clubs and cut his dick off. He was at the bridge—not on it, you won't see Douglas among all those people. He was hiding in the bushes, 'cause his mama forbid him to go. But he was there when they threw his daddy over the rail on the end of that rope and it broke his neck. See how his head is cocked almost to his shoulder? He heard people calling that man in the dark suit Mr. Kirkbride. 'There, Mr. Kirkbride, we punished the nigga molested your missus.' You understand the woman they talking about was your grandma."

Dennis watched Kirkbride staring at the photo.

"Are you suing me?"

"No sir."

"Then what do you want?"

"I wondered did you know about it."

The man seemed to hold back before shaking his head and saying no.

"The original was a postcard I had blown up to that size," Robert said. "Maybe I shouldn't have brought it. I don't mean to show you any disrespect by it."

"Well," Kirkbride said, "even though I'm not convinced the man on the bridge is my granddad—he's now deceased—I can understand how you see this and why you came. If it was an ancestor of mine who was . . ."

"Lynched," Robert said.

"Had met his end this way, I would want to know who might be responsible."

"I'm putting it behind me now," Robert said, "and I *am* sorry I bothered you. But you know something . . . ?"

He paused and Dennis had no idea what he'd say next.

"When you wanted us to join up, and you said you might have something special for me? What did you have in mind, like carry water?"

"Oh my no," Kirkbride said, laying the photo on his desk where there were long, thin scars cut into the surface.

Dennis noticed them, like a rake had been drawn across the surface front to back and varnished over.

"Nothing menial," Kirkbride said, still protesting.

"I wondered," Robert said, " 'cause I recall General Forrest had black guys in his escort. You read about that?"

Now Kirkbride was nodding. "I believe I have, yeah."

"Called 'em colored fellas," Robert said. "Told a bunch of his slaves, 'You boys come to the war with me. We win, I'll set you free. We lose, you're free anyway.' You recall that, Mr. Kirkbride?"

The man was nodding again, eyes looking off half-closed at the General Forrest print on the wall. "Yeah, I know he had a few slaves in his escort."

"You recall what General Forrest said after the war?"

"Lemme think," Kirkbride said.

"General Forrest said, 'These boys stayed with me, and better Confederates did not live.' See, I could go gray," Robert said, "as an African Confederate, or I could go blue. I seem to recall there was two regiments of the U.S. Colored Infantry, the Fifty-fifth and the Fifty-ninth under a Colonel Bouton, at Brice's Cross Roads— the one you're doing the reenactment about. I believe they held a position above Tishomingo Creek, yeah, and later on covered the Union retreat up the Guntown Road. You understand what I'm saying?"

"Yes, indeed," Kirkbride said, "it was a rout."

"Nathan 'skeer'd' the Yankees all the way to Memphis, didn't he? That's why I don't want to dress Federal for this one, even though the U.S. Colored Infantry did okay. No, I'm going South this time, wear the gray, only I don't know what as."

Dennis stepped in saying, "Walter, dye your beard. Sir, you are

General Forrest—I mean it. Hire Robert, he knows all about the Civil War and gets to be in Forrest's Escort, with the colored fellas."

"As a scout," Robert said.

"He's your scout," Dennis said to Walter. "But you really oughta dye your beard."

They walked through the front room with its displays and stacks of literature, a map of the Village and color photos of the models on the walls, a Confederate battle flag. Robert said, "I believe he'll do it."

Dennis wasn't sure. "He said he would, but the man sounds afraid of his wife."

Outside, going to the car, Robert said, "The man's a fool."

"He believed you," Dennis said.

"It's what I'm saying, the man's a fool." Getting in the car Robert said, "Even if it's true what I told him."

They were out of Southern Living Village, on the highway, before Dennis said, "What do you mean, if it was true?"

"You heard the story—did you believe it?"

"No."

"But that don't mean it isn't true, does it?"

"Wait a minute. Was that your great-grandfather hanging from the bridge?"

Robert said, "Was that *his* grampa? Was that the Hatchie River? Was a man lynched in Tippah County in 1915? Was there a blues-man name Broom Taylor?"

"Was there?"

"Take your pick."

They passed Tunica over there off the highway, heading toward the hotels.

"You came here," Dennis said, "knowing about the reenact-ment."

"Yes, I did."

"Planning to take part in it. And studied up on the Civil War."

"I already had. I did look up Brice's Cross Roads."

"Learned enough to sound like an expert."

"The key to being a good salesman."

"What're you selling?"

"Myself, man, myself."

"You never mentioned the reenactment before."

"You never asked was I interested."

"What's a farb?"

"Man that isn't hardcore about it. Wears a T-shirt under his poly-ester uniform, his own shoes, won't cook or eat sowbelly, has candy bars in his knapsack. His haversack if he's Confederate."

"How do you know all that?"

"I read."

"The picture of the lynching—"

"Man, what is it you want me to tell you?"

"You only used it to set Kirkbride up."

"That don't mean it ain't real."

Dennis paused, but then went ahead. "Already knowing you wanted to get into the reenactment with him."

"You helped me, didn't you? Telling the man he had to dye his beard? You jumped right in."

Dennis paused again. He said, "I guess you're not through with him."

Robert said, "Listen, Dennis?" and turned his head to look at him. "I have to meet some people, so I won't be at your show tonight. I'd like to, but I can't. Okay?"

Some people.

"Sure, I understand."

"You want, I could meet you later on. You can tell me how it went."

Dennis said, "Come by Vernice's for a toddy. Did I tell you she likes to talk? You might learn something can help you."

There was a silence, both of them gazing straight ahead at the highway. Now Robert turned his head again to look at Dennis.

"Trying to figure out what I'm up to, huh?"

"It isn't any of my business."

"But you dying to know."

CHARLIE HOKE SAID, "I HAVE to go to Memphis to pick this guy up? I'm not a goddamn limo driver."

They were in Billy Darwin's outer office. His assistant, Carla, handed Charlie a square of cardboard with MR. MULARONI lettered on it in black Magic Marker. She said, "Hold this up as they come off the flight from Detroit, Germano Mularoni and his wife."

"Who is he, anyway?"

"Money," Carla said. "Big-time."

Charlie had Carla down as the neatest, niftiest-looking dark-haired woman he had ever seen, not even thirty years old.

"You letter this yourself?"

Carla raised her smart brown eyes to look over the top of her glasses at him. She said, "Be careful, Charlie."

———

At the gate a heavyset guy in his fifties, his face behind a dark, neatly trimmed beard and sunglasses, made eye contact and nodded, once, and Charlie said, "Mr. Mularoni, I'm Charlie Hoke, lemme take that for you," reaching for the black carry-on bag. Mr. Mularoni jerked his thumb over his shoulder and kept walking. So Charlie said to the attractive woman in sunglasses behind him, "Lemme help you there," and was handed a bag that must've had bricks in it. He told Mrs. Mularoni, walking along with her now, he wasn't the limo driver, actually he was the Tishomingo Lodge's celebrity host. The good-looking maybe thirty-five-year-old woman, dark hair, long legs, as slim as a model in a linen coat that reached almost to the floor, said, "That's nice."

She lit a cigarette in the terminal, waiting for their luggage, and no one told her to put it out.

Charlie got them and their luggage, four full-size bags, into the black stretch and rode up front with the driver, Carlyle, Charlie half-turned in his seat so he could look at the couple way in the back.

"So, you're from the Motor City, huh?"

They were looking out the tinted windows on opposite sides through their sunglasses at the south end of Memphis.

"You have casinos up there I understand."

The wife looked up this time, no expression to speak of on her face. She didn't say anything back.

"If you happened to attend that World Series up there in '84 you might've seen me pitch. I was with the Detroit Tigers at the time, finishing up my eighteen years in organized baseball."

This time Mr. Mularoni looked up. He said, "Charlie, leave us the fuck alone, okay?"

Charlie turned to Carlyle the driver and said, "I think he remembers me. In that Series with the Padres I pitched two and a third innings of the fifth game. Went in and struck out the side. Hit a batter on a nothing-and-two count, so you know it wasn't intentional . . ."

Late afternoon, Dennis was in his bedroom taking a nap, lying on the chenille spread in a pair of shorts, no shirt. Vernice came in in her black pongee bathrobe and her white legs, the dive-caller script in her hands. She said, "Oh, were you sleeping?" Then a change of tone, looking for sympathy with, "I can't learn all this by tonight. I've never been like onstage before." Then getting a pouty look, this big girl. "I don't think I can do it."

"You read it, Vernice. Just the places that're marked."

She said, "I don't know . . ." and sat down on the edge of the bed.

Dennis said, "Let's see," drew up his knees and swung around to get next to her. He opened the script. "See, only where it's marked. The script is really for a team, three or four divers. It's the only way you can do the comic stuff. One guy, there's too much time between dives. You know? I need you to fill in. Otherwise I don't know. Get a band?"

Vernice said she wished she could help him and crossed her legs—Jesus, coming out of that black material. Hell . . . he put his hand on her pure-white thigh, plump but not too, turned his face to hers waiting for him and said, "Do you sing?"

Vernice said, "No, but I moan a lot when I make love."

It got the pongee bathrobe open to all of her flesh and that was it. They went about making love in the usual way, quick, but that was all right, they were both in a hurry to have it. She moaned a lot and then screamed.

Vernice said, catching her breath, "There. You get all that lust out of the way and the next one, that's the fun."

She left the bedroom and came back with a pack of cigarettes, her lighter and an ashtray, telling Dennis as she got in bed, "I'm an old-fashioned girl at heart with old-fashioned ways. You want one?" And said, "That's right, you don't smoke. No small vices. What's on your shoulder?" Looking at his tattoo.

"A seahorse."

"It's cute, looks like a little dragon." She smoked and said, "You like it here?"

"You mean staying here?"

"In Tunica."

"It's up to Billy Darwin."

"You can always get a casino job."

"I'm a diver, Vernice."

"You sure are, honey. You ever been married?"

"Once, a long time ago."

"Didn't care for it?"

"We were too young."

"You're not one of those fellas says 'What do I need to get married for, my neighbor's got a wife,' are you? One of those backdoor fellas thinks he's slick?"

"I wonder about Charlie," Dennis said. "You two have been together a while."

"I don't owe Charlie nothing," Vernice said, stubbing out her cigarette. She turned to him. "Hon, you think you might be ready?"

Dennis said they could give it a try.

Charlie came home—they were in the kitchen—saying he had to go all the way to Memphis International to pick up these two never said a goddamn word in the limo the whole trip. Germano something, Mularoni—think of macaroni, the way to remember it—and his wife. Looks like a movie star only she's real skinny.

Vernice, at the table in her terry-cloth robe cinched around her, said, "I 'magine you checked her rack."

"They were there, but not much to 'em that I could tell. She had a coat on."

Vernice said, "In this weather?"

"To be stylish, not to keep her warm, it was real flimsy. She wore these tiny sunglasses and was real tan, or else she was PR or Cuban, I couldn't tell."

"She look like she's trying to pass?"

"She's made it if she is. You know, playing ball I saw all kinds of PRs and Dominicans, Cubans, and some you can't tell, you'd swear were white. Didn't even have that nappy hair."

"What was hers like?"

"I guess brown, with these light streaks in it. Come down over her shoulders and she'd toss it aside. The guy, Germano, looked like a manager who'd been in the game a while, stocky, losing his hair. Had on like a golf outfit, a jacket with the cuffs turned up."

"Why would you notice that?"

"Checking out his pinky ring."

"What kind of stone?"

"Purplish. He was fooling with it waiting for the luggage. She was smoking."

"High rollers," Vernice said.

"From Detroit," Charlie said.

And Dennis, at the counter making drinks, thought of Robert. He said, "They have casinos up there," and thought of Robert saying you had to have a reason to come to Mississippi.

As Charlie was saying he didn't get a lot of conversation out of them. "She checked them in and signed the card while he went over to look in the casino. Her name's Anne, but that don't mean nothing. She said at the desk she said she wanted a suite facing east— listen to this—so she could see the diving show."

Dennis looked around. "She said that?"

"To the desk clerk, making sure she got the right view."

"How would she know about it?"

Charlie said, "You're the world champion, aren't you? Went off the cliffs of Acapulco . . . and broke your goddamn nose?"

It was evening now. Robert came in. Anne closed the door and turned to him, Robert smiling, Robert saying, "Hey, shit, huh?" They slipped their arms around each other, Robert's inside her kimono feeling her bones, Anne's under his silk sweater sliding over bare skin. They began to kiss knowing the fit and the feel, the fooling around with tongues, but cool about it, never getting too near the top. Saving it. Robert said, "You are the best kissin' I've had since I was eleven years old."

Looking into her sleepy brown bedroom eyes. Shit.

"Was it a girl?"

"It was nobody. Eleven's when I felt the need to start kissin'. It wasn't till I was in Young Boys, twelve going on twenty-one, I had any pussy. You in Young Boys you have pussy in your face all the time, big-girl pussy. You ain't had none by the time you thirteen, you homasexual."

"You think you talk street it turns me on."

"Doesn't it?"

She said, "Come on," and took him by the arm into the sitting room—Robert checking out the bottle of white in the ice bucket, two bottles of red and the basket of popcorn on the table where the lamp was on low—taking him toward the sofa in her kimono, this girl who could stride down a runway to the disco beat and turn you on.

"Did you see Jerry?"

"He's playing dice. Winning."

"He always wins."

"Wuz wrong with that?" Robert smiling again. "You ever see that interview with Miles—the man goes, 'Then we come to the lowest point in your career, when you were pimping,' and Miles says in his voice, 'Wuz wrong with that?' "

The door to the balcony was open. Robert steered Anne toward it saying, "Let's see what's happening," looked out at the night, the ladder a gray shape against the sky, the grounds around the tank dark, and said, "Nothing." Somebody was down there, maybe Dennis, but Robert couldn't make him out for sure.

Anne's hand was under his sweater again moving over his back. "Was he winning big?"

"Not enough that he'd stop."

"You think we have time?"

Across the lawn spotlights came on and Robert said, "There it is," the ladder and tank lit up top to bottom now. He saw Dennis in his red trunks and almost said his name and pointed to him. Instead, he said, "We got time."

Anne said, "It doesn't look so high."

" 'Cause we're as high as it is. Get down on the ground and look up, it's high."

She said, "What if Jerry walks in?"

"Put the chain on the door."

"Then he'd know for sure."

"You're in there taking a nap. I'm out on the balcony watching the show. He won't say nothing, he trusts me."

She kept staring at him with those eyes, liking the idea.

"We ever been caught? He trusts me," Robert said, " 'cause he needs me to make things happen." He kissed her on the cheek and said, "Go on get in the bed."

She slipped her hand from under his sweater and gave his butt a pat as she walked away, Robert looking out at the tank again.

He saw lights come on in the pitching cage, Chickasaw Charlie standing there with a young woman—the TV woman, 'cause now a dude with a video camera had come out of the cage and another one carrying a couple of black cases, yeah, the TV woman's soundman. Now all four of them were heading toward the tank.

Robert looked at his watch. Five of nine, the show in twenty minutes. He walked out on the balcony to stand at the rail and looked down to see a good crowd on the patio having drinks and people straggling out on the lawn and coming out of the trees from the parking lot, some of them carrying their lawn chairs. Chickasaw Charlie was talking to Dennis now in his red trunks, the TV woman and her technicians waiting close by to interview him.

Anne's voice reached him from the bedroom. "Hey—are we gonna do it or not?"

Annabanana's Indian love call. It was funny how his mind was always on something else when she called and he always called back, "I'm halfway there, baby."

DENNIS SAID, "I'M STUCK WITH you calling the dives again? Tell me you're kidding."

Charlie shook his head. "She's too nervous, afraid she'll screw up. You don't know Vernice like I do," Charlie said. "She has to do things her own way, how she's always done it. You give her something different, she gets confused." Charlie stepped to one side then saying, "Dennis, say hello to Diane Corrigan-Cochrane, the anchor lady at Channel Five, the Eyes and Ears of the North Delta. Diane, meet the world champion high diver, Dennis Lenahan."

Dennis smiled at her saying, "You ever call dives?"

Diane said, "Like announce what you're doing?"

Quick and perky, a cute blonde not more than thirty in her khaki shorts and white blouse, slim legs, tan feet in sandals.

"All there is to it," Dennis said. "You want to? I think Charlie has the script." Dennis turned to him. "Charlie, please tell me you brought it."

Charlie pulled the script, folded the long way, from his waist in back. "I can help her, show her what to say." He handed the script to Diane. "You read the parts that're checked. Like you tell everybody to stand back from the tank, so they don't get splashed? He's got his dives, what he'll do, numbered, one, two, three . . ."

Diane was looking at the script now. "Where will I be?"

"About where you are," Dennis said.

"I won't be on camera, will I?"

"You can have the camera go to you if you want."

She looked up from the script. "You're the show, Dennis, not me. I have a camera on me every day."

He liked her anchor-lady voice, calm and just a touch nasal. She had a cute nose and some freckles, a country girl. "You from around here, Diane?"

"Memphis. I was a deejay with a hard rock station. I hated all that chatter, so I quit."

"I trained as a blackjack dealer once," Dennis said, "but only worked a few days. I didn't like the outfit they made you wear." Letting Diane know he was as independent as she was.

"You'd rather show off your body," Diane said. "Why not? I know the girls think you're hot." She glanced at the script again. "Okay, I'll do it—if I can have a few minutes alone with you first."

"For an interview," Dennis said.

She gave him a flirty look, having fun with him. "What else would I have in mind? I'll ask how you got into high diving. What it's like to go off from up there . . ."

He said, "You know what the tank looks like?"

"I'd imagine about the size of a teacup," Diane said, "but save it till we're on."

Another teacup. It made him think of Billy Darwin and wonder if she had talked to him. But now she was walking over to the side of the tank, looking at the scaffolding that supported the three-meter board. She turned to him saying, "Is that where the guy was shot? Under there?"

Dennis hesitated. "It's what I was told."

She said, "Oh? I thought you were up on the ladder, you saw the whole thing."

"No, uh-unh. Where'd you hear that?"

She seemed to think about it before saying, "Someone heard it in a bar and told someone else. You know, passed it along. I'm trying to remember who told me. It might've been someone in the sheriff's office. I talk to the staff there a lot." Diane the TV lady kept staring at him. "If it was true—boy, wouldn't that be a story."

Robert had opened the bottle from the ice bucket and poured two glasses, Pouilly-Fuissé, Anne's drink. The red was Jerry's. They were on the balcony now, the show already going on.

Across the way in the lights, Dennis, in black Speedos, stood on the three-meter board. Over the speakers a woman's voice was telling the crowd, "Next, a three and a half forward somersault . . . And there he goes."

Robert said, "How's he have time to do all that in the air?"

"Perfect execution," the woman's voice said. "Wait until he's out of the pool . . . Okay, and now let's hear it for our world champion Dennis Lenahan, the pride of the Big Easy, New Orleans, Louisiana, where Dennis prepped at Loyola before turning professional. Dennis is going up to the forty-foot level now. I'll warn you, anyone within ten feet of the tank may be splashed. That will be our splash zone here at Tishomingo Lodge and

Casino's inaugural high dive show. Dennis is ready now. And there he goes."

"Beautiful," Robert said.

Anne sipped her wine. "How would you know?"

The woman's voice said, "A beautiful dive, perfectly executed."

Robert said, "See?"

"Our champion," the woman's voice said, "is getting ready now for what's called a spotter three and a half."

Dennis was on the three-meter board again, flexing his hands hanging at his sides.

"A spotter is a back somersault to land back *on* the diving board. And at night, under these lighting conditions, we hope Dennis will land squarely on his feet, for he'll immediately do a forward three and a half, a total of four and a half somersaults in two different directions in the same dive."

Robert said, "Hey, shit."

"Ladies and gentlemen, boys and girls, the spotter three and a half requires absolute silence."

"Watch," Robert said. And a moment later said, "Man, perfect. Did you see that?"

"He did a back flip," Anne said, "and the same dive he did before."

"You don't appreciate it," Robert said, "keep it to yourself, all right? Dennis is my man."

"I don't get it—like you're a big fan. On the phone, 'Wait till you see this guy.' "

"How many people you know can do what he does?"

"He ever saw what you get into he'd die of fright."

"Listen."

The woman's voice telling the crowd world champion Dennis Lenahan was now going off the very top of the ladder, eighty feet to the surface of the water. "Ordinarily Dennis closes the show with this dive. But because it's opening night you're in for a special treat. Dennis will do his death-defying dive twice. Now, and again at the close of the show."

Anne said, "Is he a reenactor?"

"He is, but don't know it yet."

"Wait till you see what I'm wearing. Jerry comes in while I'm packing? 'Where's the hoop for the hoopskirt?' I said, 'Tell me how to get a fucking hoop in the bag and I'll bring it.' I've never had any intention of wearing a hoopskirt. I haven't told him yet, but I'm going to be a quadroon camp follower."

"Cool. You'll be the show."

"Hang a red lantern on the tent."

"How much you charge?"

"I don't know. What do you think, back then?"

"High-class whore? Maybe two bucks. Camp follower? About four bits." He said, "Listen what she's saying."

The woman's voice telling the crowd, "Chickasaw Charlie Hoke, Tishomingo's popular celebrity host, would like to say a few words to you as our champion climbs all the way to the top of that eighty-foot ladder. Charlie?"

Now Charlie's voice came over the speakers.

"Thanks, Diane. Folks, let's give a big hand to Diane Corrigan-Cochrane, the Voice of the North Delta."

"Good crowd," Robert said. "Hundred and a half easy."

"For eighteen years," Charlie's voice told them, "Dennis has been performing as a champion, the same length of time I spent in organized baseball. Like Dennis, ready to bear down wherever and whatever famous sluggers I was facing. While Dennis was showing his stuff all over the world, I was with the Orioles organization, the Texas Rangers, the Pittsburgh Pirates, the De-troit Tigers, Baltimore again, got traded back to De-troit and finished my career with the Tigers in the '84 World Series. When Dennis started out he knew he would never give up till he was a champion in his field. Just as I bore down in the minors striking out some of the biggest hitters in baseball. Al Oliver, Gorman Thomas, Jim Rice. Let's see, Darrell Evans, Mike Schmidt when I was with Altoona, back then throwing ninety-nine-mile-an-hour fastballs. Bill Madlock, Willie McGee, Don Mattingly. And I fanned Wade Boggs twice in the longest game on record. Went eight hours and seven minutes. In other words I know and can appreciate what Dennis Lenahan has gone through to get where he's at today."

Robert said, "That man is all scam. I can't believe he's never done time."

"You haven't," Anne said. "Or have you?"

"Jail, no prison. Charlie says he's gonna reenact. Wants to be a Yankee this time."

"What about the diver?"

"Gonna be a Yankee."

"But he doesn't know it yet?"

"He don't know shit, but he's learning."

"How'd you do with the house-trailer guy?"

"Manufactured homes they're called. Got him lined up."

"You've been a busy boy." Giving him the look again.

They heard the key in the lock as Dennis went off in a flying reverse pike, Robert's eyes glued to him. Two seconds it took? Maybe two seconds falling sixty miles an hour. Robert turned, raising his arm.

"Hey, Jerry, you just missed the eighty-foot dive, man." It seemed strange, seeing him with a beard.

Jerry took a cashier's check from his pocket, laid it on the table and began opening a bottle of red saying, "How do you know it's eighty feet?"

"I either went up there with a ruler," Robert said, "or I counted the rungs. Take your pick. You win?"

"Course I won. You think I'd play if I lose?" He said to Anne, "How you doing, sweetheart? You show Robert your outfits?"

"I took a nap while Robert looked at the view."

"The show," Robert said, "it's still on." It didn't make sense to him, Anne saying she took a nap, daring Jerry to check the bed for tracks. But that's the kind she was, liked to fool with being caught. So sure of herself she didn't see it: if Jerry ever did walk in on them she'd be the one would have to go.

Robert said, "Listen, I'm gonna leave you all. I told Dennis I'd come by his house for a drink. Wants me to check out his landlady. Says she's fine." It was for Anne, but she wouldn't look at him.

Jerry was shaking his head. "You're crazy, you know it? This whole business."

"You're gonna have some fun," Robert said. "Be like olden times for you." He finished his wine and started for the door.

Jerry stopped him. "Wait. I want to show you my uniform."

They were in Charlie's ten-year-old Cadillac he'd bought used in Memphis, on their way home.

"You did it again," Dennis said.

"What I said out there? I was making the point of what you have to go through to be a winner."

"I've been diving longer'n eighteen years."

"They don't know that. I say eighteen years each, right away it's like I know what you been through."

"Charlie, it was all about you."

"Hey, didn't me and Diane keep referring to you as the world champ? What do you want? All that getting 'em to applaud? You know what I'll never understand? That business about you needing absolute quiet, like a pro golfer getting ready to take his shot, or one of those tennis players you see on TV. Somebody in the stands gets up to go take a leak as the guy's serving—Jesus, he has a fit. You see that in baseball? Hell no. I'm three and oh on a batter in his home park, I'm trying to concentrate so I don't walk him and the stands are going crazy, banging the seats. How about a batter, full count on him, they're yelling their heads off and the ball's coming at him ninety miles an hour."

"Anything you talk about," Dennis said, "you turn it around to baseball. You hear what Diane said? Somebody told her I was up on the ladder when Floyd was shot? I saw the whole thing?"

"I missed that."

"She said it started in some bar and now it's going around."

"There you are, bar talk."

"She couldn't remember who told her, but thinks it was someone in the sheriff's office. Like one of the clerks."

Charlie didn't say anything.

They got home and went in the house.

Vernice said, "You think I'm terrible, letting you down like that."

So then Dennis had to tell her no, not at all, no, don't worry about it—all that, even though he hadn't thought about her since finding out she wouldn't be there to call dives. No, what he'd thought about between dives, and waiting on the perch while Charlie gave his baseball talk, was Diane, what she'd heard. Charlie could call it bar talk because he didn't want to think about it, give it any importance;

but he could tell it was on Charlie's mind. Charlie told Vernice about Diane Corrigan-Cochrane filling in, Diane with her personality, her professional delivery, and all that did was make Vernice act more depressed. Maybe she really was. Dennis felt either way it wouldn't last.

They went in the kitchen for drinks, Vernice hanging back, telling them from the doorway she was going to catch up on her reading. She said, "I won't disturb you. I'll let you talk about the show and Diane Corrigan-Cochrane," and closed the door between the kitchen and the dining L.

Getting out the Early Times and the ice, Dennis said, "Did somebody see me up on the ladder about that time? Then learn about Floyd on TV and believe I must've been there?"

"I told you," Charlie said, "what I thought, it's just talk, pure speculation. A clerk in the sheriff's office hears a couple of smart-ass deputies talking about it."

"Or Arlen Novis told somebody," Dennis said, "one of his guys. Or Junebug was bragging about it. Charlie, I'm the one who ought to tell somebody, that CIB guy, John Rau." He said, "I'm ready to," not happy with the way he felt, like he couldn't move because this redneck ex-convict had told him to sit.

Charlie didn't care for that kind of talk. He said, "Let's don't rock the boat." He said, "Leave sleeping dogs lie." He said, "Don't duck if nobody's throwing at you." And said, "You know I was never afraid to come inside on a batter. They knew it and you'd see some of 'em at the plate with their butts stuck out, ready to bail."

By the time they were seated at the table with their drinks, Charlie smoking, Charlie telling Dennis the clubs he was with when he struck out those famous hitters—"With Triple-A Toledo playing Columbus when I got Mattingly"—they didn't see the door open or look over until they heard Vernice.

"Charlie, there's somebody to see you."

Vernice sounding like she didn't want to move her mouth.

"Yeah? Who is it?"

"Arlen Novis."

Standing right behind her in his hat. No, a different one. Arlen putting his hands on her hips now to move Vernice out of the way. He came in and she closed the door, staying out of it.

Arlen sat down at the table with them, no one saying a word, sat back in his chair staring at Dennis—Dennis staring back, getting a close look at the hat, one soldiers wore, not cowboys, military from another time, soiled and misshapen, a gold braid turned green around it instead of a band. Arlen said, "I finally got to see you dive. You're pretty good."

The man's eyes holding on him, not letting go.

Dennis stood up, turned to get the Early Times from the counter and placed it on the table. Sitting down again he said, "How would you know if I'm good or not?"

Arlen turned his head to Charlie. "You better introduce us."

"I know who you are," Dennis said. "What I don't understand is why you're telling people I was on the ladder when you shot Floyd. You make it a funny story? I'm so scared I'm shaking the ladder?"

Arlen seemed surprised. He did. But then gave Dennis his stare and was about to speak when he looked up.

Vernice was in the doorway again.

She said, "Dennis, it's somebody for you."

Robert, leaving the highway, turning that shiny S-Type front end toward downtown Tunica—where small-town friendliness was still a way of life—had been thinking about Jerry and his uniform and all the shit that went with it: the boots, the sword, the pair of revolvers, big .36 caliber Navy Colts. He had watched Jerry put the uniform on—cut by his tailor—and pose, the guinea hard-on trying to look like General Grant. The likeness was close, but not all the way there till he put the hat on. Hey, *now,* with the beard, the beard making it, the motherfucker was U. S. Grant in person.

It was the idea of getting dressed up that had drawn Jerry into the deal, the man having just enough a sense of humor the idea worked for him. Robert telling him, "Man, you get to wear a uniform, carry a sword." It might've been the sword closed the deal. Jerry saying, "You know, I never used a sword before." Then maybe thinking about the different weapons he had used, from baseball bats to car bombs. The man even knew things about the Civil War he saw on TV.

School Street.

Robert made the turn and saw he believed two cars in front of the house, coasted up the block and pulled in behind the second car, his headlights telling him it was the '96 Dodge Stratus back again. Worth five bills at a chop shop.

Hmmmm.

Robert got out of the Jag. Then reached into the back for his attaché case.

10

CHARLIE BELIEVED HE LIKED THE way this game was opening up, seeing Robert as a new pitcher coming in who didn't have a bad arm. Threw one seventy miles an hour on his third try.

"You know Dennis," Charlie said, "world champion diver. And that's Arlen Novis. Arlen was a sheriff's deputy till he went to prison." Charlie got Robert seated, facing Arlen across the length of the table, Arlen putting his stare on Robert the whole time. Neither one bothered to reach out to shake hands. Charlie motioned to the briefcase Robert held on his lap. "Can I put that out of the way?"

Robert said no, he'd set it here on the floor.

"Beer, whiskey, a soft drink?"

Robert said the Early Times would do fine and Charlie put ice in a glass for him. They were all set and Charlie said, "Well now . . ."

And Robert said to Arlen Novis in his pleasant way, "I see you're wearing the authentic Confederate slouch hat. Looks good on you. Like it's been to war."

Arlen took the hat by the curled part of the brim and adjusted it to his head, the way men did who wore hats, but didn't say thank you, didn't say anything, and Robert kept talking.

"I saw you out by the diving tank yesterday evening? That was a cowboy hat you had on. Out there with that other fella. But you didn't get to see Dennis perform his dive, did you? I saw it. Did a beautiful flying reverse pike and I gave him a ten."

Nothing like getting right into it. Charlie raised his glass and was taking a sip of whiskey as Dennis spoke up.

Saying to Robert, "We were just talking about last night. I was asking Arlen here, how come he's telling people I was on the ladder when he shot Floyd?"

Arlen was staring at Dennis with a look that drew lines in his face and made it appear rigid, like he was having a time holding back. It surprised Charlie Arlen didn't speak up.

"I asked him," Dennis said to Robert, "if he told it as a funny story. I'm so scared I'm shaking the ladder."

Arlen still held back. Cool-headed or confused, wondering what the hell was going on here.

Robert said to Dennis, "Mr. Novis and that little dude, they were the only ones out there?"

"And Charlie."

"I was in my cage," Charlie said. He believed Arlen was deciding what to do, and would come out of his chair mean and ugly once he did.

Robert said to Dennis, "Was somebody told you one of 'em is saying that?"

"Somebody who heard it spread the word around and it got to the TV news lady, Diane. She's the one told me."

"Reliable source," Robert said. "So it was either Mr. Novis here telling people you were on the ladder, or the little dude, Junebug. I would tend to think it was the Bug and not Mr. Novis. See, I was out to Junebug's place. I met him, bought some product off him. He didn't say nothing about shooting Floyd that I heard, but he seemed like the kind would tend to brag on it."

Charlie watched him looking straight ahead now at Arlen, frowning a little, like he was curious.

"Were you there, Arlen, at Junebug's? You weren't some of them came out to look at my Jag-u-ar, were you?"

Robert, the next moment, was smiling.

"I sure like that hat. I bet there's nothing farb about you, huh? Am I right? You'd take a hit before you got caught wearing anything wasn't pure Confederate. And I mean a real hit." Robert raised his hand toward Arlen's eyes, stones set in his head. "Listen, I'm not fuckin with you. I mean what I say as a compliment to your integrity. I'm wearing the gray same as you account of I'm Southron going back a ways." Robert paused and gave Arlen a serious look now. "Did you know there was sixty thousand African Confederates fought for their homeland same as white boys did? But see, nobody wanted 'em at first. I mean either side. The high-ups would say, 'We don't think these colored boys will stand and fight. They don't have the background.' The what? Over in Africa the motherfuckers are chasing lions naked, with spears—they don't have the *back*ground? You know what I'm saying, Arlen? They warrior stock, all the motherfuckers brought over here."

Robert sipped his whiskey, put the glass down, and his pleasant expression was back.

"Yeah, for Brice's Cross Roads I'm gonna be in Forrest's Escort. I heard you soldier with Mr. Kirkbride in these reenactments. That's gonna put us close in the field, huh? The field of battle. Listen, I like to show you something, prove my Southron heritage. Also show me and you have a tie to the past."

Charlie said, "I'm going Yankee this time."

As Robert reached for his briefcase and made room for it on his lap.

"I think Don Mattingly was the only Yankee I struck out during my career in organized ball."

Robert was snapping the briefcase open, raising the lid.

"But there weren't that many Yankees faced me, that I can recall."

Robert said, "Where is it?" His head bent to look in the case.

They watched him take out a file folder and lay it on the table.

They watched him take out a handful of maps and lay them on the table.

They watched him take out a pistol, a blue-steel automatic, and lay it on the file folder on the table, Robert's head still bent over the case.

Charlie saw Arlen not moving a muscle staring at the pistol now; Dennis watching the show, Dennis calm about it, not appearing anxious or surprised.

Robert said, "Here it is," and Charlie watched him bring out a photograph that looked like an old one—turning brown—people on a bridge—and watched him reach to place the photo in the middle of the table, next to the Early Times.

Robert said, "Arlen, you know who that is?"

Arlen hesitated. He leaned over the table for a moment, sat back again and said to Robert, "It looks like a nigger hanging from a bridge."

"Lynched," Robert said.

Arlen nodded. "What it looks like."

"That's my great-grandfather," Robert said. He paused to look at the photo, upside down to him on the table. "And you know who that gentleman is wearing the suit of clothes? To the right, up on the bridge?" Robert's head raised. "That's *your* great-grandfather, Arlen."

Charlie caught Robert's eyes move to glance at Dennis, Dennis still cool, no expression on his face to speak of, both of them waiting as Arlen reached for the photo and brought it to him.

He said, "That ain't Bobba."

"I believe you talking about your grandfather," Robert said. "This is your *great*-grandfather, not your Bobba."

Arlen kept shaking his head.

"Lawrence Novis," Robert said, "foreman at the Mayflower plantation, Tippah County." He said to Dennis, "Isn't that right?"

"According to county records," Dennis said.

Charlie looked from Dennis back to Robert, Robert saying, "Born in Holly Springs, Marshall County, I believe 1874."

" '73," Dennis said.

Arlen, still shaking his head, said, "Uh-unh, that ain't him. Goddamn it, I was a boy I knew him."

Robert said, "Listen, Arlen? Listen to me. I didn't mean to upset you. I thought maybe you already knew your great-granddaddy lynched that man in the picture, my own great-granddaddy, rest his soul. And cut his dick off. Can you imagine a man doing that to another man—even one you gonna lynch? Listen to me, Arlen. Lemme have the photo back before you mess it up."

Dennis took it out of Arlen's hands and passed it to Robert, Robert saying, "I wasn't gonna show you this. Then I found out we'd be soldiering together at the Tunica Muster and I thought to myself, Lookit how our heritage is tied together, going back to our ancestors. Yeah, I'm gonna show him the historical fact of it."

Arlen pushed up from the table to stand there in his starched shirt, took hold of his hat to reset it down on his eyes and said, "I'm gonna tell you this for the last goddamn time. That is not my fuckin grampa." He stared hard at Robert saying it, gave Dennis a look, then Charlie. Said to him, "You know what the deal is," and walked out of the kitchen.

"He still thinks I was talking about Bobba," Robert said. "I told him no, it's your great-grandfather . . . asshole. The man doesn't listen, does he? Got the brain of a chicken and believes whatever's in his head."

Robert sat there a moment, then jumped up and was in a hurry now, something on his mind. He laid his case on the chair and ran out of the kitchen.

Dennis and Charlie looked at each other.

Charlie picked up the Early Times and poured himself a good one. He said, "You know where he's going?"

"I imagine to tell Arlen something."

"Like what?"

Dennis shook his head. "I don't know."

"He's a talker, isn't he?"

"Yeah, but it's always a good story."

"You believe that's his grandpa was lynched?"

"His great-grandpa."

"I'm as bad as Arlen. And that's his kin up on the bridge?"

"According to Robert."

"You sounded like you knew about it."

"Not much."

Charlie let it go. He looked at the pistol lying on the table and wanted to heft it, but decided he'd better not. He said to Dennis, "Why's he carry a gun?"

"He heard there's a lot of crime here."

"In Tunica? And he's from De-troit?"

"I imagine he packs there, too."

"You know what kind it is?"

"A PPK, the one James Bond had."

"I thought it looked familiar."

There was a silence, not long, a few moments, and Dennis said, "Last night Arlen was gonna kill me. Tonight he's sitting here at the table."

"It's gonna pass," Charlie said.

"I think I should tell John Rau. Get it over with. It's on my mind all the time, knowing it's what I should do. Shit, I probably could go to jail for not saying anything."

"You heard him," Charlie said. "We made a deal."

"Keep quiet or get shot. That's some deal."

"Nobody," Charlie said, "gives a shit about Floyd. I'm telling you, it's gonna pass over."

They both looked up as Robert came in the kitchen. Dennis said, "What'd you forget to tell him?"

"That I won't say nothing about his shooting Floyd," Robert said. "You all aren't gonna say nothing, are you? I advise you, be better if you didn't."

Dennis said, "It's all I think about."

Robert shook his head. "Let nature take its course."

11

ONE OF THE WHORES AT Junebug's—two in the afternoon, the place empty—walked up to John Rau at the bar having a Coca-Cola and said, "Hi, I'm Traci. You want to see my trailer?"

"I bet it's nice," John Rau said, "but I'm waiting to see the proprietor. The bartender's gone to check."

"Junebug left," Traci said. "You want, we could party till he gets back. I don't have an appointment till three."

John Rau said, "Traci, I'm with the state highway patrol."

And she said, "Oh, was I going too fast?"

John Rau smiled at her, a cute girl in her little halter top and shorts, and that was a cute thing to say, was she going too fast. Flirting with a police officer. This place, it didn't surprise him. He'd been told they had live sex acts on the stage there in front of everybody—probably this cute girl and another one, or some farm boy with a big wang. Lock the door and hang a sign out, *Closed,* with all the cars and pickups in the lot and along the road. Junebug's had that skunky smell of beer and stale smoke, but did more business at night than any of the casino bars. The bartender, an old guy in an undershirt hanging from frail shoulders, was coming back along the bar getting ready to tell him no, Junebug wasn't here, didn't know where he went or when he was coming back or where he lived or whatever else had anything to do with him.

John Rau brought his ID case from the inside pocket of his navy-blue suitcoat and showed Traci he was with the Criminal Investigation Bureau. He said, "I don't hand out tickets and I'm not one to party, so . . ." He flipped the case closed as the bartender approached shaking his head.

John Rau nodded, accepting it, as Traci was telling him she collected ashtrays, had ashtrays from all the casinos, from places in Memphis, Jackson, Slidell, New Orleans—"let's see"—Biloxi, Pascagoula, Mobile . . . She said, "Okay then," and he watched her wander off, not going anywhere. Not more than eighteen years old. She'd go in the ladies' room and smoke a rock and one day she wouldn't be here.

He watched her turn to the door as it opened to bright sunlight behind someone coming in, a guy wearing a hat John Rau would recognize from two hundred yards, facing a line of Confederate skirmishers across a field. The figure in the doorway hesitated and seemed to change his mind about coming in—until John Rau, sure of who it was now, called to him, "Hey, Arlen, is that you?"

The trip wasn't a waste of time after all, John Rau pretty sure this was the man who'd shot Floyd Showers, or had it done.

Shit. It was too late now to duck out, the cop looking right at him. Arlen came on in raising his hand to the state cop and getting a cordial tone ready. "Hey, chief, what're you doing here, fixing to get laid? Hey, I got to piss before I wet my pants. You wait there, chief, I'll be right back." He hurried along the bar and into the back hall to the men's. He did have to piss, unzipped and stood at the rusty urinal as he got his phone out of his back pocket and punched a number.

"What're you doing? You got some little girl with you?" He listened and said, "Well I'm about to have a conversation with a state dick dropped by for a Co'Cola. When I'm through, and it ain't gonna take long, I'm coming to see you." He listened and said, "What do you think for, you dumb shit."

He punched another number.

"Fish? Drop what you're doing, we're going on a job." He listened and said, "I'll tell you on the way. Pick me up at Junebug's." He listened again and said, "No, nothing that big. Your forty-five, something you can slip in your waist."

He walked up to the state cop standing at the bar in his neat suit and tie and his Co'Cola, Arlen cordial again as he said, "I bet you're ready for the Cross Roads. You know what uniform you're gonna wear?"

This state cop didn't offer his hand. "The Second New Jersey Mounted Infantry, though I think dismounted this time. I lost a beautiful mare at Yellow Tavern. Stepped in a hole and broke her leg. How about yourself, Forrest's Escort?"

"I may as well serve under Walter," Arlen said, "since I work for him." He wished he could think of this state cop's name, so he could throw it in while they took time to bullshit each other before getting to the point. "I haven't been to the site yet to look it over."

"It'll remind you some of Brice's."

"Too bad we can't use the actual battlefield."

"Even if we could," this know-it-all cop said, "Brice's is too far away to do Tunica any good. You have to look at this muster as a way to promote Tunica."

"I guess you're right," Arlen said, nodding to the bartender, who came over in his sour undershirt popping open a can of Bud. Arlen took a long swallow, giving himself time to wonder if he should mention Floyd before the cop brought it up. Ask how the investigation was going. Show he'd talk about it like anybody else. He wished he could think of this state cop's name. He believed it was John something. Arlen had reenacted with him, remembering him going either way, gray or blue, hardcore to his buttons; and he remembered this John something testifying to evidence in court when he went down on the extortion charges. Two years of his life in the toilet.

The cop said, "I heard Dennis Lenahan, the diver . . . ?"

Beating him to it.

"Was on the ladder, way at the top, when you and Junebug shot Floyd. That's the story going around. You hear it?"

Jesus, getting right into it. Arlen said in the cop's face, "No, I don't believe I have."

"It was right here, I'm told, where it started. Either you or Junebug bragging about it."

"It was me, I'd know, wouldn't I?"

"Well, I'd lean more to Junebug saying it than you. Maybe you weren't around?"

"If what you're telling me is true," Arlen said, "then what you're saying is the diver seen who did it."

"I expect so, if he was there."

"Then whyn't you ask him?" Arlen stared right at the cop as he said it. Looked him right in the fuckin eye.

The cop said, "I intend to. You bet."

"So he hasn't stepped up hisself."

"No, he hasn't."

"Why's that, you suppose?"

"I imagine he's been threatened."

Now the cop in his Sunday suit and tie, an American flag on it, was looking him in the eye, but not giving it much. This was not like any cop Arlen had ever been exposed to. He seemed more like a lawyer.

"Tell you the truth," Arlen said, "I wouldn't have any reason to whack Floyd. He never done nothing to me. I believe that man was so miserable he mighta done hisself in, tired of living in the gutter."

"Five in the back of the head?"

"Oh, is that right?" Arlen said. "My goodness." He paused and said, "Come on, chief, why don't we quit fuckin the dog here. You gonna bring me up on a story somebody heard in a bar? When was it, the night before last? Hell, I was right here where I'm standing most of the night." He turned his head to the bartender. "Wesley, where was I the night Floyd died and went to heaven?"

"Right there," Wesley said, "where you're standing."

Arlen found out at Parchman Jim Rein was the best do-anything man you could have at your side—Jim Rein already behind that razorwire for assaulting county prisoners too aggressively. He had entered as a fish, what they called all new arrivals, but swore he'd never get hooked, become some inmate's wife. Anybody approached Jim Rein with romantic ideas Jim cracked his head open. In no time at all he was Big Fish, too mean to land. Arlen came into the population, a homeboy from Tunica, and Fish became Arlen's bodyguard, working for him just as he had when they were both sheriff's deputies.

They had the same relationship going now—driving north on 61 toward Tunica in Fish's black Chevy pickup. Fish reminded Arlen of Li'l Abner.

Arlen told him about this boy Robert last night showing him the picture. "A nigger hanging from a bridge and tells me it was my grampa Bobba lynched him."

"Your grampa, huh?"

"See, I'd have known. But I never heard of Bobba doing that. It would've been a good story to tell people. Then I'm leaving, this boy Robert come out to the car, says don't worry, he won't say nothing about my shooting Floyd. I told him, 'Stand there, I want to talk to you.' He says, 'Later,' and walks in the house."

Jim Rein said, "Where'd this boy Robert come from?"

"I have to find that out."

"Or how he knew about Floyd."

"It musta been the diver told him. I kept thinking, I'm sitting there at the table with him, he could be a federal agent of some kind. I kept my mouth shut till he shows the picture of the nigger was lynched. I have to look into this boy Robert." He told Jim Rein about his conversation with the state cop just now, as much of it as he could remember word for word and saying he couldn't think of the cop's name.

"The one come out with you? That's John Rau, the CIB man. I was talking to a deputy's on the case with him's my cousin? He says far as they's concerned John Rau don't know shit. They not doing nothing for him they don't have to."

"I should've had you do Floyd 'stead of the Bug."

"I told you I would, but I had to go to Corinth for my uncle's coming-home party. Eighteen years he was in."

"How's Earl doing?"

"Looks fine but don't know how to act now he's out. Earl's in the grocery store with Aunt Noreen? He asks can he go by himself over to where he saw the cans of Deviled Ham. Aunt Noreen says she told him, 'Earl, you don't have to ask permission no more to go someplace.' Eighteen years, man." Jim Rein turned his head. "Where we going?"

"The bughouse," Arlen said.

He watched Jim Rein think about it before starting to grin. "That's what Earl says Parchman was like, everybody in there's crazy. He was looking forward to conjugal visits, only he never had none in the eighteen years. Aunt Noreen was too embarrassed to get in the trailer there on the grounds, people watching her."

"It's where I got the idea," Arlen said, "of sticking whores in trailers at Junebug's. Ever since Rosella left him and took the kids Junebug's in there once a night with that little Traci. He sits home all day hungover smoking weed and watching TV. Or you catch him holding auditions, checking out some little girl with big titties on her wants to be in show business. Nights, when he's at the club, he'll have Eugene baby-sit the dog with a shotgun."

"It was Eugene's dog," Jim Rein said. "Junebug took care of it while Eugene was at Delta Correctional."

"I know that," Arlen said. "I asked Junebug what he was protecting the dog *from*. The dog'll tear the throat out of anybody looks at her cross. Junebug says it ain't anybody's throat he's worried about. The dog tears up the house you leave her alone."

"What kind of dog it is?"

"Farm dog. Kinda white and brown, has some setter in her."

Jim Rein said, "I didn't know Eugene was out till I run into him. He says yeah, a couple months. Did you know the dorms at Delta Correctional are air-conditioned? I couldn't believe it."

"That's account of it's private-run."

"Eugene says you tell the warden you don't like something, that state soap for instance? The warden says, 'We ain't in the business of liking.' "

They were coming on to Tunica.

"Eugene says he got rich there at Delta only never saw the money."

"Working that con on the queers," Arlen said.

"Yeah, that's what he told me but not how it worked where he was. I only got into that business far as selling my pitcher to some cons that used it. Remember that? What was that hack's name, took my pitcher in the shower?"

"Otis," Arlen said. "Dumbest spook I ever met. No, Eugene worked it the usual way. Ran personal ads in homasexual magazines. Eugene used the one, he'd been falsely accused of receiving stolen goods from his boyfriend and would like the advice of an older and wiser homasexual. Pretty soon he's hearing from a bunch of old homo sweeties feeling sorry for him. After while he gets around to saying he's up for appeal and needs five thousand sent to his lawyer in Jackson, as he can't receive the check hisself. See, the lawyer was in on it. The old homos have a stack of Eugene's letters and pitchers of this boy standing there naked and they start sending the checks."

"Pitchers of Eugene?"

"Jesus, no. Junebug took pitchers of one of the boys does the sex show, Eyetalian kid, hung like a goddamn horse, and I sent 'em to the old homos, telling 'em as a favor to Eugene, pitchers taken before he went down. He got letters from near every one of 'em saying the check's in the mail and hope to see you soon. See, the checks are made out to Eugene and suppose to go into an account the lawyer opened for him."

They were in Tunica now on Main, coming to Fox Island Road,

and Jim Rein turned right. Arlen said, "I heard that's the house the fella runs Tishomingo leased, Billy Darwin?" Arlen pointing to a big Tudor set among white oaks. "Best-looking house in town." Junebug's was up ahead on the left a half mile: one of Kirkbride's manufactured homes with a screened porch, a patio and a three-car garage, additions Junebug'd had built on.

Jim Rein said, "Eugene told me he knew it worked, but he'll never see the money, something like over two hundred thousand dollars."

"I know that was his estimate," Arlen said. "He had homos all over America sending checks. Eugene got his release—you know there wasn't any appeal, he did the whole bit, three years straight up. Went to Jackson to collect his money and the lawyer says, 'What money?' He only received ten thousand and it went for his fees."

"Lying."

"Course he was."

"What'd Eugene do?"

"He shot him."

They were coming to the house now with its new lawn and young yellow poplars, Junebug's Cadillac and a pickup truck in the drive.

Jim Rein said, "Then where's the money?"

Arlen, looking at the house, said, "That's a good question."

Walter Kirkbride would arrive in a car he borrowed from Arlen, usually the Dodge: drive around back of Junebug's to the trailer with *Traci* lettered on the door in a vivid red, the way it could've appeared on the bedroom door of an 1860s whorehouse. New Orleans coming to mind. There might not have been girls named Traci then, no Airstream trailers for another seventy years or more, it didn't matter. Kirkbride loved the feeling of the past coming here gave him. The name on the door and, once inside, little Traci in the black stockings she wore snapped onto a garter belt and no underpants. Farby, but close enough, a French whore from a time past.

She was looking at the ashtray he'd brought, a special gift today.

"Walter, I love it."

"It's from Morocco."

"Oh, wow."

"The Mamounia Hotel in Marrakech."

"It's my favorite one I've ever had."

"I'll have to tell my wife I broke it."

"She collect ashtrays too?"

"She'll see it's gone."

"Walter, you're so cute."

"But if I broke it the pieces would be in the trash."

"Hon, look up here before your eyeballs fall out."

He did, tore his eyes away from her crotch and said, "I want you to do something for me."

"I'm not gonna beat you up again, hon. I'm not strong enough."

"I want you to take part in the reenactment. I'll have a tent for you and ice chest full of Coca-Cola."

"Sure, if I can get away."

"I'll fix it."

"You want me to dress up? Like in a hoopskirt with all those petticoats they wore?"

"Just the hoopskirt. Nothing under it."

They walked into Junebug's manufactured home and Jim Rein said, "Man, we's just talking about you," to Eugene Dean watching TV with Junebug. They sat at either end of a green-plaid sofa, a dozen empty beer cans on the low table in front of them, the ashtray full of butts, the smell of marijuana in the air.

Eugene said, "Hey, Fish, how they hangin'?"

Jim Rein said, "Just like you left 'em."

Arlen turned off the giant TV and then adjusted his Confederate slouch hat to feel just right, Junebug yelling at him, "Hey, I'm watching my fuckin show. They's just about to start hitting each other."

"Arguing over the Confederate flag," Eugene said, no shirt on, showing his sunken chest and ribs. "The white guys're skinhead militia, they say it's part of our heritage. The colored guys say well, it ain't part of ours, motherfuckers. They bleep it, but you can tell what they're saying."

"Look like some gang niggers," Junebug said, "they got off the street."

Arlen said, "Bug, have you been telling people we shot Floyd?"

Junebug held a beer can on his knee looking up at Arlen. "Man, are you crazy?" A scowl on his face.

"And that diver was up on the ladder the whole while?"

"Jesus Christ, Arlen, it wasn't me told anybody, you fuckin moron, it was you. I'm behind the bar looking right at you when you told Bob Hoon and one of his boys. They'd just delivered a load of crank."

Arlen said, "You gonna stick to that story?"

"It's the truth. Ask Bob Hoon."

Arlen turned his head to Jim Rein.

Jim Rein put his hands around to his back and brought out a U.S. Army Colt .45 from under his shirt hanging out.

Arlen said, "Bust him."

Junebug tried to sit up saying, "Hey, come on—"

And *bam,* Jim Rein shot him.

A dog started barking and scratching at a door.

Arlen held his eyes on Junebug slumped back against the plaid sofa, his eyes open.

Eugene had his eyes hooked on Jim Rein.

Jim Rein said, "He ought to be dead. I shot him through the heart."

Arlen said, "You heard him lie to my face?" He looked up. "That dog don't quit I'm gonna shoot *it.*"

That got Eugene up. He went to the kitchen door the barking was coming from, telling Arlen, "I got it, I'll take care of the dog," went through the door and closed it again.

Jim Rein said, "He's more worried about that dog than hisself."

Arlen said, "Eugene didn't do nothing. Put your gun away."

Eugene came back in the room, his shoulders sagging, hesitant, saying to Arlen, "Don't look at me like that. You either, Fish. You know I'll keep it right here."

"I was thinking of something else," Arlen said. "That money you made off the homos?"

"Made, but didn't get none."

"What happened to it?"

"I don't know. The lawyer spent it or hid it someplace. I checked every bank in Jackson, wasn't one had an account in my name. I went back to see the lawyer and asked him where my money was. He kept saying I didn't have none. So I went and got a gun and shot him. Like Fish done Junebug, through the heart."

"Whyn't you make him tell where it was?"

"I lost my temper. I know, I should've caused him some pain first, but I lost my goddamn temper."

"I'm gonna ask you a question," Arlen said, "while Fish stands there with his pistol waiting on the answer. Did you get hold of the money—what was it, two hundred thousand?"

"Around there."

"And hid it yourself?"

"Who from if it was mine?"

"You owed me a third."

"Yeah, for getting me that fuckin lawyer."

"And the pitchers."

"Man, if I had that money I'd have paid you first thing, and you know it."

Arlen made him wait till finally he said, "I believe you, Ace."

They had a discussion about Junebug, what to do with him. Arlen said to leave him where he was at. Eugene said, "Arlen, this is where I *live*." Where he'd been staying since his release from Delta Correctional, it was home. His dog had to have a place to stay and she was used to living here.

Jim Rein said, "What's her name?"

"Rose."

"Yeah? That's a pretty name."

"She's a bitch, but I love her."

It meant one of them would have to take Junebug in his car someplace and dump him. Arlen picked Jim Rein. First they had to find Junebug's keys so they could bring the Cadillac in the garage and put Junebug in it. The next step was to carry him out there. They went to pick him up and saw another problem, the blood on the sofa, all over the back cushion, and the bullet hole in it. Jim Rein telling them it was why he used the .45, it was a stopper. You get hit with it you weren't going nowhere. They began to discuss what to do with the sofa. Arlen said, "Well, it ain't mine," and told Eugene to put it in his truck and get rid of it. Dump it in the river. Arlen decided that's where Junebug should go, dump him in the river, too, downstream, or state cops'd be all over them by tomorrow. The next decision to be made, what to do with the Cadillac. Eugene said, "Shit, we don't want to dump it, it's a good car. How 'bout he left it here when he disappeared?"

Arlen thought about it and said no. "Fish'll take it over to Arkansas and sell it to a nigger."

Once they had Junebug in the garage—Arlen inside watching that TV show—Eugene said to Jim Rein, "Fish, you know Wesley?"

"The bartender?"

"Yeah, Wesley. You ever talk to him?"

"If I want a drink."

"Wesley says to me, 'You want to hear a funny story?' He says one Arlen told the other night to old Bob Hoon when he was in."

Jim Rein had Junebug in his arms. He bent over to lay him in the trunk of the Cadillac, then looked at Eugene as he straightened.

"I know what you're gonna say."

"I don't care," Eugene said. "It don't make a bit of difference to me."

Jim Rein said, "Me neither."

VERNICE SAID TO ROBERT ON the phone, "Well, you sure rise and shine early. He's still sleeping, the last I heard." Robert asked if she'd have Dennis call him when he got up and Vernice said, "Sure thing."

Maybe he was awake by now. She went into Dennis' room to check and looked down at the sweet boy lying on his side, arm under the pillow, the sheet almost to his bare shoulders. She went back to the door and listened, the house quiet except for the faint sound of Charlie in the next room sawing wood. Vernice closed the door and slipped out of her robe going to the bed. She got in behind Dennis and squirmed over to press her body against his bare back. She hoped he'd have to go to the bathroom and would brush his teeth while he was in there, but if he didn't it was okay. She raised her head enough to nibble at his ear and whisper, "Hi, stranger."

He stirred and she kissed his neck. Now his hand came around to her hip, like he was checking to see who this was in bed with him.

"It's just me," Vernice whispered, almost saying "little me," hunching her shoulders, Vernice down another four pounds in the past two days. She was pretty sure he was awake now but didn't want to rush him, appear too anxious. She said, "Dennis?"

He made a sound like "Hmmmm?"

"You think a person can look good but be too thin?"

It took a moment for him to say, "I guess," sounding more awake now.

"Did you know Jane Fonda had a twenty-five-year battle with bulimia?"

"What's bulimia?"

"You eat and then throw up on account of low self-esteem. But she got over it. Estranged husband Ted Turner got Jane to believe in herself."

"I thought it was finding God did it."

"That was in an old issue."

He came around enough to look up at her and Vernice gave him a peck on the cheek. She said, "How was the show yesterday?"

"Billy Darwin doesn't want Charlie calling dives anymore. He said, 'Get somebody to introduce you, tell the crowd about the splash zone and let it go at that. No more Charlie telling stories from the old dugout.' He said do a few dives in the afternoon if you feel like it and save—he said, 'save the daredevil stuff for the show at night.' "

"You want, I'll introduce you," Vernice said. "I know I can do that."

"But then you know what he said, Billy Darwin? There's a guy standing here—the ones Charlie picked up at the airport, the Mularonis, remember?"

"Anne," Vernice said. "Charlie thought she was too thin."

"The guy tells Billy Darwin he wants to be sure I get a few days off from diving so I can take part in the reenactment. Me. I don't even know the guy. Billy Darwin says, 'Well, he knows you.' He tells me the guy laid a check for fifty grand on the casino cashier. The man's comped all the way and that includes me. If Mularoni wants me in the reenactment, I'm in the reenactment. I said to him, 'It doesn't make sense, I never even heard of the guy.' Billy Darwin says, 'It's up to you. Get in uniform or pack up your show.' Then he says, 'It's not much of a draw anyway.' "

"And you don't even *know* this person?"

They heard a toilet flush.

"Nuts," Vernice said, "Charlie's up." She rolled out of the bed, picked up her pongee robe from the floor and put it on. Going to the door she said, "Oh, that colored fella, Robert? He wants you to call him."

The phone rang in Robert's suite—all the phones. He put his hand on the one next to the bed and said to Anne, putting her warm-ups back on, "Where'd you tell Jerry you were going?"

"To work out."

"Weren't lying, were you?"

"If he ever starts, we're fucked."

"No danger, the man likes the way he is." Robert picked up the phone. "Is this Dennis I'm about to speak to?"

"What's up?"

Robert said to Anne, "It's Dennis."

So Dennis would say, "Somebody's there with you?"

"The maid. She's getting dressed."

"Come on—"

"See, what you do, believe everything I say and you won't have to mind-fuck yourself thinking about it. Listen, I want to introduce you to somebody."

"His name Mularoni?"

"Hey, how'd you pick up on that?"

"Billy Darwin. I do the reenactment thing or the gig's over."

"He didn't need to put it like that—shit. You were gonna do it, weren't you? All we wanted, make sure you got some days off. Mr. Mularoni's the kind of man can make it happen. You understand what I'm saying? I want you to meet him."

"How about Anne?"

Robert put his hand over the phone and watched Anne sitting on the bed putting on a tennis shoe. He took his hand off the phone and said, "Dennis, you got chops working now I hadn't noticed. That was cool, that 'How about Anne?' Damn."

"I'm diving at two."

"You can if you want. But Mr. Billy Darwin agreed you could cut that one."

"Why?"

"Have time to get the uniform and the gun and shit. We meeting in their suite at one o'clock, have some lunch."

"What if I'd rather dive?"

"Dennis? Listen to me. You're hungry. You eat, wait an hour and then you can dive all you want."

He hung up, Anne looking at him now, ready to leave.

"How'd he know about me?"

Robert was already thinking about it. He said, "Gimme another minute or two."

Mularoni was introduced to Dennis as Jerry, not Germano. In his fifties, shorter than Dennis with a head of thick dark hair and a

beard, a poser with the cigar, the dark sunglasses. He seemed pleasant enough, but also the boss, saying, "Dennis, come here," put his
arm around Dennis' shoulders and brought him to the balcony, the
doors wide open.

"The ladder stands eighty feet high. That correct?"

"Exactly," Dennis said. "Eight ten-foot sections."

"But how does anybody know for sure?"

"Some people actually count the rungs."

"That's what I thought," Jerry said, "the skeptics. You know
what you could do? Have a couple of the ladders, the ones you put
on top, make the rungs six inches apart instead of a foot. From the
ground you'd never be able to tell, but now you're ten feet lower up
there."

"Jerry thought of that last night," Robert said, "watching the
show."

"But whether you go off from seventy or eighty feet," Dennis
said, "it doesn't make that much difference."

"Either one," Robert said, "you can kill yourself, huh? You want
champagne, beer, vodka tonic—what's your pleasure?"

Dennis said champagne. Robert popped a bottle of Mumm and
poured two glasses. Jerry had red wine.

Anne came out of the bedroom in what looked like a beach cover
mostly yellow, almost see-through, smiling at Dennis and extending
her hand. She said, "I've watched you perform twice now, both
times with my heart in my mouth. Hi, I'm Anne."

Sounding like a TV commercial. Charlie was right, she could be
a fashion model, the long, streaked hair, the way she moved, sure of
herself. She took his hand and kissed the air next to his cheek, giving him a whiff of scent that was the best thing he'd ever smelled.
In his life. Up close she could be thirty-five.

For lunch there was cold shrimp, a mixed salad, marinated

calamari, fried chicken, Anne saying, "Nothing fancy." Robert saying, "And a nod to regional chow, the river catfish and the mustard greens."

Dennis said to Robert aside, each taking a shrimp on a toothpick, "What's going on?"

"It's lunchtime," Robert said. "Don't you eat lunch?"

"Come on."

"They're my friends and you're my friend."

Anne got around to asking about high diving and Acapulco, standing close to him with her scent, bikini under the beach cover hanging open, saying it must be harrowing and Dennis telling her the rush was worth it. "Every day," she said, "living on the edge." Dennis shrugged. "It's dive or get a job." She looked right into his eyes, making him wonder if it was there for him. He wasn't sure how to handle it. He asked if she and Jerry had any children—stupid, trying to think of something to say—and it turned off the look she was giving him. She said, "Jerry and I aren't into children."

He wanted to ask what Jerry did for a living—Jerry on the balcony now with a plate of calamari. But Robert came over with a vodka tonic for Anne, saying to Dennis, "You might want to thank Jerry for getting you off to play war."

Anne said, "I'm going as a camp follower," looking right at him again, "but no hoopskirts."

"A quadroon," Robert said, "so I won't be the only darky."

Dennis watched Robert give her a look, part smile, part something else going on between them.

"What's Jerry gonna be?"

"A Yankee," Robert said, "who gets his ass whipped. Remember I told you, Forrest put the skeer in the Yankees, chased 'em all the way back to Memphis?"

Dennis had his next question ready and asked it. "What kind of business is Jerry in?"

Anne said, "Land development."

Robert said, "Big projects, all over the Midwest. And you know what kind? Manufactured home communities." Robert waited, looking at Dennis like he was giving him time to decide on the next question, how to put it.

"Jerry knows Kirkbride?"

"Knows of him."

"But if they're in the same business—"

"I'm out of this," Anne said, and walked away.

Dennis watched her go in the bedroom, Robert saying to him, "It's Jerry's brother runs the business. Jerry's made his, he's semi-retired, consults is all." Robert said, "You gonna ask me a lot of questions now, aren't you? All right, what's the name of Kirkbride's company? Was on the sign in the village he's doing."

"I don't remember."

"American Dream, Incorporated. Kirkbride makes 'em in Corinth and sells 'em all over the country. Jerry's brother looked into American Dream as a source. You know, to buy from. One reason or another it didn't work out. They deal with the same kind of company up by Detroit makes homes you put together."

"You didn't mention this to Kirkbride."

"Why would I? Jerry's not dealing with him."

"But they're in the same business."

"Jerry's like Anne, he's down here to have some fun, not talk business—shit. I'm the one, I told you, looked up Kirkbride, see what he's like, what else he might be into."

"Like playing war," Dennis said, "and now you and Jerry want to get in on it."

"And Anne. She's nice, huh?"

"But you don't want Kirkbride to know anything about you, or what Jerry does."

Robert said, "There's no reason for him to. Man, you know there's always more to what you see going on than meets the eye. Be patient."

"But why bring me along?"

"You're my straightman, Dennis. Come on, have some of this lunch."

They stood around the two room-service tables pushed together picking at the lunch. Dennis made himself say to Jerry, "Hey, thanks for getting me off."

"You ever reenact before?"

"No, but I can't wait."

Robert said, "Don't overdo it."

Anne said, "These two haven't either."

Jerry said to Anne, "But we know all about the war, Queenie. You don't know shit."

"I'm looking forward to the sowbelly," Robert said. "The hardtack."

The phone rang.

Jerry stepped over to the counter and picked it up saying to Robert, "We're getting around that, don't worry," and said into the phone, "Yeah? . . . Send him up." Coming back to the table Jerry said, "Tonto's here."

Robert went to the door saying to Dennis, "His real name's Antonio Rey, but Jerry calls him Tonto, so that's what it is now." Robert opened the door and stood waiting, telling Dennis, "He's part Tonto-Mojave but related to Geronimo going way back to when Geronimo raped his great-great-grandma, in Oklahoma. Tonto's part Mexican-American, too, from Tucson, Arizona."

"And part African-American," Jerry said, "from Niggerville."

"Be nice," Robert said, serious, like he was giving Jerry an order. His expression changed then as the guy appeared, Robert grinning now saying, "My man, Tonto."

Dennis watched them high-five and hug each other, Tonto with dark skin, dark hair to his shoulders coming out of a bandanna he wore pirate-fashion, a man you had to notice and look at.

Jerry and Anne didn't seem taken with him, though Anne said, "That's what I'm wearing with my costume, a do-rag," and Jerry raised his hand to him.

Robert said, "Dennis? Tonto Rey, man."

Dennis, holding a piece of fried chicken, gave him a nod.

Jerry said, "How'd you do? You get everything?"

"Some from the Dixie Gun Work," Tonto said, with an accent from down Mexico way. "Some from the place in Corint." He brought out folded sheets of paper from his denim jacket and opened them, Robert hovering, asking if he wanted a drink, something to eat—"Yes, of course"—Robert finally getting him seated with a straight vodka and a plate of food on the table in front of the sofa. Dennis saw he was wearing scuffed brown cowboy boots. Jerry had taken a chair, Anne had gone in the bedroom and closed the door.

Robert said, "You want to eat your lunch first?"

Jerry said, "I want to know what the fuck he got, okay?"

Tonto Rey took his time, looking at Jerry and then at the sheets of paper he was holding. He said, "I got everything Robert tole me. I got four Navy Colt revolvers, thirty-six-caliber, like the ones you have," looking at Jerry again.

Jerry said, "Extra cylinders?"

"Two for each revolver. Also I got four of the big fucking Enfield rifles, fifty-eight-caliber. I got cartridge boxes, canteens, cooking pots, the lanterns, the sacks . . ."

"Knapsacks," Robert said.

"Yeah, those."

Jerry said, "The tents?"

"I got three of the big wall tents with the awnings, and I got the stakes, the cooking irons, pots, a table that folds up."

Robert said, "Anything you couldn't get?"

"Everything you tole me. Is all in the truck."

"What about Dennis' uniform?"

"At the place in Corint. Is ready, he can pick it up."

Dennis looked at Robert. "How's he know my size?"

"I told him same as mine be close enough. This place in Corinth, you can pick out your hat, too. Have a choice, a forage cap or the kepi."

Jerry got up from his chair saying, "I'm going to take a nap. You guys finish and get out of here." He went in the bedroom and closed the door.

Robert said to Tonto, "You bring some good weed?"

"Only the best."

"What they have here's not too bad."

"Where they get it?"

"Mostly Virginia."

"I hear is okay."

"We'll go to my room," Robert said and looked at Dennis. "You want to puff some?"

Dennis said no. He had a question, but now Robert was asking Tonto what he'd like to do after.

"Get laid," Tonto said. "They any girls around here?"

"Cute ones. They say, 'You want to see my trailer?' You tell the one you want, 'You betcha.' " He looked at Dennis. "You want to come?"

Dennis shook his head and Robert said to Tonto, "I believe the man has all he needs. Hey, man? You can blow your whistle, you can ring your bell, but I know you want it by the way you smell. Know what I'm saying?"

Tonto said, "I hear you, man."

Dennis watched them grinning at each other. He said, "I know where you've got something going too." Robert's grin didn't fade away, but did weaken. "Tell me," Dennis said, "why you need all the guns."

"We got more reenactors coming," Robert said.

Vernice had let him use her Honda. He pulled up to the house and saw her waiting for him at the front door, Vernice looking worried, anxious. "Your car's fine," Dennis said, "still in one piece."

"You have a visitor."

"Don't tell me Arlen Novis."

"From the state police. What in the world have you been doing?"

"I wish I knew," Dennis said. He walked through the empty living room and dining L to the kitchen.

John Rau, wearing his dark suit and the tie with the flag, was at the table with a cup of coffee. He said to Dennis, "Sit down." He looked past him and, in a milder tone, said, "Vernice, would you mind leaving us alone for a few minutes? Thank you."

Dennis heard the door close as he took the chair facing John Rau stirring his coffee but looking this way.

He said, "Guess who's dead?"

"Do I know him?"

"I think you do. Junior Owens."

Dennis started to shake his head.

"Better known as Junebug."

"I never met him."

"He was fished out of the river this morning."

"He drowned?"

"You know better than that. Cause of death, gunshot."

"How many times?"

"You want to know if it was the same gun that did Floyd. No, he was shot once, in the chest, looking at the man who fired a bullet that went through and through."

"Have you talked to anybody?"

"You're top of the list, Dennis. Like you were on top the ladder when those fellas killed Floyd. Have you heard that story?"

"I have, yeah."

"Is it true?"

"I've been advised not to get involved in this."

"By a lawyer?"

"Or talk about it with you."

"You've been threatened."

"I'm not going to say anything."

"But you want to. Don't you?"

"How can I be involved based on a story going around, a rumor?"

"One of the fellas that did Floyd started it. You think it was Arlen Novis or Junebug?"

Dennis could picture them walking toward the tank, even before it was done, and he'd say the one in the hat, Arlen. That was easy. But he didn't say anything; he shook his head.

"Can you imagine why Junebug was killed? If you were Arlen and you heard the Bug was shooting off his mouth?"

Dennis didn't say anything.

"You know Arlen?"

"I met him."

"What do you think of him?"

"He acts like a sheriff's deputy."

"I know what you mean. But he didn't shoot anybody till he came out of prison." John Rau waited and then he said, "Why don't you help me put him back in?"

THEY WENT UP TO MEMPHIS and took 72 East to
Corinth, a two-and-a-half-hour drive from Tunica, most of it dipping down into Mississippi and across the top of the state, the sound
of blues in the car all the way. "A medley of De-troit bluesmen,"
Robert said. "Johnny 'Yard Dog' Jones, mixing soul with his blues,
Alberta Adams, been doing it seventy years. Sang with everybody
who's anybody. Got Robert Jones on there, he'll make you think of
another Robert, the great Robert Johnson, Son House, too. And,
let's see, Johnnie Bassett, plays a kind of jazz blues."

Dennis said, "Why you live in Detroit?"

"Everybody's got to live someplace."

"Yeah, but Detroit—"

"It's a no-shit town, man, it jumps. Look at Motown, Kid Rock,
that wigger Eminem. All kind of sounds come out of Detroit."

"You grew up there, went to school?"

"In my youth," Robert said, sitting low behind the wheel of the Jag, "you know what I did? Worked for Young Boys, Incorporated, street-corner entrepreneurs, sell a dime bag of heroin for thirteen dollars and keep three. Started when I was twelve years old working for Mr. Jones. That was his name. He goes, 'Want to make three hundred a day? Hustle you can make three thousand a week?' What do you think I said to the man? There were a couple hundred of us doing it. They give you these little envelopes marked with brand names like Murder One, Rolls-Royce, you take out to your corner, or to the projects for home delivery. Yeah, Young Boys showed how it was done, then other gangs came along, like Pony Down was one."

Out in the country cruising past cornfields, cows in a pasture, signs on trees that said JESUS SAVES . . . Dennis said, "You were twelve years old?"

"Thirteen, I bought a Cadillac."

"You weren't old enough to drive."

"I drove. Got pulled over every block, so I had the car put in my mama's name. She sold it. I was fourteen I bought a Corvette, kept it to use at night till it got jacked on me. You sell over two grand a week, Christmastime they take you to Las Vegas and get you laid by your first white lady."

"Did you use drugs?"

"Weed is all. Look at the people you selling to, you know you don't want to get hooked on the heavy shit. No, I even put money away, bought my mama things. I was fifteen I left Young Boys to try Pony Down and got a knife put to my throat. So I retired from the business."

"You went to school while you were doing this?"

"A Catholic school, but they didn't have many nuns left. It was too bad, I liked the nuns. They give it to you straight, no bullshit."

"They know what you were doing?"

"No, man. I'd get brought up in Juvenile Court, my mama'd call the school, say I had a sore throat."

"She didn't mind you selling drugs?"

"She'd look the other way taking the money. I never got sent down. I went to Oakland University three years and did some dealing to pay for my tuition and books and shit, but only weed. I wouldn't sell heroin to students, fuck up their young minds. Lot of 'em were fucked up to begin with, worrying about what they gonna do when they got out."

"You weren't worried?"

"I took eighteen semester hours of history—ask me a question about it, anything, like the names of famous assassins in history. Who shot Lincoln, Grover Cleveland. I took history 'cause I loved it, man, not to get a job from it. I knew about the Civil War even before I saw it on TV, the one Ken Burns did. I stole the entire set of videos from Blockbuster."

Robert looked over at Dennis staring out the window.

"You go to school to get a job?"

"I knew the first time I saw a high diver go off that's what I wanted to do."

"There you are. What'd you take?"

"I quit after two years and joined the Great American High Dive Team."

"How long can you keep doing it?"

"I'm running out of time."

"Then what?"

"I don't know."

"You ain't ever been to jail, have you?"

"I was held one time while they searched my truck."

"Thought you were trafficking?"

"I wasn't."

"The kind of nerve you have," Robert said, "when you quit diving you ought to get into something, you know, edgy."

"When I was on the dive team, I was the edge guy."

"There you are."

"But with divers," Dennis said, "they say the better the performer, the less stable the personality."

They came to Corinth, to a wide, open area of railroad tracks on the south edge of the town's business district, and Robert stopped the car.

"This is Civil War City, man, Corinth, the rail center all the fighting around here was about. You looking right at it. The Memphis and Charleston line went east and west, the Mobile and Ohio the other way. You listening to me?"

Dennis said, "You came here to meet Kirkbride?"

"To see what he had going. His plant's south of here, across 72. But he was already in Tunica putting up his Village. It wasn't a wasted trip 'cause I also came to visit Jarnagin's and look at uniforms. Can I go on?"

"You're driving."

"I mean with your lesson, telling you about what happened here. Musta been thirty thousand, at *least*, killed, wounded, died of cholera or the shits fighting over these railroad tracks. I'm counting Shiloh, north of here across the Tennessee line, Iuka, a place where they fought east of here, and the Battle of Corinth itself. Was October 1862, the Confederates trying to take it back from the Federals." Robert pointed. "Over that way not too far I'll show you where the meanest fighting was, the Confederates trying to take Battery

Robinett. It's now a historical landmark, some of the earthworks still there."

Dennis said, "Yeah, Battery Robinett. I believe one of the heroes of the assault was a Colonel Rogers of the Second Texas. Shot seven times charging up the redan."

Robert turned his head and stared at Dennis before he said, "You sneaky, aren't you? Every now and then flash your chops at me." Robert smiled. "Shows your potential. Tells me I'm right to bring you along. But the way I heard it, was a drummer boy picked up a pistol and shot Colonel Rogers. It's a better story, the big hero getting popped by a kid. You ever imagine what it would be like?"

"What, getting shot?"

"No, being in a battle. Walking across a field toward a line of men shooting at you. Or charge this Battery Robinett, big Parrott guns, twenty-pounders, firing canister at you."

"What's canister?"

"I think it's like scrap metal packed together, but I'm not all the way sure. I know I wouldn't want any parts of it. Man, you have to be brave keep walking into that shit. But they did, both sides." Robert shook his head. "How, I don't know. I went up to Shiloh? This Park Service person, Ranger Diana, cute girl, took me around in her uniform and Smokey the Bear hat. Showed me the Sunken Road, the famous Hornet's Nest, like a woods. She said they fought in there for hours, the black-powder smoke so thick they shooting their own people by mistake. The trees caught fire and there's wounded in there can't get out. She said you could hear 'em screaming and smell burning flesh. Yeah, Ranger Diana, she was good, put you right there at the scene."

For maybe a minute the air-conditioning was the only sound in the car.

Robert said, "Right over there across the tracks was the original

Tishomingo Hotel. They used it as a hospital. You can take a walking tour of historical sites, see where General Beauregard stayed, visit a war museum, or we can skip it, get your uniform and something to eat. Beer and wine, but no booze in this county. What else you want to know?"

There was no showroom or retail shop here. Dennis stood before the mirror in Jarnagin's stockroom wearing a Federal infantry shell jacket, the one with sky-blue piping on the stand-up collar and the cuffs, nine buttons down the front, the jacket Robert had ordered for him. The sky-blue trousers were a disappointment—Dennis staring at the almost shapeless cut—but good enough for a couple of days. He tried on a kepi. Yeah . . . ? Then a forage cap, like the kepi but with a higher crown that David Jarnagin told him was worn with the crown falling forward on the leather bill. Dennis put on the kepi again. David Jarnagin said that regulars in the Union Army normally wore the forage cap. Dennis said, "If I have a choice . . ." and went with the kepi, seeing himself in the mirror 140 years ago. He liked the look and tried the kepi a bit closer on his eyes. Yeah. The shoes were something else, plain black ankle-high brogans with blunt toes, four holes for the shoelaces; they were called bootees. David Jarnagin told Dennis they'd soften with shoe oil; but don't put them close to a fire, the soles would dry up and crack. Dennis picked out a belt, a bugle infantry insignia for the cap, sky-blue corporal chevrons to add some color. He looked at the Civil War underwear, flannel longjohns, told himself he could always cut the legs off, looked at Robert, Robert shrugged, and Dennis said he'd skip the official underwear. He didn't think David Jarnagin cared one way or the other; he put Dennis' uniform in a box and said, "Thanks for your business," as Robert wrote the check.

Outside, Dennis asked him how much it cost.

"Don't worry your head about it."

"I know the shell jacket was one-twenty, the shoes around a hundred."

"You get a present from somebody, you ask how much they spent on you?"

"This isn't a present. How much?"

"Little under four bills."

They were in the Jaguar now going back to Tunica by way of Memphis, into the sun, both wearing their shades.

"You understand," Robert said, "reenactors are serious people. I mean whether they all the way hardcore or not. They go to the trouble to get to the place, put their uniform on, sleep in a tent on the ground, cook their food over a fire, they're serious people do that. They have no patience with farbs wearing Speedo skivvies under their wool pants. You know what I'm saying?"

"They're serious."

"They are ser-i-ous."

"Not just about reenacting."

"About everything."

"Like you and Jerry. And Anne."

"Going as a quadroon hooker—shit, huh?" Robert grinning. "She walk down that row of tents you see the heads come popping out."

"And she's serious."

"Me and Jerry and Anne—hey, and you—we all part of this agenda."

Dennis said, "I'm not gonna ask what it is, so fuck you."

Robert glanced over. "You don't like me playing with your head.

But you're cool, you can handle it." He said, "Listen, what I was saying about these people . . . I went to two different reenactments up in Michigan. One near Flint, a small one, only a couple hundred people dressed up, one cannon. And the other reenactment near Jackson, home of America's biggest walled lockup, five thousand inmates in there messing with each other. This Jackson reenactment had a couple of thousand counting people dressed as civilians, women and children, General Grant, Robert E. Lee, the cavalry, lot of cannons, people selling Civil War memorabilia, kielbasa and grilled Italian sausage, and all the people I spoke to, man, were serious."

"So you were serious, too," Dennis said.

"Yes, I was."

"They didn't know you were only acting serious."

"No. I *was*. I found myself being serious with them and it was a strange experience."

"Being in the real world for a change."

Robert said, "Yeaaah," in a dreamy tone of voice. "That's what it's like, huh?"

Dennis fell asleep. He missed going through Memphis, opened his eyes to see they were in the country going south, blues coming out of the speakers.

"Robert Johnson," Dennis said.

"You passed the test. Eric Clapton will speak to you."

They went by a US 61 road sign and Dennis said, "Do we come to 49?"

"Other side of Tunica, down by Clarksdale, the most famous crossroads in the history of blues. Shit, in the history of music."

"Where Robert Johnson sold his soul to the devil."

"You remember—that's good."

"But I don't know what it means."

"Like Faust, man. Sell your soul you get anything you want. They say Robert Johnson made that kind of deal. He didn't say it, they did. But now *Tom* Johnson's a different story. This was when Robert Johnson was still a child. Tom Johnson tells people he sold his own soul at the crossroads. I say maybe, maybe not. The man drank poison, canned heat, that Sterno. What kind of deal is that? Now Robert Johnson—one day Son House tells him he ain't gonna make it, ain't good enough. Robert goes to the crossroads—the way the story is told—meets Satan in the form of this giant black dude. Satan takes Robert's guitar and messes with it, hands it back, and from then on nobody can believe the way he plays. They say to him, 'How you do that?' Robert won't tell. See, but if he didn't sell his soul, why did he write 'Hell Hound on My Trail'? Why did he write 'Me and the Devil Blues'? Everybody's saying he musta gone to the crossroads and made the deal, 'cause listen to him, his wailin' chords, man, crawling up your spine. No doubt about it, was the devil gave him his mojo."

"Like a charm?"

"Mojo—yeah, like a charm, an amulet, something you use to get what you want, or be what you want. Something that's magic for you. You keep it in your mojo bag."

Dennis said, "It sounds like gris-gris."

"How you know about gris-gris?"

"New Orleans."

"Yeah, I forgot. Voodoo City."

"You have a mojo?"

"Wouldn't be without it."

"You keep it in a mojo bag?"

"Yeah, little bag made of flannel, has a drawstring. You want to see it, don't you?"

"I wouldn't mind."

"It's in the room. I'll show it to you."

"What's the charm that's in it?"

"Strands of Madonna's coochie mop."

"Strands? You're kidding."

"Am I?"

Shit, this guy—Dennis kept his mouth shut. He swore he wouldn't get into it any deeper.

But then Robert said, "You ever think about selling your soul?"

And Dennis bit; couldn't help it.

"How do you do that?"

"You stand up and say, when the time comes, Enough of this shit, I'm gonna do what I want. Or I'm gonna get me what I want. It's how you turn your life around."

"What if you don't know what you want?"

"You have to be cool, wait for it to be offered. But when it comes, you only have the one chance to grab it. You know what I'm saying?"

"Like a job? What I've always wanted, a regular job."

"You're feeling edgy now, huh? You like to be eighty feet in the air about to do your number—a thousand fans watching and you know you have 'em in your hand. And for that," Robert said, "they pay you three hundred a day?" He stared at the highway now as he said, "Man, I can make you feel like you way higher than eighty feet. Up on an edge you won't believe."

There was a silence, Dennis telling himself to leave it alone. But there was a question he had to ask.

"How'd you get it?"

Robert turned his head. "What?"

"Your mojo."

"I bought it."

"How do you know it's the real thing?"

"I believe it. That's enough to make it work."

14

WALTER KIRKBRIDE CALLED THE MEETING, in his office at Southern Living Village, Walter in casual clothes, his beard still gray, a Cuban cigar in one hand, a Confederate cavalry saber in the other. Arlen Novis, Eugene Dean, Bob Hoon and his brother Newton filed in and took seats: Arlen wearing his slouch hat, Eugene holding a sixteen-ounce bottle of Pepsi-Cola, Bob Hoon with a cigar stub showing in the thicket of his beard, Newton showing tobacco juice in his.

They all assumed this meeting was about the reenactment.

Walter corrected that notion. He brought up the hilt of the saber even with his eyes and hacked the blade down on his oak desk, hard, and their shoulders jumped, all four of them sitting right in front of the desk. Walter said:

"Do I have your attention?"

Loud, as they were looking at the new scar on the desk, next to the ones that had been varnished over. Walter lowered his voice but kept grit in it saying to Arlen, "You shot Floyd telling me it was a personal thing that had to be done. You shot Junebug without telling me anything, and I want to know why."

"Don't think I wanted to, Walter."

"You had Fish do it?"

"He's my shooter."

Walter said, "Where is he?" looking beyond them, as if Jim Rein might be lurking back there.

Eugene said, "He's minding my dog."

Now Walter had to stare at Eugene. He heard himself say in his head, He's minding your dog? With a tone that required an explanation. He heard himself say, Minding your dog is more important than . . . ? What he said was, "I told all five of you to be here."

Eugene said, "My dog don't have somebody with her she chews up the house."

Walter had never seen this dog and was curious, but kept to his purpose. He said to Arlen, "Why Junebug?"

Arlen said, "I had him put down 'cause he was getting drunk and talking too much."

"But you let an eyewitness to your shooting Floyd walk down the street, do whatever he wants."

"I set him straight. He knows what'll happen he's called and testifies."

"And Charlie Hoke?"

"Charlie knows better." Arlen cleared his throat and said, "I don't see this has anything to do with business. It come out of our dealing with Floyd. So I don't see it has anything to do with you?"

"It's business," Walter said, "because it brings the police. I can say to myself there is nothing they can find that would tie me in with what you're doing, but I can never be absolutely sure, can I? What

I think about is any one of you facing a conviction—doesn't matter what it is—could roll me over to get a reduced sentence. Or name all the names, all your friends and associates, to get immunity from prosecution."

Arlen turned his head to Bob Hoon on one side of him and then to Eugene on the other. "Walter sounds like he's running the business."

Bob Hoon said, "I thought he was," and nudged his brother, Newton.

"As I see it," Arlen said, "we hired him."

"At gunpoint," Walter said.

The gun a photograph of Walter naked in color, Walter in a trailer tooting crack with a naked whore named Kikky. Some party till the camera flash went off. They showed him the photo and asked for two hundred and fifty thousand, saying they had taken over the drug business here and needed cash to buy product, buy sugar for the stills, buy the stuff you made the methamphetamines with.

"Listen to Bob Hoon," Walter said. "He's our in-house manufacturer of speed, the only one of you even close to knowing anything about business. You can't be the louts you are and exercise any good sense. How long did it take me to get your cash flow set up, show you the need to run a balance sheet, how to make a steady profit and hide it? What was the first thing I told you, Arlen?"

"I must've forgot."

"I said get rid of your fifty-thousand-dollar automobile. You're a security stiff working for ten an hour."

"We let you in," Arlen said, "and you felt right at home's what happened."

"You know why?" Walter said. "Because business is business. I said to myself, If this man is forcing me to become involved, then I'll study up on his trade and see how it works. Okay, then see how my expertise can make it work even better. The first thing I look at, what to do with the profits. Okay, why not launder it through my own subsidiary, Southern Living Village, Incorporated, and pay it to suppliers who only exist on paper."

Eugene said, "I never understood that part."

"You don't have to," Walter said. "We have a CPA who's one of the great chefs at cooking books. He has no idea where the money's coming from and doesn't want to know. You fellas are a bigger risk than he is. Now you're shooting people, bringing the police around. Arlen, what did I say to do with the nigger, this boy Robert? I said scare him, run him off."

"What I was thinking," Arlen said, "have a deputy stop him out on the road and find that pitcher. Bring him in and accuse him of using it to con people out of money."

"He doesn't ask for money."

"We can say he did."

"You want to testify?"

"Walter, you know it's some con he's working. The man on the bridge can't be both our grampas."

"No, but it could be yours *or* mine. Didn't he know things about your family? Where your granddad worked? You said he did. What'd I tell you to do? I said run him off. *You* do it, not some deputy'll fuck with the nigger's civil rights."

"Another way I was thinking," Arlen said, "shoot him accidentally during the Brice's reenactment."

"Except he's on our side," Walter said. "Guns are inspected anyway, make sure they're not loaded."

"But it happens," Arlen said. "Wasn't there one at Gettysburg a few years ago?"

"During the one-thirty-fifth," Walter said, "you're right. A fella with the Seventh Virginia was shot in the neck. Doctor removed a ball from a forty-four-caliber pistol. It was ruled accidental. The ball must've been stuck in the barrel, since the pistol had been inspected, the chambers clear."

"How about that diver," Eugene said. "Is he reenacting?"

"There'd be an investigation," Walter said, "anybody gets killed." But now he was thinking about it.

Arlen was too. Arlen saying, "Do 'em both at the reenactment, the diver *and* the nigger. Draw 'em off into the woods there and shoot 'em. Dump the bodies in an irrigation ditch. Come back after dark and bury 'em in the levee. Who'd miss 'em? Nobody'd know where they went or care."

"That's how to do it," Newton said, leaning forward to look past his brother at Arlen and give him a nod. "You want, I'll do the nigger."

Walter said to Arlen, "You're full of ideas, aren't you? What'd you say to John Rau when he asked about Junebug?"

"I said he disappeared on me, didn't know where he was at."

"He come to the house," Eugene said, "looks around and wants to know where was the sofa. I guess on account of the coffee table was sitting there with nothing behind it. I said, 'What sofa? I only board here.' "

Bob Hoon said, "He asked us where we was. Newton told him, 'Out in the country making speed, where you think I was?' Kidding with him. This John Rau's a serious person. He says, 'I'm gonna send the North Mississippi Narcotics Task Force after you.' I said, 'What's that? I never heard of it.' Lot of those law enforcement people you can kid with, but not John Rau, he takes it serious."

They were winding down.

Arlen asked Walter how come he hadn't dyed his beard. Walter said you look at photos of Old Bedford in uniform, taken during the war, his beard was black as coal. But in photos less than ten years later his beard was pure white. Walter said it led him to believe the wartime photos had been retouched to make the general look fierce, "and the beard actually wasn't any darker than mine."

Arlen said, "Wasn't 'cause your wife'd get after you if you dyed it?"

There was a time a remark like that would disturb Walter. Not anymore. Walter could say to Arlen, yes, his wife was recognized as a self-righteous pain in the ass, set in her ways, two married daughters in Corinth still under her foot. If she were ever to see that photo of him tooting in the buff with Kikky, would she howl for his blood and leave him? He could say to Arlen, yes, of course she would. But so what? He could say to Arlen, show her the photo if you want. Walter had drug profits put away, scattered from Jackson to the Caymans, that Arlen and his morons would never find in a million years. Walter believed that at a moment's notice he could walk away and become someone else.

What he did say to Arlen was, "Leave my wife out of this. Please." Keeping it light, a gesture to Henny Youngman, saying it as Jim Rein walked in. Walter said, "Fish, grab yourself a chair."

And Eugene was on him. "Jesus Christ, don't tell me you left Rose alone."

Jim Rein held up his hand wrapped in a dishtowel. "She bit me."

"Fish, I told you you can't leave her. She'll tear up the curtains, the chairs, eat the carpet—"

"The house is okay," Jim Rein said. "I shot her."

Carla came out to watch him dive and they sat for a while in lawn chairs, in the shade back of the tank, talking, beginning to get to know each other.

In the days that followed his meeting the Mularonis, Dennis was diving again in the afternoon: climbing to the perch and looking for a cowboy hat among the scattered crowd watching, doing his flying reverse pike, then wearing his shades, a towel around his neck, as he stood among girls from Tunica and told them what it was like to risk death or serious injury every day of his life. He could turn it on and the words would come out in a quiet tone of voice. But in the past week he had seen a man shot to death and had met Robert Taylor and watched him perform and the daredevil act from eighty feet had gotten old. When he was with Robert he felt like a stooge—as Robert even said, his straightman. Dennis no longer the star. But now the past couple of days he hadn't seen Robert at all, Robert out doing his act with his Indian buddy Tonto Rey, and that was fine, Jesus, why would he want to get close to a con artist? Even one who said he could take him higher than eighty feet, show him an edge—risk, excitement, thrills?—he wouldn't believe. And that business about selling his soul—come on. Ask him what all that meant and Robert said wait and see.

Carla came along and the Tunica girls, no match, took off.

She said, "You know you don't have to do a matinee." Dennis said yeah, but it was what he did, and Carla said, "We haven't talked much, have we? Hardly at all."

Sounding as though she wanted to tell him something, confide. They moved lawn chairs into the shade of the tank, the private area where Floyd was shot, Carla wearing shorts and a loose tank top, dark blue against her slim arms and shoulders. She said, "I don't have anyone to talk to."

Dennis offered Billy Darwin. "I thought you two were close."

"Why?"

"You came with him from Atlantic City."

Carla said, "You don't talk to your boss. You know what I mean, goof around, say anything you want, unless you have something going. And we don't."

Dennis took another step closer saying, "I thought you two might be hot for each other."

"It's there, but we both know it wouldn't work. Billy's into casinos and I'm not. I may go back to school and get my MBA. Billy's happy, he has a girlfriend who comes down from New York to see him. She was a showgirl in Las Vegas when they met."

"I see him going for a different type."

"Guys are guys, Dennis."

"Does he fool around locally?"

"Why do you want to know?"

"You said you need someone to talk to, that's what we're doing, talking. I'm in the same boat. Where I'm staying we talk about baseball or losing weight."

"You've been talking to the police lately."

Dennis felt they were getting to it now.

She said, "And you talk to Robert Taylor."

"How do you know?"

"He told me. He was in to see Billy with his jam box and played a record for him. Marvin Pontiac. Have you ever heard of him?"

" 'I'm a Doggy'? 'I stink when I'm wet'? Yeah, I like Marvin. He's different."

"Robert said the rights to the songs are available and Billy could get in on it if he wanted."

"What'd he say?"

"What do you think? He said no."

"Doesn't like the music?"

"It's Robert. Billy says Robert has a criminal mind. He isn't even sure Marvin Pontiac exists."

"He's dead. Run over by a bus in Detroit."

"You know what I mean. You can never be sure where Robert's coming from." Carla showed her smile. "But you can't help liking him."

"You talk to him much?"

"He stops by the office to chat. He thinks you were up on the ladder when the guy was shot"—holding Dennis with her dark brown eyes—"and saw the whole thing."

"I came down, that's when I first met Robert."

"Were you?"

"What?"

"On the ladder when the guy was shot?"

Dennis hesitated.

She said, "You were, weren't you?"

He didn't answer because he didn't want to lie to her, but wasn't sure why. Because they were talking? Confiding?

She said, "One of the security guys told me about the story going around, that you were there."

"Why am I still here?"

"Robert said you were threatened."

"How would he know that?"

"I suppose he's guessing. He said, 'You know Dennis, the way he makes his living, ain't afraid of nothing.' " Carla doing Robert, and it was close. " 'But he ain't gonna mess with anybody shoots people they don't like.' "

"That wasn't bad."

"I do Charlie Hoke, Billy . . ." She cleared her throat and said, " 'I went to the top of the ladder today,' " in Billy Darwin's quiet, unhurried voice. " 'The next time I think I'll go off.' "

"I can hear him," Dennis said.

"And he's serious," Carla said. "He'll try it."

"He's crazy if he does."

"He said he'd jump."

"But doesn't know how to enter the water. He could break his legs."

"He'll do some kind of study," Carla said. "Billy never takes risks without checking it out first. I have to investigate the background of nearly everyone he hires. I looked into yours, Dennis. I wondered why you got married at such a young age."

"She was a very cute girl."

"But what?"

"People born and raised in New Orleans only move if they're forced to."

"And you didn't love her enough to stay."

"And get a regular job for the rest of my life, no. You check everybody out, huh?"

"Pretty much. Charlie was the most fun."

"You check on guests?"

"Some."

"What about Germano Mularoni?"

"And his lovely wife, Anne? Yes, I did."

"What does Germano do for a living?"

"He's a gangster. I thought you knew that."

It surprised Dennis that she said it though not to hear that he was.

"Detroit Mafia?"

"No, but that's rather murky. He was in prison once, for tax evasion."

Dennis said, "So Robert—"

"He works for Jerry, but that doesn't really tell you where he stands, does it? Take this battle reenactment coming up," Carla said, "why is Jerry on one side and Robert on the other?"

HECTOR DIAZ ARRIVED FROM DETROIT and Robert
and Tonto picked him up in Memphis. There he was coming out of
the jetway in a black suit buttoned up, Hector less primitive than
Tonto but not much. Hector was tall for being Mexican and liked to
pose in his sunglasses, the ring in his ear, his hair pulled back into a
pigtail, a *coleta* that was like a matador's. Hector, a long time ago,
had caped bulls in Mexico City but never made it to Spain; he was
older than Tonto by twenty years, somewhere in his late fifties. And
was tired now from sitting around Detroit Metro when the flight
was delayed. Robert told him to sit in the backseat of the Jaguar,
stretch out and take it easy.

On the road south Tonto gave Hector a Navy Colt cap-and-ball
pistol he got out of the glove box. Give him an idea of the kind of
weapons they would be playing with. Hector checked it out, spin-
ning the cylinder, thumbing back the hammer.

Robert said to the rearview mirror, "Be sure what you doing, man, it's loaded."

They picked up Jerry in front of the hotel after waiting close to an hour. Jerry came out in a black windbreaker and all four of them were in dark clothes—Robert in dark brown, Tonto in his denim jacket and a black bandanna—because Jerry said you always dressed dark you're going to confront somebody; you dress in light colors you looked like a fuckin twink. Tonto went in back with Hector to let Jerry ride in front. They got on Old 61 again, south, down to the Dubbs turnoff, left, and pulled into the lot in front of the club, Jerry saying, "This is it?"

Not impressed by this big run-down barn of a place, JUNEBUG'S painted to fit across the entire front where cars and pickups were angle-parked. "It's a honky-tonk," Robert said, "what Loretta Lynn sings about." He crept the Jaguar past an open spot and backed in to face out. Robert said to Hector, "Stay where you are, man, and rest. Know what I'm saying? You watching my auto."

It was after ten, the club the only lights out here in the country on a dark night.

They were out of the car now, Robert and Tonto slipping on their shades, Robert saying to Jerry, "They gonna be looking us over."

Jerry said, "Yeah . . . ?"

"Don't say to anybody the fuck you looking at, till we do our business."

"Say please and thank you," Jerry said, "and wash my hands after I take a piss. Come on."

Robert followed him inside, Tonto watching their backs: the three walking in to country swing coming from the sound system but no two-steppers out on the floor, Robert observing country dudes at the bar and some of the tables on this weeknight, not much of a crowd, a drum kit and speakers on the empty bandstand

straight ahead, only a few women among the beer drinkers, that little blond whore . . . Toni? No, Traci, talking to a dude at the end
of the bar that was to the left and ran all the way back. Robert followed Jerry toward the near end where a young dude stood resting
his back against the bar, elbows on the round edge, baseball cap
curved down around his eyes inspecting Jerry coming toward him,
the kid hanging in, but then bailed to give Jerry room, Jerry not
even looking at him. Jerry had his arm raised, calling to the bartender, "Hey, come here," to Wesley in his undershirt, maybe the
same one from the other night. Robert said, "Wesley, how you doing, man?" Wesley looking but not knowing shit who he was looking at. Jerry handed him a business card saying, "You don't have to
read it, Wesley. Give it to your boss." They watched him walk
down the bar with the card, looking at it again. Jerry said, "Fuckin
Wesley. Beautiful guy."

Robert imagined Arlen Novis somewhere in the back, maybe an
office, looking at the business card that said *Germano Industries,* and
smaller, *Manufactured Home Specialists,* a Detroit address and the
name at the bottom, *Caesare Germano.*

Jerry said, "You think he can read?"

"There he is," Robert said as Arlen came out of the doorway next
to the bandstand, "the one in the Confederate hat." Following him
was a dude with a build, short sleeves tight on his arms, the shirt
hanging out. "The other one I'm gonna say is Arlen's gun, Dennis
told me about, they call Fish."

Arlen was looking at the card again as he reached them. He said,
"Who's Ceezur German-o?" fucking up both parts of the name.
Robert thought of helping out, but Jerry stepped in.

Jerry telling him, "It's Che-za-ray," and Arlen, trying to understand what that meant, shook his head.

"Like Julius Caesar," Robert said to him. "Mr. Ger*man*o's name.

Call him Caesar, be close enough. He wants to talk some business with you."

"What kind of business?" The man suspicious.

"Why don't we sit down at a table," Robert said, "have Wesley bring us some cold drinks? Caesar likes rum and Coca-Cola, working for the Yankee dollah, as they say." Arlen looking at him, not knowing shit what he was talking about. But it got all five of them sitting around a table by the dance floor, away from people watching them, Jerry saying to Arlen, "You're at Southern Living, right?"

He said yeah? Still holding back.

"You do all right?"

"What is it you want to know?"

"You have building materials you don't need?"

"I'm head of security," Arlen said.

"That's why I'm talking to you," Jerry said. "I'm asking do you have anything you want to move, yes or no? I'll make you a good offer."

Robert watched him, the man tempted, thinking of what he could move in the dead of night—shit, a whole house, take the motherfucker apart—but was still suspicious.

Saying to Jerry, "You want to show me some ID?"

They were wasting time. Robert moved on him. He said, "Arlen?" in a quiet tone, almost soothing. "I know what you been up to, don't I? What we talked about in Vernice's kitchen? You got deals going you have to protect. The reason you had Junebug pop Floyd. The reason you had this man here—Fish, they call you?— pop Junebug for telling people your business. Arlen. Haven't I kept all this to myself, as I told you I would?"

Robert paused, giving Arlen, both of them, a chance to speak if they wanted to.

No, they both stared, Arlen looking cold but had to be wondering, shit, what was going *on* here? In his place of business, people around, Shania Twain belting out country.

"You have to trust *some*body, the kind of deals you must have going—and it ain't hard to speculate about that. I imagine, for instance, you run the drug business in Tunica County. I bought some fine weed here the other night and could've bought anything, Junebug going down the list—what do I need, crank, blow? All I had to do was name it. I understand why you popped him, the man was dangerous. But there always people you have to trust. You can lose all the Junebugs around as long as you have a man like Kirkbride with you. Am I right?"

Robert laid it out there to see what the name would bring and watched Arlen take his time before saying, "Well, he ain't a bad guy to work for." Shoved that aside and said to Jerry, "Who am I talking to here, Caesar, you or him?"

"What's the difference?" Jerry said. "You haven't said a fuckin word yet. I ask you about a Midnight Sale, what you can move, you don't say yes or no."

Arlen said, "If I'd been able to get a word in—"

And Robert cut him off. "Let's wait, Arlen. You got your mind on the reenactment. We're getting ready, too. We ain't about to move anything right now anyway." He said to Jerry, "Me and Arlen are in the same outfit, Forrest's Escort. We both gonna be shooting at you, man." Robert turned to Arlen again. "Caesar's going as General Grant. Can't miss him."

Jerry got into it with, "How you decide who wins?"

"Whoever won the real battle," Arlen said. "Brice's it was us."

Robert, one of Forrest's colored fellas, said, "That's right, man, *us*."

———

They left. Got in the car and drove off, Hector Diaz telling them a couple of guys came by and looked in the car.

Robert said, "They wake you up?"

"No, man, I was awake. I cocked the pistol and they left."

Jerry said to Robert, "You find out what you wanted to know?"

"I have to think on it," Robert said, "but I'm pretty sure, yeah."

He dropped the three off at the hotel and got back on Old 61 to Tunica, to Vernice's house.

It was late now, the house dark as Robert pulled up and parked in front. No, a light showed in the yard, he believed coming from the porch. Robert walked around to the side and there was Dennis on the porch by a lamp, reading. Robert scratched on the screen and watched Dennis jump. "Jes' me, man, the nightstalker."

They sat down and Robert said, "You learning anything?"

"Rap rivals Lil' Kim and Foxy Brown were involved in a shootout, in New York."

"The place to have it. My money's on Lil' Kim," Robert said, "even though she's chubbier than I like."

"One was going in a radio station," Dennis said, "when the other was coming out and their posses started shooting at each other."

"Nobody killed, huh?"

"One guy hit, a minor wound."

"They think they gangstas, the hangerons, the en-tou-ragers, shit. All they are's unemployed niggas. Ask me where I been."

"Where?"

"Junebug's. I took Jerry and Tonto to see the place and another one's joined us, Hector Diaz from Mexicantown in Detroit. Use to be a bullfighter."

"What's he do now?"

"What we all do, man, help Jerry develop land."

Dennis said, "Land or territories?"

Robert didn't speak for a moment, looking at him.

"You know what you talking about?"

"Carla says Jerry's a gangster. She said, 'I thought you knew that.' From my hanging around with you."

"Bad influence."

"You told me yourself you sold drugs."

"When I was a child."

"Young Boys, Incorporated," Dennis said. "I think you have your own young boys now, your own crew."

Robert was shaking his head. "Gangs, Dennis. You recruit the gang, walking around in their colors, nothing to do. They Young Dogs now I send on the road. Go to Fort Wayne, South Bend, Muncie, Kokomo. Was in the paper, two out of three dealers in Muncie, Indiana, are from Detroit. We move over to Ohio, set up Young Dogs in Lima, Dayton, Findlay. You ever hear that joke, the traveling salesman gets laid in Findlay, Ohio, and goes to confession?"

Dennis said, "And then gets laid in New York and goes? Yeah, I heard it."

"Canton, Ohio, man, there's a neighborhood there, projects, they call Little Detroit account of all the Young Dogs operating there. There's gangs from L.A. working into the same territories. It's how come you have your drive-bys. Mostly the trade is crack, 'cause you make more cooking and then cutting a hundred-dollar gram of coke into a hundred rocks you can sell for ten each. The Young Dogs go to a town, set up crack houses. It's like a franchise, Dennis, the McDonald's of drugs."

"What do the Dogs need you for?"

"The product, man. Where these kids gonna score it in quantity?"

"They could skim on the profits."

"I sell 'em the hamburger patties, the McNuggets. They sell it and come to me for more."

"Now you're looking at Tunica County? Working south, setting up your franchises?"

Robert said, "Dennis, you approaching your crossroads. You know what I'm saying? You come a long way, baby, and you almost there."

"Playing your stooge. I make your con game look legitimate. The con throws them off while you look into the drug business here."

"Having some fun with 'em. But listen," Robert said, "tonight I took Jerry and Tonto and Hector to Junebug's—"

"You took Tonto the other night."

"We didn't make it. Tonto saw a hooker in the hotel bar looked good to him. This is tonight, we sitting at a table talking to Arlen. Also the one you said was his shooter, Fish."

"Vernice said that."

"I accept her word," Robert said. "This young dude, the Fish, sits there, Tonto staring at him through his shades, Tonto seeing if the man would stare back. And he did, almost the whole time. You understand? The two of them getting on a personal basis. But see, what I wanted to know was if Arlen worked for Mr. Kirkbride or Mr. Kirkbride worked for Arlen."

Robert waited, giving Dennis time to think about it while bugs hit the screen going for the lamplight. All kinds of bugs making noise down here in the summer.

"You told me," Dennis said, "Kirkbride's a fool. I took that to mean harmless."

"It was a hasty call. See, then I got to thinking, this Arlen is too dumb to run an outfit. What's he do with all the money they make? I said to Arlen, we're sitting there—" Robert paused. "See, I had already fucked with the man's head, saying I knew he ran the Tunica drug business. I said to him, Junebug wasn't any loss, was he? Long as you had a man like Kirkbride with you."

"What'd he say?"

"Was what he didn't say. Mr. Kirkbride? You crazy? Any kind of shit like that. No, what he said, Kirkbride wasn't a bad guy to work for."

"He didn't get it. What you meant."

"He got it. I watched him. He skimmed over it and went to something else."

"You're telling me Walter Kirkbride's in the drug business?"

"Yes, I am."

"And you're gonna take over whatever they have going?"

"Yes, we are." Robert paused and said, "You ready?"

"For what?"

"You at the crossroads, Dennis. I'm about to make an offer to buy your soul."

Dennis said, "How much?"

And Robert beamed.

"You're my man, Dennis. Hundred and fifty thousand the first year, two hundred the second and so on. Plus what you make off your business. That's yours, too."

"What business?"

"The one we set up for you."

"I'm the front."

"You the Mr. Kirkbride of the deal. Look at him. Nobody knows what he's up to except one that knows one. You'd have the same deep cover. You the store that local business goes through. You take over Junebug's and clean it up, get rid of Wesley. Put a man in there wears a red vest, he's the seller. You're playing golf, you don't know shit what he's up to."

"I run a honky-tonk," Dennis said.

"You keep an eye on things. But your main business . . . You ready? You set up a traveling high-diving show, a big operation, Dennis Lenahan's Dive-O-Rama, bunch of young good-looking dudes, some cute girls that dive, but you're the name, World Champion Dennis Lenahan, been doing it twenty-two years."

"The diving show," Dennis said, "cleans the drug money."

"Distributes it here and there—that's something we'll get into later. Jerry wrote the book on how to do it."

"And went to jail."

"For not paying his taxes. He was into something else then, burning down buildings people wanted the insurance on. Jerry's good with high explosives, too. He put a man out of business was fuckin with his brother. I'll have to tell you about Jerry sometime."

"And the lovely Anne."

"You picked that up from Carla, didn't you? That Carla's as cool as Mr. Billy Darwin, you know it? I look at the two of them—they must have it going."

"They don't," Dennis said. "I asked her."

It brought Robert's smile. "You working in there? Never mind. But if you gonna be staying here and she's here . . . ?" He could see Dennis taking his time now, looking at the offer.

"I don't handle any product? Drive around with drugs under the seat?"

The man just got himself a car.

"What kind you want, Mercedes, Porsche? No, man, you never touch the product. Not directly. Tonto's the one gets it up from Mexico and Hector Diaz sees to where it goes. We get you a

Dive-O-Rama accountant to handle the business, keep the books. I imagine the same as Mr. Kirkbride, if he knows what he's doing."

"There's still risk," Dennis said.

Robert liked him saying that, the man leaning, looking for a way he could accept the offer. Robert answered him straight. "Sure there's risk. That's why I picked you out. You know all about high risk, it's your friend, it's what keeps you going. Soon as I saw you up there on the ladder, the other evening, I said to myself, that's my man. I didn't even need to speak to you, I knew it."

"You sound like you already have the business here."

"It's sitting there waiting on us."

"How do you take it away from the Dixie Mafia?"

"That's the fun part," Robert said. "Remember you asking—we just met, I'm driving you home and you ask me, being funny, if I'm checking out the historical points of interest? And I said history can work for you, you know how to use it."

"I don't get it."

"We using the battle reenactment to put the rednecks out of business. Draw the motherfuckers into the woods and shoot 'em."

"But you'll be with them, playing a Confederate."

"So I can be close," Robert said. "I'm the spotter. I point out which ones to shoot."

16

THEY HAD CHOSEN THIS ABANDONED farmland for the site and stood in the opening of a barn loft looking out at what would be the battlefield: John Rau, Walter Kirkbride and Charlie Hoke representing Billy Darwin, who couldn't make it: all three in shirtsleeves this sunny afternoon, at least ninety degrees out in that empty pasture.

Charlie listened to them deal with the weather first, Walter saying they'd sweat to death in their wool uniforms. John Rau saying it wouldn't be any hotter than it was June 10, 1864, at Brice's. Walter saying he would leave his longjohns at home if John Rau would and they'd keep it between them. John Rau said, "I didn't hear you say that, Walter." Charlie didn't own a pair of longjohns and kept it to himself. He saw Walter now gazing out at the pasture again.

"You think it looks like Brice's?"

"A big open field," John Rau said, "mostly, I believe, blackjack oak on one side, that old orchard on the other. Not as wide as Brice's but it'll do."

Walter said, "You don't know blackjack from a trash berry thicket and box elders. That's all that cover is, till you get toward the levee. It isn't nothing like Brice's. All you have is a field."

"In this case it's all we need," John Rau said. "Walter, you know it has to be in plain view of the spectators. They'll be down right in front of the barn where the ground slopes. We have a good two hundred yards out there to play with. You send your Third, Seventh and Eighth Kentucky Mounted Infantry out of the orchard over there and charge them straight across the pasture. I'm over in the thicket with the Seventh Indiana Cavalry and my own Second New Jersey shooting you down with our Spencers. You fall back and regroup and come at us again, and that's the Sunday-afternoon show."

Sounding to Charlie like they were going to actually refight the battle.

"We stop there," Walter said, "it looks like the Federals won at Brice's."

"Charlie will be making the announcements"—John Rau turning to him as he said it—"right?"

"Yes sir, I'll be happy to."

"And describe the action, who's who."

"I can do that."

"Charlie'll tell the crowd who won."

"I'll send skirmishers out first," Walter said, "and draw fire."

John Rau said, "Don't you have those fellas that like to take hits with canister?"

"Some of Arlen's bunch. Yeah, they practice all of 'em going down together."

"Best diers," Charlie said, "I ever saw."

John Rau said, "I hope that woman brings her cannon. I don't know her name. Wears the big straw, kinda fat?"

"*Kinda?*" Charlie said. "She's got a butt on her like a mule in a pair of bluejeans."

John Rau said, "She'd have to be Federal to keep it authentic. Forrest didn't have cannon to bring up till late in the day."

Charlie said, "Who's gonna know that?"

And got a stern look from John Rau saying, "Walter and I know it."

"When we did bring 'em up," Walter said, "we rode the limbers in close and raked you with grape."

Listen to him, like he was there. Charlie saw John Rau nodding.

"That young cannoneer—what was his name?"

"John Morton, my artillery commander, twenty-one years old."

Now John Rau was saying, "Did you know there was a woman fought at Brice's?"

"She the one went by Albert something?"

"Private Albert Cashier, Ninety-fifth Illinois, her real name was Jenny Hodges. Everyone thought she was a man," John Rau said, "till she was run over by a car in 1911."

Walter said, "It's too bad we can't put on a show in the thicket, along the Federal line there."

"The spectators wouldn't see anything."

"I know, but that's my favorite action in the battle. I send Tyree Bell's troopers charging in there firing their Colt Navies. John, they had extra cylinders capped and loaded in their pockets. More firepower'n even your Spencer repeaters."

John Rau said, "I did get hold of some Second New Jersey fellas, they're coming with their Spencers. I hope to have a couple of Illinois groups, the Eighty-first and One-oh-eighth Infantry. I talked to a fella may bring as many as fifty. He said, 'You want Ninth Kentucky or First Iowa?' They do it either way. I said, 'First Iowa, we're gonna need Yankees.' I told Billy Darwin about the Fifty-fifth and Fifty-ninth U.S. Colored Infantry. He said he'd dress as many of the hotel help as volunteers. And there's a fella staying at the hotel wants to be General Grant. Has never reenacted, though he does look like him."

"Grant wasn't at Brice's."

"Everybody knows that, Walter. I don't like it either, but you know people'll want to have their pictures taken with him. Is Lee coming—that fella always plays him?"

"I believe he died. I haven't seen him since Chickamauga. I got hold of the Seventh Tennessee and the Eighteenth Mississippi Cavalry. Some are coming, but hardly anybody's bringing horses. We let Billy Darwin rush us into this," Walter said. "We got started too late."

Charlie said to John Rau, "I recall you lost a horse at one of these."

"Yellow Tavern."

"I'll be astride King Philip," Walter said. "Parade around on my sorrel and let the kids pet him. I never feel so alive as when I'm Old Bedford."

Charlie said, "I hear Robert Taylor wants to be in your escort."

"If he'll feed and wipe down King Philip," Walter said, and then to John Rau, "Have you met this Robert Taylor? Colored fella from Detroit."

"Yeah, with General Grant." John Rau looking surprised. "I assumed he'd be a Yankee. Why's he want to wear gray?"

"He heard Forrest had colored fellas in his escort," Walter said. "He seemed to know what he was talking about, but he's slippery. I don't know what exactly to think about this Robert Taylor."

"Arlen met him," Charlie said. "He tell you?"

Now Walter looked surprised. He said no, and seemed ready to ask about it, but then John Rau was speaking.

"You know there were African Confederates. Not only slaves brought along by officers and put in uniform, but volunteers, too." He said to Walter, "Arlen's coming?"

"He wouldn't miss it."

"He will if he's in jail."

"For what, Floyd Showers? Everybody knows Junebug shot Floyd, and then one of Floyd's friends must've shot Junebug. It makes sense."

"Walter, do you actually believe Floyd Showers had a friend?"

"It's none of my business," Walter said. "What I'm concerned with is bringing off this event, making it work. How many you think we'll have altogether, counting women, children and dogs?"

"Our first muster?" John Rau said. "I'm hoping for as many as four hundred. Maybe fifty or so women and children dressed the part. Half-dressed anyway, little boys running around in kepis. I'm afraid the majority of the reenactors though will be UOs."

This was one Charlie hadn't heard of. "What're UOs?"

"Unorganized Others. We'll assign them regiments, so when you're telling the crowd who's who out in the field, they'll be accounted for. We'll do that Saturday morning."

Walter said, "How do we handle farbs?"

"With patience," John Rau said. "All we can do is point out the error of their ways. And I will be wearing longjohns, Walter." He looked at his watch saying, "I have to go," but lingered to mention the Porta-Johns were coming Friday afternoon, food vendors Saturday morning. Moving toward the ladder he said something about a sutler's store, drums and bugles . . . Walter behind him saying he'd wait for the crew coming to stake out the areas where the camps, the civilian tents and stores would set up, something about parking across the road . . . Charlie waited for them to go down the rickety ladder ahead of him.

Out in the barn lot John Rau was looking up at the weathered side of the old barn saying, "We'll have a banner up there, 'First Annual Tunica Muster' and so on." He turned to the farmhouse rotting away across the yard. "I wish we didn't have that eyesore." Walter said he'd have his crew clean up around it. Charlie said, "I'll see you," and walked over to his Cadillac.

By the time he'd turned out of the barn lot and was heading west on the county road, he saw in his mirror John Rau's maroon Buick Regal swing out of the lot behind him. Charlie was coming onto 61 when he saw a car approaching, a black one as it whipped past him and then past John Rau in the mirror, a black Jaguar—Robert Taylor heading toward the site.

Robert saw one car in the lot, some kind of big SUV, and Kirkbride shielding his eyes from the sun with his hand, watching him drive in. Robert got out and walked toward him noticing the man hadn't dyed his beard.

"Mr. Kirkbride, how you doing? I called your office, the young lady said you were out here."

The man stood there squinting in the sun.

"Hot enough for you?" Robert giving him white talk. "I sure hope it lets up some by the weekend. I was wondering, it rains, we postpone the battle or what?"

"It rained the entire week leading up to Brice's," Kirkbride said. "You don't mind getting wet, do you?"

Giving him some hardcore reenactor shit without answering the question. Robert said, "No, I like to get wet," and heard the rest of it, *you dumb fuck,* in his head. "I been out driving around the area, see what's over the other side of the woods. Not much, a farm road . . ."

"The levee road," Kirkbride said. "There's canebrakes back there, cottonwood and willow oak. It's too bad we have to keep the battle out in the open. I think it would be interesting, at least for the reenactors, to put on a fight in the woods."

Robert said, "They any snakes back there?"

"Cottonmouth's the poisonous one to look out for, the one you see the most of. The worst things are the ticks and the red bugs."

Robert said, "Ticks and red bugs."

"And mosquitoes," Kirkbride said. "Did you know Field Marshal Erwin Rommel, the Desert Fox, came here and studied this battle? Impressed by the way Old Bedford put it to the Yankees?"

"Yeah, I read that. But I wondered did either of 'em know Hannibal pulled the same kind of shit on the Romans back in the B.C.s. Jammed 'em in a pincer move till they were stumbling all over each other. With their spears and shit."

It didn't look as if Kirkbride knew it either, standing there squinting at him. He said, "I've got a crew coming."

Making it sound like reinforcements.

Robert wasn't sure what he meant and said, "I got one coming, too. Or I should say my buddy General Grant has, since we gonna be fighting against each other."

"I mean this afternoon," Kirkbride said, and looked toward the road. "They'll stake out the Union and Confederate camps and what'll be in other areas."

"Arlen coming?"

Kirkbride said, "I understand you two have met," still not answering questions.

"He tell you?"

"I believe was Charlie Hoke mentioned it."

"Yeah, I met Arlen the first time with Charlie and the diver, where they're staying. Then I brought General Grant out to Junebug's to meet him. He didn't tell you about it?"

"Why would he?"

"You know the man's a criminal to look at him, huh?"

Kirkbride only stared, not biting on that one, or interested in who General Grant was.

So Robert said, "I know it's hard to tell, gangstas down here not looking much like gangstas in the movies. You know what I'm saying? Your gangstas all have that Jimmy Dean country way about them." Robert zinged one in now saying, "I asked Arlen were you in business with him. He tried not to say but told me yeah, you were, whether he knows it or not." Robert paused to see what that would get him. Nothing. He said, "Mr. Kirkbride, am I going too fast for you?"

The man said, "Maybe if you told me what the hell you're talking about—"

"The drug business. All that shit you move through Junebug's into the countryside. You the drug czar of Tunica County, man. What surprises me is nobody seems to know it."

Now the man took his time, not saying shit as he walked toward him, Robert believing the man was thinking if he should explode with some Southron indignation. Like, did he know who he was speaking to? No, the man walked up till they were looking each other in the eye, the man doing all right so far, the way he was handling it.

Robert said, "You haven't dyed your beard."

And that threw him off some.

He regrouped and said, "No, I haven't, and I don't intend to."

"You playing Forrest, aren't you?"

"Yes, I am. But I don't want to dye my beard, so I'm not gonna dye it." Going with a tone of voice that was straight on, like he was his own man and had nothing to hide. He said, "You talked to Arlen about *me,* and you think you found out something?"

Like what would Arlen know.

"Ain't he head of your security?"

"That's all he is."

"I asked him did he want to sell any your materials, supplies, out the back door."

"My security man."

"That's the one you see. 'Specially one that makes a living as a criminal. Yeah, I believe he was ready to do business," Robert said, "but I was jes' messing with his head. See, I already knew he had Junebug do Floyd and then did Junebug himself or had somebody else do him, the consensus leaning toward the one you all call the Fish. See, Arlen knows I'm not gonna say nothing about it or use it on him, hold him up with it. I don't do that."

Kirkbride, eye to eye, said, "What makes you think he's involved?"

"Come on, man, everybody knows it. The CIB man knows it. He'd be deep into the case, hounding Arlen, it wasn't for the reenactment. Listen, by now he'd have talked to the hotel help and all the guests still around, check on anybody might've been looking out the window besides me. You realize I jes' missed seeing it by a minute or two? But we talking about John Rau now, the man so deep into this Civil War gig coming up he's already living it, can't wait. I bet you anything you want he wears his longjohns. He won't even cut the legs off. I'm told you can do that in the summer, it's okay. But to John Rau, man, that would be edging toward farbness. After, though, I expect he'll be back on the job. That is, if Arlen's still around."

Kirkbride jumped on it. "Still around—where else would he be?"

"I mean if he's still alive," Robert said. "Arlen has the kind of personality, there must be people would like to shoot him. You know what I'm saying?"

It wasn't a question the man was likely to answer, but Robert saw him looking at it.

"The point I'm making, Mr. Kirkbride, everybody knows he did Floyd and everybody knows he deals drugs. You go out to his store, that honky-tonk, and buy all you want."

"You been there, huh?"

Why did that stop him?

"Haven't you?"

"Not in a while."

"What I'm thinking," Robert said, "it must be easy to deal here. Pay off whoever you have to and go about your business. But it can't be easy for Arlen Novis 'cause Arlen's a nitwit, and that makes him dangerous. Somebody's directing him, else he'd be living high, driving around the country in a Rolls-Royce, have all kinds of federal people checking him out. He'd hide the money someplace, like under his bed."

He had Kirkbride listening, paying close attention, the man appearing almost to nod his head in agreement.

"See, first I ask myself, why would you hire a man everybody knows is a criminal to run your security? It must be you don't have nothing to say about it. Like Arlen's got some kind of hold on you. Stays close by so he can keep an eye on you. You're the front, you're—" Robert stopped, a lyric coming into his head, and he said it again, "You're the front . . . you're the Colosseum. You're the front, you're the Louvre Museum."

Robert kept his expression deadpan.

Now he had the man staring at him, mouth not quite open but almost. Robert believed he could fuck him up some more, tell Mr. Kirkbride he was the Nile, the Tower of Pisa. He was the smile, on the *Mona Lisa*.

But the man still wouldn't get it.

So he said, "What you do is hide the money for him. Put it to work." He said, "I'm telling you this for two reasons. One, so you'll know I know what you're doing. And two, so you'll be ready to make a decision when the time comes."

The man was doing all right, listening and keeping himself in control. He said, "You want to tell me what you're talking about?"

"Look at it," Robert said, "like you're coming to a crossroads and you know you have to make a turn. You don't decide quick enough, what happens? You end up in the ditch."

Robert stepped to his car and opened the door.

"I have to make a decision about what?"

The man wanting an answer. Robert turned to him.

"Where you want to be," Robert said, "when Arlen goes down."

17

AS SOON AS ROBERT GOT back to his suite he called room service and asked for Xavier. He waited, punched the remote to turn the TV on and said, "My man Xavier. *Dos margaritas.* Ten dollars for every minute you get 'em here under fifteen. You *sabe* what I'm saying? . . . Then go." He laid a fifty-dollar bill on the table and took a quick shower. Robert came out in the hotel robe to see two margaritas on the table and the fifty gone. Robert had Xavier going through his Basics with incentives, getting the waiter in the right frame of mind to deliver meals from the hotel to the campsite. There was no way they'd get Anne to cook. She had never in her life slept in a tent and knew she'd hate it. Jerry told her she was gonna sleep in the fuckin tent, so forget it. Robert didn't believe in sleeping in tents either; he believed people who camped out must be as serious as people who put on uniforms and became Civil War soldiers, and here these people were doing both.

He watched TV as he called Jerry's suite, knowing Anne would pick up.

"I have two ice-cold margaritas sitting here."

"He's taking a nap."

"I thought he was going down to roll the dice."

"He changed his mind. He'd rather play at night."

"Wake him up. Tell him that Australian, the one fucks with poisonous snakes, is on TV. Jerry likes that show."

"You ever wake him up?"

"Doesn't like it, huh?"

"Even when he wakes up himself, in the morning? You can't talk to him for a couple of hours."

"I'll come by later."

He watched the Aussie fuckin with the poisonous snake, his chin down on the ground talking to it in a nice tone of voice, the snake hissing, the snake trying to tell the man, get the fuck away from me, fool.

Robert could picture Anne right now looking down at Jerry sleeping with his mouth open, zoo noises coming from him, Anne wondering if what she got out of being his wife was worth it.

Jerry had picked her out of an auto show, Anne on the carousel with a car she said was all new from its high-concept styling to its heart-stopping performance, Anne dealing out adjectives with a dreamy smile. Robert was there. He watched Jerry walk up and ask the standard question auto show models got a hundred times a night, "Do you come with the car?" He did, and she said, "You can't afford me, with or without the car." She told Robert, after Jerry had put her into a high-rise on the Detroit River, "You're supposed to smile and act coy, but I knew this guy was real and I made the first move to get him. I thought he looked like a gangster."

Robert said to her that time, "Not many girls wish for a gangster and get one. You challenged the man and he stepped up."

Even dumped his wife, left her behind with three kids in college. It cost him, but must've been worth it. Germano attentive at first, acting like he was in love. Was he still in love? It was hard to tell with a gangster. Robert believed he loved her the way he loved a pair of good-looking alligator shoes he'd never let go of. Anne said, "Of course he loves me, don't you?" Saying it with the same high opinion of herself she had when she told Jerry he couldn't afford her, even though her modeling career hadn't left Detroit and there she was working an auto show.

Robert admired girls who were determined and worked hard on getting what they wanted. It didn't take nothing but a look to get her to slide over.

Anne's situation, once she had it, she didn't want it. But couldn't walk out on account of the prenuptial agreement gave her zero if she left during the first five years. But Jerry's personality was even more threatening than the agreement. Would he let her walk even if she decided to?

They were kidding around one time and she said to Robert, "But when Jerry dies, like if he got popped? Which could happen, right? That's different, I get what I deserve." Robert thinking that was a funny way to put it. She mentioned it another time in bed saying, "I worry about Jerry getting popped." Robert thinking, Women that worry about it don't say it that way. Robert having heard a number of women, not even counting his mother, express this kind of worry about him but using much softer words.

Still another time after being intimate and still bare naked, when she talked the most, Anne said, "Robert, I'm gonna be honest with you. If something happens to Jerry and we can be together? I won't ever marry you."

Like he'd ask her.

"How come?"

"I wouldn't be able to handle the racial thing."

Robert gave her his puzzled look that time. "Why? I can take you to black clubs, nobody'll say nothing. You'll be safe."

She said, "I don't mean *that.*"

See, she didn't get it.

Anne had style and was mostly with it, but not all the way on the same level of cool as he was. Those three-quarters of white girl in her held her back. Like being seen out in public with him would jeopardize her having passed. It was the reason she told Dennis she wasn't into having kids. Careful not to. A child with black features was to emerge, Jerry would throw both of them out on the street. Her dressing as a quadroon whore for the reenactment wasn't a risk. Robert saw it as showing off for him, something between them, no chance of Jerry catching on. Robert told her one time, "You want Jerry to let you go? Tell him your grandma was high yella." She told him he wasn't funny.

He wasn't trying to be. Robert looked at situations straight on, didn't color them in his mind or change his personality to meet the occasion. He liked to look around, believed he could get something going with Carla, but would have to meet her in New York. Carla, without you realizing it, would run you like a company and you wouldn't own yourself no more. He liked to grade women, see how they'd measure up as wives, but without seeing any need to ever marry. He didn't need kids. He was still a Young Boy.

Robert punched his way through channels with the remote and came to a movie he liked and could see anytime, *All That Jazz,* a behind-the-scenes movie, Robert's favorite kind, this one taking you backstage to show what putting on a musical was like, Roy

Scheider playing the choreographer based on Bob Fosse, Roy smoking all the way through the picture, smoking while a doctor examines him, has a heart attack and the cute nurse is in bed with him in the hospital, the man living every minute of his life till the way he's living kills him. Beautiful.

Watching the movie Robert twisted one to smoke along with Roy, and somewhere before it ended he fell asleep.

When he opened his eyes he clicked the set off, he sat low in the chair staring at the dark screen, staring for maybe a minute before he reached for the phone and called the hotel operator.

"Helene, how you doing? You know the number for Junebug's? I don't have a phone book, somebody stole it." He said, "I'd appreciate it, dear, thank you." He waited ten rings before a voice came on. "Wesley, how you doing? Listen, this is Robert. Is Walter Kirkbride there? . . . Well, can you take a peek, see if his car's in back?"

"He don't use his car," Wesley said, "he uses one of Arlen's."

"I forgot. Wesley, is it Traci he sees or the other one?"

"I think Traci. Yeah, the little bitty one."

"You see Walter, tell him I called, okay?"

Wesley said, "Who's this again?"

At nine, Robert got dressed and stepped two doors down the hall to Jerry's suite. Anne let him in and went in the bedroom. Jerry was standing in front of the TV watching a baseball game. He turned the set off saying, "Braves and the Cards—who gives a shit."

Robert said, "I talked to Kirkbride. Told him we know what he's doing."

"You're sure about this?"

"Five to one I'm right."

"You told him—what'd he say?"

"Nothing. But he listened. You know what I'm saying? The man listened to every word. Took it in. Almost seemed to nod his head like he was saying yeah, that's how it works."

Jerry had his hand on the doorknob.

"Can we use him?"

"Have to wait and see."

"For what?"

"My man Dennis."

Jerry shook his head as he opened the door.

Robert said, "Walter wants to stage a fight in the woods, dying to."

It caught Jerry before he could walk out.

"But we won't be able to do it and still have the spectators watching us. See, they did fight in the woods at Brice's Cross Roads and Walter likes to do it right, make it look authentic."

Jerry waited, holding the door open.

"Or he wants to get me and you and Dennis in the woods and take us out with nobody seeing it. I don't mean make it look like an accident. I told you, they inspect the weapons before you take the field. It can still happen—there was a man shot during a reenactment one time, but it was a strange situation, not one you can pull any time you want. So they'd have to set it up some other way, get us out of sight of the crowd, the people watching."

Jerry looked like he was thinking again, concentrating this time. He said, "You tell this guy what we know, him and the redneck, Arlen, and give 'em a reason to want to take us out."

Robert nodded, the man catching on.

"So instead of us thinking of a way to get *them* in the woods,"

Jerry said, "you have them thinking of how to get *us* in the fuckin woods."

"And chase us," Robert said, "all the way to a levee road back there—I checked it out—where we put the truck."

"I forgot about that part, the truck."

"Doesn't work without it, Jerry."

He looked like he was thinking again, but about what? It was hard to tell. All he did then was shrug. He said, "Okay," and raised his voice toward the bedroom. "Annabanana, I'm going now."

Robert wondered was she gonna come out to kiss him goodbye. Uh-unh. Her voice came back, "See you later."

"One other thing," Robert said. "The CIB man, John Rau? He lives for this reenacting. He's gonna be on your side, with you the whole time, and he won't leave till it's over. You hear what I'm saying? We don't want him anywhere near when we start shooting people. And we sure don't want to shoot *him*."

Jerry said, "Whack a cop—only if your life depends on it."

"We want him far away when it goes down."

Jerry said, "How do we work that?"

"I'll have to think about it."

Jerry said, "I'll leave it up to you," the way he left everything, and was gone to roll dice.

Robert glanced toward the bedroom as he walked to the balcony. He opened the doors and heard a woman's voice coming over the speakers, the TV woman, Diane—what was her name?—calling the dives again, Diane telling the crowd they'd have to clap real loud if they wanted world champion Dennis Lenahan to hear them way up on that eighty-foot perch.

There he was in the spotlight climbing to the top.

Robert moved to the railing to watch him: Dennis looking down at the crowd looking up at him, mostly white people from around here, small groups of teenagers, the older crowd in their lawn chairs. How many, a hundred? Close to it. Dennis deciding what to show them. Or thinking about his crossroads, way up there alone in the night. Thinking about money. Thinking about years to come and where he'd be. No, right now he was cool, he was haughty seeing himself in the air. Come on, flying reverse pike.

Anne's voice came from the bedroom. "What're you doing?"

"Watching my man."

"Are you coming?"

"In a minute. He's about to go off."

Every day honest people got into dealing drugs, it wasn't so unusual. Dennis wouldn't even be dealing, strictly speaking.

He had his arms raised, ready to go. Then lowered his arms and held on to the ladder with one hand as he leaned out and yelled down something and now Charlie was looking up at him. Now Charlie picked up a pole, the skimmer they took bugs out of the tank with, and mounted the ladder to the narrow walk that went around the tank and now Charlie was waving the skimmer over the surface of the water to make waves. Robert decided it was so Dennis could judge where he would enter the water, the man not taking any more risk than he had to. Good.

Anne's voice said, "Are you coming or not?" sounding closer.

He stepped toward the doorway, quick, to see her coming out of the bedroom in her kimono, open, nothing on under it. He thought, *The Open Kimono* by Seymour Hare, and said, "Wait. Don't move." And turned back in time to see Dennis go off twisting and somersaulting to slice the water and come up with his hair slicked back in the spotlight. Hey, shit. How'd he know to make all those moves in two seconds? Maybe even less.

He felt Anne's hand slip under his shirt and move up his spine.

He said, "I love to watch people who make what they do look easy. No flaws, nothing sticking out."

"God, I hope you're not queer for him. Are you?"

"No, I never tried that. Like I never tried the opera. Or never roller-skated. I've ice-skated and I've skied. Steve Allen says to Jose Jimenez standing there with a pair of skis, 'So, you're a skier. Is that right?' And Jose Jimenez says, 'Yes,' with his accent, 'I'm a skeer to go down the hill.' "

He felt her hand slide down his back and out from under his shirt. Her voice, off in the room now, said, "You want a glass of wine?"

"I'm trying to think . . . Yes, I would, please. I'm trying to think of what else I haven't done that people do. One comes to mind— haven't camped out."

Anne said, "So you've never gotten laid in a tent," coming out with a glass of white in each hand.

"I have other strange places."

"Movie theater?"

"Many times, in my youth."

"Airplane?"

"Once, on a red-eye. How about you? What's the strangest place you ever did it?"

"You mean straight fucking?"

"What else we talking about?"

"You don't count a blow job."

"*Blow* job, you get that anywhere."

She said, "Let me think . . . How about on the floor?"

"Everybody does it on the floor now and then. You think that's a strange place?"

She said, "I don't want to play this anymore."

Like that. Like when she and Jerry argued . . . Robert picking them up to go to some function, a wedding, and Jerry's yelling at her for never in her fuckin life being ready on time and Anne would say, "I don't want to talk about it." Jerry would look ready to smack her, but never did. He'd cool off and later on be calling her Queenie.

She said she didn't want to play anymore and Robert said, "That's cool," not caring one way or the other. He looked down at the crowd breaking up and Dennis, out of the tank now, talking to Diane Corrigan-Cochrane—that was her name—the Eyes and Ears of the North Delta, Robert thinking Dennis should have him some of that. Cute woman in her little shorts.

Anne said something.

"What?"

"I said is this going to work? What we're doing?"

"Gonna work fine."

"Jerry thinks you're crazy."

"He's told me that. But he's here."

She said, "I have a bad feeling about it."

Robert said, "Want me to hold you? Tell you everything's gonna be all right?"

"I'm serious, and you make fun of me."

He could tell her she was easy to make fun *of*, any time she became serious like that, having the bad feeling. But he didn't. No, he showed her he was as sensitive as he had to be, saying, "What's wrong, baby? What you worried about?"

"I keep thinking," Anne said, "something's going to happen to Jerry."

What she meant was *hoping*. Robert said, "Like he could get popped?"

"It's possible, isn't it?"

"You play the grieving widow till the lawyer cuts you a check?"

"You're not funny."

"Wear a black thong bikini around the pool?"

She walked away from him.

Robert said after her, "My sensitivity stretches so far and it snaps back on me."

Dennis asked the TV lady if she'd have a drink with him, the least he could do, telling Diane she was the best dive-caller he'd ever had, and the best-looking—as she followed him around behind the tank. He said he had to change first and she said, "Go ahead, I won't look." He watched her bend her head back to gaze straight up the ladder, then at the ground beneath the scaffolding where Floyd was shot, and then at him as he stood naked stepping into his underwear.

"I thought you weren't gonna look."

She said, "I lied."

They brought chairs from the patio bar out to the edge of the lawn, away from loud voices, a party going on, and sat next to each other with summer drinks, in the dark, Dennis' gaze on his ladder that rose against the sky and stopped, not going anywhere.

Her voice, close to him, quiet, said, "How long have you been hauling it around?"

"Four years."

"Are you tired of it?"

"I'm getting there."

"Then what?"

"I don't know."

"Where're you staying?"

He turned his head to see the soft expression in her eyes, waiting.

"I have a landlady who stays up late."

"You want to go to Memphis?"

"Is that where you live?"

She nodded. "After I do the news?"

He said, "There's nothing I'd rather do than go to Memphis," and let it hang.

She said, "But there's a lot you have to think about."

"If I told you, you wouldn't believe it."

She said, "You were on the ladder that night, weren't you?"

He nodded, their eyes still holding.

"Arlen and the Bug?"

He nodded again.

She looked away, toward the ladder, before turning to him again. "I don't understand. Why you're telling me now."

"I don't know either. You asked. . . . If you hadn't I probably wouldn't have said anything."

"You needed to tell somebody."

"Who doesn't know? It's not like getting something off my chest and now I feel better. But you're the one to tell—maybe that's it— the TV lady, if I'm gonna tell anybody. Outside of a lawyer. But don't put it on the air yet, I won't admit it. You have to wait."

"Until what happens?"

"Till you see how it ends."

"What do you think will happen?"

"I haven't any idea."

It was only a few minutes later Robert showed up.

He said, "You all like to be alone?"

In that moment Dennis had to make up his mind. If he said yes, they'd like to be alone, he risked Diane bugging him until he told her everything that was going on. But if he said no, they wouldn't, he might never get to Memphis. All that in his mind when Diane said she had to go get ready for the eleven o'clock news. So Dennis said he was tired, he'd find Charlie and go on home. Robert said he'd drive him, but why didn't they relax and have a drink first. "There's something I want to tell you."

Now Dennis sat staring at the ladder with another vodka collins and Robert instead of Diane.

"You haven't made up your mind yet, have you?"

"To sell my soul? No, I haven't."

"You can't beat the deal."

"I don't have any offers to compare it to."

"There's poverty. What you gonna do when you can't dive no more? Listen, I'll answer any your questions and I'll be honest with you. What we in is a dirty business, but it's where the money's at. I want you in so I'm upping the pay schedule. Two-fifty the first year. Five the second. We jump now like Regis does on his show to one million the third year. Also bonuses, also what you make off your Dive-O-Rama. Wuz wrong with that?" Robert grinned and sipped his drink. "How Miles Davis says it. 'Wuz wrong with that?' In his voice."

"What about Jerry?"

"Yeah, what?"

"What's he do? You said he use to be into arson."

"And high explosives, he learned about in the Nam. Jerry shipped home a footlocker full of C4 when he got out and was in business."

"With the Mafia?"

"Detroit, they call it the Outfit. Jerry did some work for them till they got involved with his brother. Two of the Outfit dudes wanted a cut of the land development business, the manufactured homes? The next time they went to see Jerry's brother, they come out of the office, get in their car and it blows up. From then on Jerry had an understanding with the wiseguys. Leave him and his brother alone and he won't blow up any more their cars."

"How'd he get away with it?"

"Jerry's a hard-on, doesn't give an inch. Also he was related, like a second cousin, to the guy running the Outfit at the time. One of those blood things where they have to get along. The way I met him," Robert said, "I'm running Young Dogs and there's a rival gang, the Cash Flow Posse, giving us trouble. I hire Jerry—this was back ten years—to throw some pipe bombs in their crack houses. Worked better than a drive-by, it put 'em out of business. So then I bring Jerry in as the muscle. You know what I'm saying? The enforcer, keep the Young Dogs in line, thinking straight. Pretty soon we partners. Then he steps up another level saying he's the boss, gonna run the show. He's the five-hundred-pound gorilla and what am I gonna fuckin do about it? But I owed him, 'cause he set up how to maintain the money, ways he learned from his brother to keep it away from the tax people. He did take a fall, went to Milan for a couple of years and that's where he got his master's degree. Learned from the big boys, the Wall Street types, how to hide money without leaving tracks."

Dennis said, "That's why he's the boss?"

"He's the boss 'cause he says he is."

"You're smarter than he is."

"I know that."

"Does he?"

"Yeah, he knows it."

"It must piss him off."

"Uh-unh, 'cause he knows he can beat me up."

"But he needs you to run things."

"Yes, he does."

"Do you need him?"

"We all answer to a higher power, Dennis."

"One that blows up cars and makes pipe bombs?"

"That kind you answer on the double."

"What're you telling me?"

"I'm not around, watch out for him."

SATURDAY MORNING DENNIS GOT UP at seven-thirty.
He put on his corporal's uniform—Vernice had sewed the chevrons
on for him, the bugle insignia on the kepi—set the cap straight over
his eyes, and looked at himself this way and that in the full-length
mirror on the closet door. He said to himself, Is that you?

He said, The hell are you getting into?

He said, Nothing. I'm not.

He said, But it could work, couldn't it?

He saw in the mirror the impression of a Union soldier 140 years
ago while his mind played with Robert's proposal. He would put it
out of his mind. There, I'm not doing it. But it kept coming up again
and again. The idea that it could work: he could run an international
diving show that as far as he was concerned had nothing to do with
the sale of drugs. Or, was related to it, but in a very minor way.
Robert had asked him what was the problem.

"You can smoke it but can't sell it?"

"I don't do cocaine, any of that other stuff."

Robert said he didn't either. Robert said, "We don't force anybody to use it."

"You get them hooked."

"They get themselves hooked. Like alcoholics who can't drink without making a mess."

"Come on—it's against the law."

"So was booze at one time. Nobody stopped drinking."

"You can go to prison."

"You can go off the ladder wrong and break your back."

There were ways to look at it and it was okay. He'd be doing something with his life. He'd be offering steady jobs to high divers looking for gigs. He could help out his mother, seventy-two years old, living in a dump on Magazine Street with his sister the alcoholic, a disease inherited from their dad, who drank till he died of it. He could get his mom a house out in the Garden District. Look at all the good he could do. Spread it around. Help the needy.

Pay off his conscience.

Shit.

He told himself he had made up his mind, so forget it. Don't think about it anymore. He went out to the kitchen.

Charlie, wearing one of his LET'S SEE YOUR ARM T-shirts, was having toast and a cup of coffee.

Dennis said, "I thought we were going early."

"A reenactment being put on for the first time," Charlie said, "on a location never used for it before, you get there anytime before noon, or even a little after, you're early. You want to be put to work driving tent stakes? I do my bit later on this afternoon, make announcements, then tomorrow I tell what's going on when they do the battle."

"Who asked you?"

"The committee, who you think?"

"They want to hear baseball stories?"

"I've been reenacting nine years, Dennis, I know what it's about. Doing a battle play-by-play isn't like calling dives." He said, "Step back, lemme look at you," and began nodding his head. "You'll pass muster, you look good. How the shoes feel?"

"Stiff, but they're okay."

"You said the other night they were tight on you."

"I put on lighter socks."

"You can pull the socks up over the bottom of your pants if you want. Some argue whether blousing is authentic or not. You'll hear serious discussions about such things. Are your buttonholes hand-stitched? They say if you're Confederate you don't have to be so goddamn hardcore. Somebody else says they were as GI as any Federal troops. You know what, though? They say most girls go for farbs, guys who don't give a shit."

Vernice came in ready for work in her fringed cocktail waitress uniform, the feather sticking straight up behind her head. She said, "Well, look at my soldier boy. Honey, don't get hurt, okay?"

Charlie said, "You know how many was killed in that war, both sides? Six hundred twenty thousand."

"I'm coming out after I get off," Vernice said. "Have to serve the early crowd their Bloody Marys. What's on later, the battle?"

"This afternoon you can watch 'em drill," Charlie said. "If there's a skirmish they didn't tell me. There's a ladies' tea if you're dressed for it, period dance instructions and tonight a military ball."

"You're kidding," Vernice said.

"I make an announcement that cavalrymen are to remove their spurs."

"What's on tomorrow?"

"Period church service, some more marching, a pie-baking contest, and the Battle of Brice's Cross Roads."

"I may wait for tomorrow," Vernice said. "It's gonna be hot out." She turned to Dennis again. "You look so cute in your uniform. You gonna camp out or come home tonight?"

Dennis said he hadn't made up his mind. "I'll have to see how it goes."

"I don't sleep outside," Charlie said. "I don't eat sowbelly either. I asked Vernice how in the hell you make hardtack. She said buy some rolls and let 'em sit out on the counter a few days."

"I'm going," Vernice said, but then picked up the latest *Enquirer* from the counter. "Another reason Tom might've dumped Nicole? She's so full of herself. It says she'd go in a Ben and Jerry's for an ice-cream cone and walk right up to the front of the line."

Charlie said, "And I bet nobody cared, either. You're a movie star, you don't have to stand in line." He looked at Dennis. "You stand in line?"

"I see a line," Dennis said, "I keep walking."

Charlie said, "I can't think of the last time I stood in line."

Vernice dropped the *Enquirer* on the breakfast table. She said, "I'll see you movie stars later," and left.

Dennis had an egg and onion sandwich while Charlie was getting dressed. When he came in the kitchen again he was wearing a black slouch hat and a uniform John Rau had given him and Vernice had let out. Charlie still talking.

"You know what Arlen's people will be doing at this thing? Drinking. I never was at a reenactment with 'em they didn't get smashed. Then what'd they do is take a hit early in the skirmish, preferably in the shade, else they'd crawl to a tree and snooze till it's over. You watch 'em. They put a lot into dying, making it look real. You want to stop and get some breakfast?"

"I just had a sandwich."

"I mean some real breakfast."

"We got us a good crowd," Charlie said, steering his Cadillac past a quarter mile of cars and pickups parked along both sides of the county road. The field across from the farm property, reserved for reenactors, was full of cars, trucks, motor homes, even a few horse trailers. They turned into the barn lot, reserved for VIP parking, and stopped so Charlie could show his pass to the security people. Dennis spotted Robert Taylor's Jaguar in a row of cars by the barn and said to Charlie, "Look who's a VIP."

Charlie said, "Wouldn't you know," and asked Dennis if he was registered.

"I didn't know I had to."

Charlie said, "Go on over to that table sitting just inside the barn. Give the girl ten bucks and you're a reenactor, you can sleep outside with the bugs tonight." He told Dennis the battlefield was on the other side of the barn, the military camps over there on opposite sides of the field. It was north. The civilian campsites and stores were over there to the east. He said, "Start that way to look around and you'll be back in Civil War times before you know it." Charlie would catch up with him later; he had to hang around, find out when he'd be making announcements.

Dennis walked off among spectators and reenactors arriving, a Confederate shouldering a musket asking him who he was with and Dennis told him the Second New Jersey Mounted Infantry, and felt himself beginning to play the part. He came to a row of food vendors along the edge of the barn lot, the sides of their cooking trailers open to offer fried chicken, catfish, hot dogs and hamburgers, different kinds of sausage, popcorn, soft drinks. He came to a row of blue portable toilets and was approaching tent stores now and the civilian campsites, grouped about to form a semblance of streets in the shade of old, shaggy oaks. He began to see more uniforms, mostly Confederate, a grungy-looking bunch in mismatched uniforms, different shades of gray, a few wearing kepis but most of them favoring slouch hats, some black ones, no shape to them. They stood around talking, their rifles in several tepeed stacks. One of them called to him, "Hey, Yank, who you with?" and it gave Dennis kind of a thrill. That's what he was, a Yank, and told them Second New Jersey as he walked past.

He came to a sutler's tent, a big one with the front flaps tied back, a military store that offered uniforms and arms and everything that went with them, insignia, belts, cartridge boxes, canteens, a sign that offered BLACK POWDER RELOADING SUPPLIES. Next to the sutler's place was a tent store that sold Confederate battle flags and bumper stickers, statuettes of Jefferson Davis and the more famous Confederate generals; Robert E. Lee and Stonewall Jackson salt and pepper shakers. There was a photographer's tent with backgrounds to choose from, flags, cannon, palm trees. And a shelter tent with a sign that said ENLIST NOW! FIFTH TEXAS VOL. INF. CO. E, DIXIE BLUES.

Union soldiers were wheeling a cannon through the shaggy oaks.

Dennis came to Diane, the TV lady, and her crew interviewing a couple in mid-nineteenth-century civilian dress: the woman holding a parasol that matched her light-blue dress with its hoopskirt; she wore a little peaked hat with a snood, and sunglasses; the man with a cane, white gloves and tall beaver hat. They played their part with dignity, walking around the grounds, stopping to be photographed, interviewed, Dennis wondering why they went to the trouble. He could listen to the interview and maybe find out. Hang around and talk to Diane. He decided to catch up with her later and moved on.

He saw drummer boys in gray kepis and remembered Robert

talking about the one at Battery Robinett who picked up a pistol and shot the Rebel officer. He could not imagine kids this age, twelve years old, in combat. But they were. He saw a squad of Union soldiers, all in the same dark blue except for the three in Zouave uniforms, the red fez and the blousy red trousers tucked into pure-white puttees. He'd have to ask John Rau about Zouaves. Or Robert, who knew everything. Where was he?

Dennis came to the civilian campsites, a street of wall tents with awnings, canvas chairs sitting in front by grills set up with cooking irons, coffeepots hanging from the crossbars over the fires. There were camp tables of utensils, tinware, tin candle lanterns, wooden buckets, the women all in long skirts and aprons, some with hoops underneath, some wearing sunbonnets, Dennis again wondering why they would go to all the trouble. Unpack all this stuff, lay it out for two days, pack it up again and go home.

He saw the women as womenfolk off farms or from small towns doing chores and having a good time with each other, enjoying what they were doing. He came to a woman rolling out dough on a camp table: dark-haired, her face drawn, no makeup but nice-looking, thin compared to most of them.

"What're you making?"

Her head raised and she took time to look at him.

"Naughty Child Pie."

"Yeah? What's in it?"

She said, "Green tomatoes," picking up her apron to wipe her hands.

"Why's it called Naughty Child?"

"You find out, let me know. I never made one before."

Dennis started to ask her why, if this was her first try at it . . .

She told him it was her husband's favorite, the woman bringing a pack of cigarettes and lighter from the pocket of her apron. "His ex-wife use to win all the big pie-making contests with Naughty Child. Till she left him."

"He's hardcore, huh?"

"To the bone." She lit a cigarette and looked at him again. "Brand-new uniform—this must be your first muster."

"First and last."

She said, "Mine, too. I'm Loretta."

"I'm Dennis. Who's your husband with?"

"Seventh Tennessee."

"Does he like to sleep out in the field?"

"Loves it. He prays for rain so he can have the experience. Do you sleep out?"

"I haven't yet."

She said, "Stop by tonight, I may have a piece of Naughty Child for you."

He found General Grant's headquarters, three wall tents with awnings in the shade, Jerry sitting in a striped canvas beach chair smoking a cigar. He was in shirtsleeves but wore his general's hat with the gold braid. Standing near him were Tonto and a Latin-looking guy Dennis believed would be Hector Diaz, and two black guys he'd never seen before, all in Federal blue.

Dennis walked up to Germano Mularoni feeling for the first time in his life an urge to salute, and he did, he saluted.

Jerry said, "Jesus Christ, you too? I've worn out my arm saluting. These people I never fuckin saw before in my life, they come by throwing me salutes. Where's Robert?"

"I just got here," Dennis said.

The one he believed was Hector Diaz said, "There," looking off. "He's with Missus. By those guys out there. Now they coming."

A group of mangy-looking Confederates, seven of them, were standing out in the open in sunlight with their rifles, some with their arms resting on the upright muzzles, all watching Robert and Anne walking away from them.

Robert in gray, Anne in black, the skirt, the shirt unbuttoned in front, her streaked hair coming out of a red bandanna. She wore sunglasses. And now Dennis saw a Colt pistol holstered on her hip. They were closer now, Robert showing a checkered shirt under his open shell jacket. He was holding a cavalry saber, now and again swiping at clumps of brush with it. Walking up to them he said, "Hey, my man Dennis, you made it. I was afraid maybe you deserted and we have to hunt you down and shoot you."

Jerry said, "Where you been?"

"I saw those Johnnies going by, I wanted to know was Arlen with them. The Fish was there but no Arlen. Me and Annabanana are being sociable till this one says to me, 'Who's you-all's hero, Martin Luther Coon?' This primitive one with tobacco juice in his beard. I said, 'No, my hero's Muhammad Ali, asshole.' He wants to know what did I just say? So I had to repeat it. 'Muhammad Ali, asshole. You don't hear so good?' Then he says he's gonna take my head off."

"And stick it up your black ass," Anne said.

"That's right, he did. I said to him, 'You talk like that to a man has a sword in his hand? You want to fuck with me, take it up with my buddy General Kirkbride.' "

"He did," Anne said, "really. I had my hand on my gun the whole time."

Jerry said, "What'd you give her a gun for?"

"Let her bust some caps, see what it's like."

Jerry said, "Queenie, put it away. You're gonna shoot somebody."

Anne said, "It goes with my impression."

Jerry said, "I never knew any hookers that packed," and looked
at Robert. "Have you?"

"Yeah, I have," Robert said. "Long time ago." He looked up at
Dennis with a grin and said, "Dog, say hello to Hector Diaz, man
with the *coleta*. You know Tonto Rey. That's Cedric, from the fields
of Virginia come to be with us, and the cool one there is my man
Groove, from the Motor City."

They gave each other a nod and Dennis said well, he was going
to move along, see you later. He started off through the trees, heading for the battlefield, and Robert caught up with him.

"You having fun?"

"It's like a county fair without the rides."

"I got weed, you want to pick up your mood. Me and Annabanana slipped away from the general to share a joint. She come
back with Chinese eyes, the man's too lazy to notice."

"Jerry doesn't do any drugs?"

"Sticks to his red wine, the Sicilian in him."

"How'd you get a VIP parking spot?"

"The Jag-u-ar, man. General Grant in the front seat and one of
those little American flags taped onto the fender. Pulled in there like
it was the official car. The security man saluted."

"I did too when I saw him."

"Everybody does. Jerry's a show and don't know it." He touched
Dennis' arm and said, "Wait up."

They were on the crest of a slope that fell gradually to what
would be the battlefield.

"We got lunch coming from the hotel pretty soon. My man
Xavier bringing it disguised, in tin pots."

"I want to find my camp," Dennis said. "Report to John Rau and
get that done."

"You into it, aren't you? Going around saluting—I'd like to see that. Well, you get hungry come on back."

"I'm surprised," Dennis said, "Jerry came out."

"He might not last. I told him, 'Man, you have to be seen, so people will think you're all the way into the gig.' That's his cover, being out front, serious, loving it."

"Who're the new guys?"

"The tall one, Groove, came out of Young Boys about when I did, known him all my life. Groove's gonna stay here and do the buying. On the side he'll see to making Ecstasy for the lovers, the E-tards, and find somebody knows how to make speed without blowing himself up. Cedric I found in my travels to Virginia. Knows the business, did his apprentice work under a man sold weed out of a church in Cincinnati called Temple of the Cool and Beautiful J.C. A skinhead Nazi come along and blew it up with a rocket gun. You imagine? I lined Cedric up, he's gonna deliver a chronic type of dojo weed once we set up."

Dennis said, "Tonto and Hector?"

"Old pros. They stay close to Jerry for the time being, their Colt guns capped and loaded. Case Arlen pulls any sneaky shit in the night."

"So Arlen thinks Jerry's the boss."

He could see Robert caught what he meant.

"Yes, he does."

"If he can scare off Jerry you and your guys will go with him."

"He calls Jerry Caesar. I told him like in Julius."

"Why'd you antagonize Arlen's guy, call him an asshole?"

" 'Cause that's what he is. 'Cause I had a big fuckin sword in my hand."

"Come on—"

"I want him coming after me once we in the woods. Get him riled. You gonna be with us?"

"Is that part of the deal?"

"Noooo, man, do what you want is cool. Hang out with the county fair people, learn the period dances. You notice what I told you, everybody being so serious? Hey, maybe they'll let you judge the pie-making contest."

"I met a woman was making one," Dennis said, "rolling out the dough . . . Only she doesn't know what she's doing here."

It caused Robert to pause, looking at Dennis to catch on to what he meant.

"What kind of pie?"

"Naughty Child."

"You're kidding me. They call it that?"

"Has green tomatoes in it."

Robert paused again.

"You gonna have a piece?"

"I might."

DENNIS CROSSED THE SLOPE WHERE the spectators
would sit to watch the battle, no one else out here yet. He reached
the pasture, headed for the thicket over to the left, and saw he'd have
to watch his step as he moved through the coarse grass, the ground
underneath broken and rutted, years of grazing cows leaving their
marks. Man, but it was hot in the wool uniform, the sun still high.
There was a crackling sound and a voice over the PA system.

"Four score and seven years ago . . . Wait a minute, somebody
gave me the wrong speech."

There was no mistaking Charlie Hoke. Dennis continued toward
the edge of the field as Charlie said, "Here we go. Hi, I'm Charlie
Hoke, the old left-hander, welcoming you to the First Annual Tunica, Mississippi, Civil War Muster. What it reminds me of, folks, is
opening day at the old ballpark. Any park, there's nothing like
opening day." He said, "What?" His voice sounding faint then,

away from the mike, and Dennis heard him say, "I'm coming to it." Charlie's full voice returned to say, "You all are taking part in a living history, commemorating a period of our heritage that united us once and for all as Americans."

And a Union soldier stepped out of the thicket in front of Dennis, a young guy no more than eighteen, holding his rifle at port arms. He said, "Identify yourself, name and regiment." Dennis told him, and the sentry said, "Pass." Man, dead serious.

Dennis walked by him into the thicket, the ground sandy now. He could still hear Charlie's voice as he made his way through the growth. About fifty yards into it he came to the camp: two-man tents in a clearing, stacked rifles, Union soldiers in and out of uniform, most of them with their shell jackets off, but all wearing their forage caps, a look of seasoned campaigners, a couple of them smoking pipes. He heard Charlie's voice saying they were reliving the past today in the present, and it was what Dennis felt and knew he would remember, passing through the scrub to find himself 140 years back in time.

Except for the pickup truck.

An old one, but not nearly old enough.

A group of twenty or more soldiers, apart from the ones he saw first, were looking up at John Rau, who stood in full uniform on the tailgate of the pickup, the truck bed loaded with cardboard cartons, a 55-gallon wooden barrel and what looked like a pile of shelter halves and bedrolls.

John Rau was saying, "I'm not going to make an issue of authenticity, criticize trifles, the way your uniform happens to be made. Point out that the top stitching on the fly of someone's trousers is too wide."

Sounding like he was making a speech, all the soldiers in front of him looking up, paying attention.

"Take it too far," John Rau said, "the ultra-hardcores will next be insisting we use real bullets and hope that some of us take actual hits, or at least come down with dysentery. Obviously in a reenactment we will never experience the sheer terror of actual combat. We won't see our pards drilled by minié balls and blown to pieces by canister. So let's not make too much of authenticity. But, I do not want to see evidence of candy-bar wrappers or empty soda-pop cans lying around this bivouac. That's the one thing I insist on."

Dennis moved in to stand closer to the group and John Rau spotted him, Colonel John Rau looking cool, right out of the book in his cavalry officer's uniform, the brim of his hat pinned up on one side. Dennis, about to nod and say hi, stopped as John Rau said, "Soldier, where's your rifle?" No sign of recognition there.

Robert had the guns. Dennis almost said he forgot to get it, but changed it quick to, "I haven't picked it up yet."

Colonel Rau said, "Do you mean, '*Sir*, I haven't picked it up yet?'"

Dennis said, "Yes, sir."

"Why haven't you?"

Jesus, he was serious. Dennis said, "I was anxious to report to the camp. Sir."

"This is a bivouac, soldier, not a camp."

"Yes sir."

"The next time I see you, you will have your rifle. I will never see you again with*out* your rifle. Unless of course it's stacked, as it should be."

Dennis said it again, "Yes sir," getting a feeling for it, like watching a war movie he was in.

John Rau turned to his audience, looking over his troopers before saying, "My first sergeant will see to the issue of rations for two days, courtesy of the Tishomingo Lodge and Casino. I'm sure it's their hope that once we stand down, you'll go over there and lay your money on the gaming tables. Do any of you know what the pay of a private in the Union Army was during the Civil War?"

A voice from the troops said, "Sir, thirteen dollars a month, *sir*."

Dennis wondered if the guy was overdoing it.

"That's correct," John Rau said. "Now then, I want this truck off-loaded so we can get it out of here and settle into a proper bivouac. We have extra shelter halves here and bedrolls consisting of a gum blanket and a wool blanket, all any soldier needs on a summer campaign. It won't be nearly cool enough for any spooning, so I don't expect to see any evidence of it, as I might get the wrong idea."

John Rau smiled and it got a laugh, but Dennis didn't know why.

"Your food rations, here in these boxes, are the authentic fare: hardtack, coffee and salt horse. Also potatoes, cornmeal if you want it—mixed into a gruel and fried can be very tasty—and dried fruit. What's commonly referred to as salt horse is, more often than not, salt pork—though fresh horse meat would have been a gourmet treat to a man in the field during the war. Nor am I referring to the salt pork you buy in the market, a hunk of bacon. That wouldn't hold up even for a reenactment weekend."

Dennis noticed men in the group beginning to stir and glance at one another as John Rau, not sounding much like the CIB man, continued.

"I know you first- and second-timers are anxious to learn all you can about what it was like, have it in your head. I've often said an authentic attitude is more important than how regulation you are in your uniform. On this subject of salt pork I might mention that table salt is never used for curing because of the filler in it. You use kosher salt as your base and cut it with a sweetener. I prefer brown sugar myself, though you can use honey or molasses. To spice it up add onions, garlic and pepper. But the main ingredients, say for a hundred pounds of meat, would be eight pounds of kosher salt and two pounds of brown sugar. What the process does, of course, is thoroughly dry out the meat. Let it sit in a cool place—the reason farmers always butchered in the winter—for up to six weeks and you've got salt horse. I'll warn anyone who wants to try preparing it himself, it does make quite a mess as the moisture is drawn out."

Dennis, listening, thinking yeah, that was good to know, in case he ever lost his fuckin mind and felt the urge to make some. Jesus. Ask Vernice if he could use her kitchen. He saw some of the troopers in the back of the group starting to edge away and heard John Rau raise his voice.

"Men, eyes front. I'm not yet finished. We have a water barrel here, so you can keep your canteens filled. Also, you'll be interested to know, I ordered six hundred and fifty rations to feed a hundred men, my original estimate, and any stragglers who might come along. If this were a three- or four-day event and we took prisoners, we'd have rations for them, too. My projection now is that we'll have no more than seventy in our ranks, if that. I was hoping for as many as fifty of the First Iowa joining us, but it looks like only ten to fifteen will be able to make it. I'm expecting them at any time now. What it means, there will be at least three and a half extra rations per man." John Rau paused. "If I had said that to you at Brice's Cross Roads on June 9th, the eve of the battle, you know what you'd do? Give out a cheer, a spirited 'Huzzah,' and throw your forage caps in the air. Anyway, you'll be able to eat your fill. You might see how inventive you can be with the rations. I've always liked my salt horse diced and put in a pot to boil with a potato. I've found that recipe works best when you're good and hungry."

Dennis tried to imagine pieces of pork fat cooking in a pot and remembered Robert asking him to lunch, brought from the hotel.

He looked up again to see the first sergeant handing John Rau a clipboard, Colonel Rau looking at it as he said, "I have the duty roster here. Anyone who hasn't been assigned, raise your hand."

Dennis, not knowing shit about duty rosters, raised his. In the next moment, as John Rau looked right at him, Dennis realized you never put your hand in the air.

"Private Lenahan," John Rau said, glancing at the roster again, "you'll be going on picket duty."

Dennis said, "Sir, I'm a corporal," hoping that would get him out of it.

John Rau said, "Is that right?" and took time to study him. "Tell me how you achieved your stripes?"

It was in Dennis' mind to say, The same way you made colonel. But he didn't. He said, "Sir, I thought I could be anything I wanted."

"Soldier," John Rau said, "you have to earn your advancement in rank."

He didn't say, By putting up with this shit. But that's what Dennis was thinking. He saw John Rau waiting for him to say:

"Yes sir."

Now he said, "Corporal?"

And paused. Dennis believed to make him say it again. See how many times he could get him to repeat it.

"Yes sir?"

"You'll draw perimeter picket duty tonight, eight to twelve. See the first sergeant before the hour and he'll assign you to a post."

One more time.

"Yes sir."

John Rau looked out at his troops and then right away turned to him again. "But before you draw rations and prepare your meal, I want you to get your rifle."

It took Dennis a moment to realize he was free. He could leave. He could have some of that lunch Robert had coming from the hotel, Dennis in his mind until he realized John Rau was staring at him, waiting.

"Soldier, did you hear what I just said?"

Dennis saluted. He said, "Loud and clear, *sir,*" the way Red Buttons said it to John Wayne in *The Longest Day* before they made the jump and Red's parachute got caught on the church steeple.

20

"JERRY WON'T EAT OUTSIDE," ROBERT said, "and Anne says it's too hot in the tent, so Tonto and Hector ran them back to the hotel."

"Get to do whatever they want," Dennis said.

"Like Mel Brooks said, 'It's good to be the king.' "

Dennis said, "I bet they never stand in line."

"For what?"

"Anything."

"Same as I'm offering you, man. Never having to stand in line again in your life."

"They coming back?"

"I told Jerry he has to spend the night out here at his command post. I want to see if Arlen's got the nerve to slip over here and fuck with him."

"What's Jerry say about that?"

"I only tell him he has to sleep here, not he's the bait. Anne, I told her to stay at the hotel."

"So you'll be going back there tonight."

Robert didn't say yes or no, he told Dennis to come on, have something to eat, and got him seated under the tent awning with a plate of crawfish étouffée and a cold beer. Robert, his checkered shirt hanging open, popped one for himself. He asked Dennis how was the crawfish and Dennis said it took him home. He told Robert then:

"Charlie says Arlen and his guys always get smashed they come to one of these. They're probably drinking right now."

"So either it jacks 'em up to become active," Robert said, "or they get shitfaced and don't even think of it."

"The next day they're hungover. Charlie says they take hits early in the battle and sleep till it's over. He says they're really good at taking hits."

Robert started to smile. "Come on, what're you telling me?"

"The way they go down. They practice getting shot."

Robert said, "I don't believe you," smiling just a little. "They practice? Go out in their yard and fall down? Sounds like a bunch of redneck Monty Pythons. Well, you know these dudes can be funny they with each other. What I'm saying, they can't *all* be stupid. See, you forget these Dixie Mafia people are mean motherfuckers. I started thinking, after I showed Arlen the picture of the lynching? Shit, I could be putting ideas in the man's head. Next thing he wants is to hang my ass from a tree."

"Tell me the truth," Dennis said, "where'd you get the picture?"

"I told you, was from a postcard old Broom Taylor gave me."

"But it's not your great-grandfather hanging from the bridge."

"It's somebody's."

"How many times have you used it?"

"Only since I'm here. See, I'm being truthful, 'cause I want you to trust me you come to make up your mind."

"I've already decided."

"No, you haven't, so don't tell me nothing yet."

"What I came to get is a rifle."

It turned on Robert's smile. "You want to be there tomorrow, don't you? In the woods."

Dennis didn't answer, but he said, "Colonel John Rau doesn't want to see me again without a rifle."

Robert turned his head to the tent next door, to his left. "Groove? Fix this man up with an Enfield. The cartridge box, the pouch, all the shit goes with it." He said to Dennis, "Or what happens, he puts you on KP, makes you peel potatoes?"

"You cook your own meals. We don't have to cure the salt pork, but he told us how, in case we want to fix it at home."

"Dry it out good, lot of salt, some molasses and a tangy hot sauce."

"Colonel Rau likes brown sugar."

"I have to think of what to do with him," Robert said. He looked up and then rose from the chair. "Here's your gun. You know how to shoot?"

Dennis said, "You pull the trigger, don't you?"

Groove came with the Enfield, Groove wearing shades with the uniform pants, but no shirt covering his slim build.

Robert said, "He needs to know how to load it."

Groove held the rifle upright against him, the muzzle at his chest. He showed Dennis a white paper cartridge about the size of his thumb, raised it to his mouth and tore off one end.

"You don't have teeth," Robert said, "you can't shoot. Now he pours the Elephant black powder down the barrel. See, the minié ball, the bullet's in there too, in the paper. You drop it down the muzzle and take your ramrod—see where it's attached—Groove pulls it out and runs it down the barrel to tamp the ball in there good. Now he picks the gun up, opens the breech. Now he takes a percussion cap—you know what I'm saying? The thing makes it explode, and puts it on the nipple there. Groove, tell him how straight this gun shoots."

"Good up to nine hundred yards," Groove said. "What the man said taught me all this shit. You hit your enemy up to that distance with the fifty-eight slug? The motherfucker is dead."

Robert said, "We gonna keep this rifle and give you another one you load how Groove showed you only without the bullet. So you don't shoot somebody during the reenacting part." Robert said, "Don't move." He went in the tent and came out with a joint and a drugstore lighter he placed next to Dennis' plate.

"I'm on picket duty tonight."

"Then you got what you need. You want, I could bring you a cold beer later on."

"I don't know where I'll be. I might as well sleep out there when I get off, in the camp."

"Don't let nobody spoon on you."

"Rau said something about spooning. I didn't know what he was talking about."

"It's what it sounds like. What they use to do. Cold night, a bunch of 'em would sleep fitting against each other on their sides. Nobody's washed or brushed their teeth in a month. Imagine the stinky smell. Like swamp gas hanging over you. Imagine some dude's bone sticking in your back all night."

Dennis said, "You're going back to the hotel, aren't you?"

"I may as well," Robert said, "I don't plan to see General Kirkbride—" He stopped and said, "Hey, shit, I forgot to mention, he came by here a while ago on his horse. Jerry was gone by then. He wants to know where I'm at. Groove and Cedric tell him they haven't seen me. Walter says, 'Soon as you do, send him down to my camp. I finish my ride, I want him to rub down my horse.' "

"Where were you?"

"In the tent having a smoke. But then later I'm thinking: he didn't come to get his horse rubbed down, that was his excuse to get next to me. The man's nervous from the bug I put in his ear and wants to talk."

"What'd you tell him?"

"Was out here, the day before this got going. I told him I knew he was in the drug business. See, then I put the bug to him. 'Where you want to be when Arlen goes down?' The man's the only one we met isn't all the way stupid."

"John Rau isn't either," Dennis said, "and he'll be there when you pull your stunt."

"That's what I said before, I have to think about."

Dennis said, "Why don't you take him prisoner?"

Robert's smile took a few moments coming, and when it did it wasn't much of a smile, just enough to let Dennis know he was looking at the idea. He said, "Out in front of everybody." He said, "Yeah, I wonder could that be done."

The bivouac area looked more lived in when Dennis got back with his rifle, a cartridge box, cap pouch, canteen and bayonet hanging from his belt and a sling over his shoulder. There was smoke from cook fires, more gear lying around, clothes hanging from stacked rifles, and civilians roaming through the camp, people in shorts and T-shirts among the blue uniforms, though not much visiting going on.

The first sergeant, giving Dennis a couple of blankets and his rations in a paper sack, did not hold with spectators hanging around a military camp. "God almighty, people walking by with Confederate flags on their T-shirts. It disturbs the mood. Makes it hard to maintain the right attitude of being in the field."

Dennis said, "Colonel Rau's over there telling a group how to cure salt pork."

"He's a detail man," the first sergeant said. "He means well, and he's a dandy battalion commander in the field, but he tries too hard to be helpful. Like the tents. We were out on an actual campaign, you wouldn't see any tents. You wanted some cover you built yourself a shebang. You know what I mean by shebang?" Dennis shook his head. "Like a lean-to, the weather side made of brush. I been out with old-timers all you saw in camp were shebangs, most of the boys sleeping in the open, the way they actually did. You think we had tents at Brice's Cross Roads? Hell, we're on the line, the supply wagons are still a day's haul to the rear. There'd been a lot of rain all week and it was slow going through the mud, engineers laying down timber all the way. No sir, you traveled light in that war, threw away everything but your musket and a blanket."

Dennis said, "You ever spoon?"

"If we're going by the book and are told not to keep the fires stoked? Hell yes. Hell, Virginia one time in May, you spooned or you froze." He said to Dennis, "You don't need a tent. You want shelter, go on over to that fella with the First Iowa. He's looking for a pard."

The fella with the First Iowa, in limp and graying longjohns, told Dennis sure, he could bunk with him.

Dennis said, "You don't spoon, do you?"

The First Iowan said, "Not in this weather." He said, "I don't snore or let farts either, if I can help it."

Dennis said he'd leave his gear, but was thinking of sleeping outside.

He'd done it enough times between gigs, always a sleeping bag in the setup truck, the last time on his way to Panama City and the Miracle Strip amusement park. That hot sun all day long and not much to do but go to movies. The nights weren't bad. Put on his show and then hang with people who liked to party. It could get old, but then he'd move on and look for the same people at the next stop. There were the good-time girls who loved daredevils, and there were more serious ones, divorced, trying to get by with a couple of little kids, young girls in their thirties starting to fade, not having the time to be themselves. They would invite him to dinner. They would put on makeup and music and open the door in their coolest outfit and sit across from him in candlelight and there it was, a chance to fall in love, and every once in a while he was tempted. But what would happen to the daredevil?

The First Iowa fella said, "I brought beans I cooked with the salt pork and some molasses you're welcome to."

Dennis had a plate and another scoop of beans with a cup of coffee, but couldn't eat the hardtack; it had no taste. He stretched out on the ground to rest, using his blanket rolled up for a pillow: the daredevil camped out with a bunch of guys playing soldier as they played cards, swore a lot, told jokes, talked about guns, deer hunting, battles, reenactments of Franklin, Chickamauga, Cold Harbor, generals good and bad, sang with a harmonica about rallying 'round the flag, boys . . . and Dennis dozed off.

A brogan nudged his ribs and he looked up to see the first sergeant standing over him. Dennis sat up right away. It was dark, the camp quiet, it had to be later than eight. He said, "What time is it?" getting to his feet. The sergeant told him it was going on ten.

"We got more people than duty time, so the colonel's cut the watches in half. You're on perimeter ten to twelve."

"Where's my post?"

"I'll take you. Pick up your rifle."

He asked the first sergeant what he was supposed to do here. The sergeant said watch for Rebs sneaking up in the night to attack the camp or take prisoners. He said they liked to snatch pickets who weren't alert and ship them off to Andersonville to die of dysentery.

Dennis stood at the edge of the scrub looking across the pasture, way over to the dark mass of trees, seeing flickering pinpoints of light in there. Confederate campfires. And the music coming from the barn up on the slope might be the military ball, though the squeaky fiddles sounded more like bluegrass.

He had told the First Iowa soldier he had picket duty and the man said, "Good." Imagine you're at Brice's and you can feel the Johnny Rebs close by, you can smell 'em. You see something move out there, put your rifle on it. Get your mind to believe what you're doing, else why're you here. He didn't tell the soldier he didn't *want* to be here. The man would ask, then why was he.

Standing here in the scrub swinging his free hand at insects buzzing around him. He took the joint from his pocket and lit it, sucked on it hard to get a good draw and blew smoke at the bugs, hoping to send them off stoned. He wondered if Civil War soldiers smoked weed, the way they did in Vietnam. He wondered if they said "this fucking war" like soldiers in war movies, more saying it in Vietnam war movies than World War Two flicks. He would have to ask Robert. Robert probably wouldn't know but would have an answer. Robert was the most in-control person he had ever met in his life. Like the way, in front of Arlen staring at him, he laid the gun on the kitchen table without looking at it. Just something that happened to be in his briefcase. The weed had his mind flashing on Robert highlights. Robert with Walter Kirkbride, wanting to be one of his colored fellas. Robert making whatever he did look easy. Robert taking his time, days, to build toward the crossroads, what it meant, before making his offer. Robert saying, "No way could you ever be indicted on a drug charge, you'd be hidden from view. Your Dive-O-Rama accountant ever got picked up? You'd be shocked." Robert saying, "Man, if a daredevil couldn't handle that . . ."

The daredevil standing in the dark holding a ten-pound replica of a Civil War rifle. Not anywhere near an edge.

He walked off with the rifle toward faint lights showing in the civilian camp.

A LANTERN HUNG FROM THE tent where the pie lady, smoking a cigarette, sat in a low-slung canvas chair at the edge of the awning. She watched him walk up to her, not smiling, not saying a word.

She was wearing lipstick.

She was wearing, he believed, eyeliner. Her hair was combed from a part and fell to her shoulders in a white shirt with a few buttons undone and a long skirt; but it didn't look period either.

He held out the joint, half of it left, and watched her look at it and then look up at his eyes before she took it, pinched it between her fingers and leaned forward in the scoop of canvas to the flame on the lighter he offered. She inhaled and held it, her body straight, before she blew out a cloud and sank back in the chair and smiled.

"You made it."

"I'm on picket duty."

"You mean right now?"

"At this moment, in the scrub."

She said from down in her chair, "You left your post for a piece of Naughty Child?"

There was an answer to that and he tried hard to think of what it was while she sat waiting to hear it. Finally all he did was smile.

She didn't, she kept looking at his eyes looking at hers.

"How'd it turn out?"

"The mister came up from his camp to pick up the pie and take it back. I told him it burned and I threw it away. He wanted to know where, so he could check on me, not trusting I even made the pie. I told him go on over to the Porta-Johns, it was in the second one to the left."

"Did he check?"

"He thought about it."

"Did you make the pie?"

"I rolled out the dough, got that far."

Dennis propped his rifle against the table. He pulled a short straight camp chair over next to hers, sat down and took off his kepi, settling in with things to say to her.

"You didn't want him to have any Naughty Child."

"I suppose."

"I run into girls all the time," Dennis said, "feeling trapped in a situation they don't know how to get out of. They're young, they're divorced, they have kids and the former husbands are all behind in their child support. Some of 'em look at me, the girls, I can see 'em wondering if it might work this time."

She said, "What are you wondering, how to get out?"

"Not always." He could feel the weed and was comfortable and wanted to talk. "I've met girls—I always think of them as girls instead of young women because it's my favorite word. Girl." He smiled.

"What's your least favorite?"

"Snot. What's yours?"

"Bitch. I get called it a lot."

They could go off on that, but he wanted to make his point before he forgot what it was. "I started to say, I've met girls I feel I could marry and we'd be happy and get along."

"How do you know?"

"We can talk and like the same things. Being able to talk is important."

She said, "Tell me about it," and said, "What do you do, you meet all these girls?"

"For a living? Take a guess."

She said, "You're not a salesman," and kept staring at him. "You're not from around here, or anywhere close by. You're not in law enforcement."

"Why do you say that?"

"I mean like a sheriff's deputy. You seem intelligent."

"You don't think much of cops?"

She said, "Having known a few."

"Why'd you marry this hardcore Confederate?"

She said, "I was going through one of my stupid periods. I started writing to a convict—he was related to a friend of mine and she got me into it. Girls do that, you know, write to convicts. They come to believe theirs is really a nice guy—look at the letters he writes. The idea is to make him see his good side and be comfortable with it." She raised the joint to take a hit but then paused. "Well, mine doesn't have a good side, and by the time I found out it was too late, we were married."

"Leave," Dennis said. "Walk out."

"I'm working up my nerve to file. What I'd love to do is move to Florida. Orlando. I hear it's the place to be, a lot going on."

She was a country girl—Loretta—trying hard not to be, but stuck with who she was. Her goal, to live where there were theme parks.

She said, "Anyway, I'm guessing what you do, meet all these girls that fall in love with you," staring at him again, slipping back into her soft mood; but then seemed to straighten in the camp chair as she said, "You're a croupier, at one of the casinos. No, you're a professional gambler, a card counter."

Dennis shook his head. It sounded good though. He caught a glimpse of himself at a poker table, very cool.

"You're not a business executive."

"Why not?"

"Your hair."

"I could be in the music business."

"Yeah, you could. Are you?"

"No."

"Then why'd you mention it?"

"I'm trying to help. You like blues?"

"Yeah, I guess. You're some kind of musician?"

Dennis shook his head. "How about Drug Enforcement, something like that, a federal agent?"

Looking at him she half-closed her eyes in the lantern glow. "Yeah, you could be working undercover. But you wouldn't give me a joint, would you?"

"What if I was a dealer?"

She studied him again, their faces only a couple of feet apart. "I suppose. But you look too, like, clean and healthy." She narrowed her eyes now, suspicious. "You ever been to Parchman?"

He shook his head. "That where your husband was?"

"Two years."

It came to Dennis all at once. He said, "Your husband was a sheriff's deputy before that and now he works for Mr. Kirkbride . . ."

She said, "Oh, my Lord."

"And runs the drug business."

She said, "You're the diver."

Dennis waited.

She said, "Why don't you tell on the son of a bitch and have him put away?"

Everybody knew he was up on the ladder when Floyd was shot. She said it herself and Dennis asked if Arlen had told her. She heard it in a casino bar and when she asked her husband about it, yes, he told her. Loretta said he got drunk and told her all kinds of stupid things he did.

Dennis was in the pasture now with his rifle, heading back to his post, every now and again stumbling over ruts and clods of earth in the dark.

She wanted to know why he didn't tell. He said to her, "I'm going to next week, unless something happens I don't have to." She didn't know what he meant. "Like what?" Now he was talking the way Robert did, with no intention of spelling it out. He said to Loretta, the way Robert would keep you hanging, "Don't file yet. You may not have to." Picked up his rifle and got out of there.

He trudged along toward the dark mass of the thicket. Finally when he was getting close he saw the figure standing in the open. Dennis thought it was another sentry and he was off course from the direction he should be heading. When he'd walked off from the post he had turned around and lined up with the round top of an oak back in the thicket. There it was, he was heading toward it. But also toward the sentry, who didn't look like he had a rifle.

No, because it was Colonel John Rau—shit—his hand on the hilt of his sword.

He said, "Corporal, you left your post."

Dennis said, "Yes sir," because, well, why not.

"You know you could be court-martialed and shot?"

"Sir," Dennis said, going along with it, half-turning to point toward the dark pasture, "I thought I saw something out there."

It stopped him, John Rau with nothing in his head ready to say.

"I thought it might be a Confederate raiding party," Dennis said, "looking to take prisoners."

John Rau said, "Corporal—"

But Dennis was already saying, "Get shipped off to Andersonville to die of dysentery."

"Corporal?"

"Yes sir."

"You've been gone over an hour."

"Colonel, you want to know the truth?"

"Tell me."

"I'm not a reenactor. I don't feel it in me."

"Are you quitting?"

"When this is over. I doubt I'll ever do it again."

"But you'll be here tomorrow."

"Yes sir, for the battle."

"And you know Arlen Novis will be coming out of the orchard over there with his boys. I can't say they're Dixie Mafia, that name doesn't mean anything to me. I do know they're thugs, they're vicious, and as soon as they wake up in the morning they'll be drinking again. By the time they cross this field they will have worked themselves up, they'll come with that Rebel yell like they're ready to kill. During battle reenactments they get into fistfights with Union soldiers all the time. They're warned beforehand, they still do it, 'cause they become out of control. I remember both at Franklin and at Corinth last year they met our line swinging rifle butts at us. My impression at those events, I was a captain with the Ninety-fifth Ohio, acting as an infantry officer for a change. Though I prefer cavalry. I was Stuart at Yellow Tavern when I lost my horse, a beautiful mare." John Rau paused to look for the point he was making. "You understand, Arlen and his fellas could come tomorrow with every intention of taking you out of the picture, for good."

Dennis was ready. He said, "If I told you right now I saw them murder Floyd Showers, would you go over there and arrest him?"

John Rau took a moment before saying, "He'll still be around Monday."

Here was a chance to play Robert with him. Say something like, Oh, are you sure? Or, You sure about that? But in Dennis' head it didn't sound anything like Robert. Jesus, trying to be clever. What he said was, "So you're giving Arlen a chance to take me out of the picture, as you say."

John Rau shook his head. "Don't report for tomorrow's muster."

"I know a person," Dennis said, "Arlen *told* they killed Floyd, and wants him put away."

John Rau said, "I *have* Loretta Novis. She'll tell it if my eyewitness testifies. But if he does, I don't need her, do I?"

Dennis said, "I'll talk to you Monday."

John Rau said, "You know I can have you subpoenaed and put on the stand under oath."

Dennis said, "Sir, I have to get back to my post."

Thinking he was smart. But John Rau had the last word.

He said, "You take part tomorrow, I don't want to see you wearing those chevrons, private."

They had it worked out that Arlen would come up from one end of the tent street and Fish and Newton would approach from the other end. He'd picked Newton 'cause he was the one had sassed this Robert when he was with the girl showing some of her tit, and would have gone after him he didn't have a goddamn sword in his hand. Newton'd worked the wad around in his mouth, messy as hell, beard all stained, and said he would settle with the nigger, don't worry.

They'd meet at General Grant's tent and see what was doing. See if they could stick a gun in the man's mouth, this Caesar German-o, and tell him to go on home. It gave Arlen a chance to stop and see his wife. If he saw any green tomatoes it'd mean she never made the goddamn pie she burned.

The first thing he said to her was, "Jesus Christ, is that a roach on the table?"

Loretta looked over from her sling chair. "It looks like a roach to me. Doesn't it look like one to you?"

"I *know* what it is."

"Then what're you asking me for?"

"What is wrong with you?"

"Nothing."

"I told you, don't ever bring none from home. Have these women sniffing the air, saying things about you."

"They're so scared of you they don't come near me. I wasn't even invited to the tea. I wouldn't have gone, but they could've asked."

Arlen said, "You disobeyed me."

"I didn't bring the pot, sweetheart. A soldier boy came by, a Yan-kee, and left it for me."

"Who was it?"

"I don't want to get you upset."

"I'm asking you who it was."

"And I'm not telling, so go fuck yourself."

This was not the girl used to write sweet letters to him in the joint. They changed on you, all of 'em. Set 'em up with a nice house and a car and turned into alligators.

"You're trying to get me to smack you," Arlen said, "so you can scream and get people looking out their tents. I'll ask you again we get home, you can scream all you want."

Now she was giving him her sleepy-eyed reefer grin, like she knew something about him he didn't. She did it all the time and it liked to drive him crazy.

Arlen said to her as he always did, hoping for an answer but never getting one, "What is wrong with you?"

An hour or so before this, in General Grant's camp, Germano had come out of his tent sweating in his underwear, growling, telling Hector and Tonto, "That's it, fuck it. I can't sleep in there, I'm going back to the hotel."

There was no way to argue with him if that's what he wanted to do. Hector said, "Of course," and said he would get Groove and Cedric to take him. It didn't matter to Germano who drove him, but it did to Hector; he wanted to be here if the Confederates came to visit.

Germano asked if Robert was sleeping. Hector said no, but he was around someplace. Germano said, "Tell him I've gone back."

When they had left, Hector said to Tonto, "There was no way to stop him. Now, what if he finds Robert in bed with his missus?"

Tonto took time to think about it, but all he said was, "I don't know. I guess we have to wait to find out."

They were sitting by the table in front of Germano's tent now, the lantern hanging above them from the awning. Both Hector and Tonto, when they thought of Jerry or would mention him, it was always as Germano. They couldn't understand why Robert allowed him to be the boss. They would protect the man's life, not having much respect for him, but because Robert would say to do it, okay? You mind? Not the way Germano the hard-on said to do something. Robert made you feel close to him. "Working for Robert," Hector said, "was like being in the fucking movies." Robert had imagination. Go on down to Mississippi and take over a deal from the Dixie Mafia. What? First get you some Civil War uniforms. What? And Civil War guns. Yeah? And you get to play war like when you were kids. Yeah? No kidding.

Sitting in the lantern light, Hector said, "He could have been a killer of bulls, a good one with his own style. But I believe he would have someone else plant the sticks.

"You know why? Because he likes to have people with him who know what they're doing. Planting the sticks looks difficult, but requires far less nerve than to go over the horns with the sword. I believe he can be anything he wants that catches his eye."

"Don't you know what he wants to do?" Tonto said. "He wants to dive off that ladder."

"He told you that?"

"No, but he would like to."

"How do you know?"

"See the way he watches that quiet guy dive off the ladder, that Dennis. Look at Robert's eyes, man, when he says 'Hey, shit,' and shakes his head. He would give up something to do it. The guy high in the air, twisting and turning, is in control of himself, showing how cool he is. And Robert's cool. He keeps Dennis around because he respects him as a man."

"You believe he wants to," Hector said, "but you don't know it."

Tonto said, "No, not the same way I know that guy down the street, the Confederate guy, is coming here. But the feeling I have about Robert is that I know it."

"From the other way also," Hector said, "two of them coming."

Jim Rein, the Fish, saw the two sitting in the lantern light. The one behind the table had the pigtail in his hair. The one at this end of the table had the bandanna covering his. He was looking this way. Jim Rein said to Newton, "That one there was at Junebug's with the general and the nigger." Meaning Robert, the one Newton was looking for.

Newton said, "Ain't those two niggers?"

Jim Rein said, "I think they's Mexicans."

Newton said, "What's the difference? They look like smokes to me."

They saw Arlen, who'd come from the opposite end of the tent street, facing them now, Arlen's Navy Colt stuck in his belt near to the front. Jim Rein and Newton wore their revolvers in military holsters with the flaps cut off. Jim Rein saw the one wearing the bandanna staring at him the same way he'd stared at Junebug's without ever saying a word. As Jim Rein and Newton came up to Arlen, Jim Rein saw the two Mexicans or whatever they were bring out their own Colt revolvers from wherever they kept them and lay them on the table—at the same time without saying anything or nudging each other.

Hector Diaz looked at the three Confederate soldiers in their hats with no style to them, no personality, three guys, Hector believed, who were used to scaring people by the way they looked at you. But now the expression on the face of the leader changed. This was the one called Arlen. He said, "How you boys doing this evening?"

Hector looked up at him. Tonto looked at the other two.

"Getting yourselves some air?"

They didn't answer that one either.

"Can't get you boys to say nothing," Arlen said. "How about your general, Mr. German-o? How's he doing?"

Hector smiled a little; he couldn't help it. He said, "Our general is asleep."

"You his guard dogs?"

"No, what you said, we getting the air."

"Ask him to come out here," Arlen said, "so I can speak to him. Or I can step inside the tent."

"I tole you," Hector said, "he sleeping."

Arlen nodded at the table. "Those pistols loaded?"

"Yes, they are," Hector said.

"You know you're not suppose to put loads in your guns?"

"Yes, we know it," Hector said, "the same as you know it."

Arlen said, "What're we getting to here?"

Hector turned his head to Tonto. "Fucking *High Noon,* man."

Arlen said, "I didn't hear you."

"I tole him," Hector said, "you want to pull your guns, but you don't have the nerve."

The one with the tobacco stains in his beard said, "What'd he say?"

But the one, Arlen, was louder, telling them, "You think that's what we come here for? To shoot you? Jesus Christ."

"Our Lord and Savior," Hector said. "No, I don't think to shoot us. Maybe scare us so we go home."

"We gonna see you tomorrow," Arlen said, "when we do Brice's, and run you off with rifle butts and bayonets."

Hector said, "And swords?"

"You want to sword-fight?" Arlen said. "I got a sword. Shit, we'll do 'er any way you want, Pancho."

Hector turned to Tonto again. "You hear this guy?"

Tonto only shrugged.

But then the one with the stained beard said, "Where's the nigger at?"

Tonto looked at him and said, "He left. He went to fuck your wife."

Hector could see the guy with the beard was about to go crazy, but Arlen stopped him, took the hand reaching for the pistol and twisted it behind him the way cops know how to do it, and that was the end of the visit. Arlen said one word to them before they marched off with the one still on the edge of being crazy. He said, "Tomorrow."

Hector looked at Tonto. "Tomorrow okay with you?"

A FEW MINUTES PAST SIX the next morning, Sunday, the big day, Anne left Robert's suite to go down the hall sleepy-eyed to get in her own bed.

The one—*Oh, shit*—Jerry was in.

Jerry snoring away, the sound, that drone, coming from the bedroom. It stopped Anne in her slides as she entered the suite and got her thinking, Quick, where were you?

But first she'd have to know what time Jerry got back. Now she was saying things to herself like, Are you out of your mind? You actually believed he'd sleep in a fucking tent? She should never have listened to Robert with that baby, it's cool, nothing to worry about. "You don't want him walking in on us, we do it in my bed." Anne saying, "But if he comes back and I'm not in *my* bed—" Robert saying, "Come on, baby, have us a quickie and call it a night." Except that Robert was a slowpoke making love, kept slow-poking till they both fell asleep for almost six hours.

Fooling around could have its hair-raising moments, especially cheating on a gangster, and she'd tell herself it wasn't worth it. But then Robert would give her the look and she'd give him the look and they'd be back fooling around again. She slipped into the king-size bed next to Jerry to lie there waiting for him to wake up.

The phone rang at eight, the phone on Jerry's side of the bed.

Anne reached across him, stretching, for a moment her face close to his, lifted the receiver before it rang again and laid it back in its cradle. Slipping back across Jerry she came to his face, his eyes, inches away, open, looking at her. She kissed him on the mouth, a peck, and rolled back onto her pillow.

"Who was that?"

"I've no idea."

"Why'd you hang up?"

"It's too early to talk."

She waited, hoping that fucking phone would not ring.

"Where were you?"

Here we go.

"Where *was* I? When?"

"All fuckin night."

"I don't know what you mean."

"I come back, you're not here."

"What time was it?"

"What's the difference—you weren't fuckin here."

"Jerry. What *time* was it?"

"Twelve, twelve-thirty."

Anne said, "Yeah . . . ?" taking her time, and said, "I was out on the balcony," adding a note of surprise to her voice. "I fell asleep on the lounge. You didn't see me? Yeah, I came in and looked at the clock. It was one-thirty, you were asleep . . ." She said, "I knew you weren't gonna spend the night in that tent."

"You were out on the balcony."

"Yeah, I can't believe you didn't see me."

There was a silence, Jerry lying there with nothing more to say. But now she was home free and couldn't let it go.

"Where did you think I was?"

Walter Kirkbride had started to get dressed with every intention of slipping out of the tent early, unobserved, before the women in camp were out there cooking breakfast. And he would have, if he hadn't looked over at little Traci turning onto her side on the cot, the little sweetie pulling the blanket with her to show him her bare white bummy. It lured Walter out of his longjohns to express his love. And then had to rest.

While he was getting dressed the second time little Traci lit into him in a pouty way, moaning about being mostly all alone yesterday, and having to wear that dumb hoopskirt.

"I walk around here, everybody looks at me."

"Well, sure they do, you're cute as a bug. Aren't you my little Barbie?" He'd call her that in the trailer and she'd call him Ken, only in her countrified way it would come out sounding like "Kin."

"Those fat women'd ask me who're my people. Where was I from. Do I want to help them make johnnycake. What was I suppose to say? I told 'em I had to go to the bathroom. But you try to get in one of those little shithouses with a hoopskirt on. You have to lift it up in front real high and go in sideways. But then you're in there the skirt takes up all the room. What I did was get up on the seat and squat over it to pee."

Walter was pulling his boots, straining, trying to hurry. That, and hearing her talking about peeing, gave him the urge.

"I went in that store where they have all the little statues of famous generals and stuff? I have all kinds of ashtrays with Confederate flags on 'em, so I bought a plate I thought might be used as one, had Robert E. Lee, Jefferson Davis and Stonewall Jackson on it, and the flag, of course. I use to have a G-string with a Confederate flag on it guys liked a lot when I was dancing go-go. They'd salute it. I was only fourteen but already had my tits."

Walter stood at the back of the tent relieving himself, feeling calmer as the flow hit the sand, not making a sound.

"Sweetie, you get dressed, put on your bluejeans. We may leave here in a hurry."

"You mean it?"

"I think today's gonna be different than any reenactment I've ever been to." He would approach it carefully, alert, keeping on the front of his mind what the colored fella Robert had said. *Where you want to be when Arlen goes down?* Seeing it more as a warning than a decision he had to make. Robert telling him to stay out of it and he wouldn't get hurt. Keep to one side and maybe this Robert would come see him after about doing business. It seemed all he had to do was stay alert and not get too near to Arlen.

"After," Traci said, "can we get something to eat?"

"Anything you want."

"You know who Arlen sent with my supper I would never've eaten anyway? All that pork fat? Even if he hadn't spilt it on the ground? Newton Hoon, the stinkiest man I ever met in my life.

He'd try to come in my trailer? I said, 'You filled a tub with wash powder and soaked in it all day I still wouldn't let you in.' "

Walter, getting into his wool coat, said, "That's my girl."

"I couldn't buy anything for supper, I didn't have no money with me and you didn't give me none. I was lucky I stopped to talk to this lady down a ways smoking a cigarette? She'd snuck in some Stouffer's frozen dinners, only defrosted, the Chicken and Vegetables Pasta Bake, threw 'em in a pot and pretended she was cooking. It was good, too. She talked funny. She said she'd been stuck in a hard life, but believed her redeemer was about to cometh."

"A religious woman," Walter said, strapping on his sword. He picked up his hat and a voice came from outside the tent.

"Walter, goddamn it, you coming?"

He opened the tent flap a few inches to see Arlen's dirty look, one that seemed imprinted on the man's features.

"What's wrong?"

"I was thinking," Arlen said, "it was time we set our minds on what we're doing here. Except you're with your whore, Eugene and Fish are fighting over a dead dog, and all Newton wants to do is lynch the nigger."

It was in Walter's mind that he might not have to listen to this man, this lout, ever again after today. And to make it come true he should help Robert any way he could.

Arlen said, "The hell're you looking at?"

It brought Walter back. He turned his head to Traci on the cot. "See you later, Barbie honey."

She lifted her head from the pillow. "Okay, Kin."

Walter stepped outside.

Arlen said, "You got a new one in there?"

Anne got up from the room-service table to answer the door. Jerry didn't move, looking at the Sunday paper, the *Memphis Commercial Appeal,* as he ate his breakfast.

Robert was in uniform. Coming in he said, "That was me called." Anne opened the door all the way and now he saw Jerry at the table. "And you two were sound asleep, huh? I'm sorry I woke you up."

Jerry said, "How was it?" dipping his spoon into a soup bowl of soft-boiled eggs.

Robert estimating there were three eggs in the bowl, runny, maybe four when Jerry started eating. That took up part of a moment in Robert's mind, the rest of it was thinking, How was what? And realized Jerry meant sleeping in a tent. "We missed you, Jer. Yeah, that camping out's fun. We built a fire, sat around it and told ghost stories."

Anne said, "Did you sing camp songs?"

She stood with her orange juice now by the open doors to the balcony.

"We didn't know any. Tonto did sixty days in one of those tent jails that's like a camp, in Texas? But he said they didn't sing any songs."

Jerry said, "What time's this thing today, the battle?"

"Two o'clock. You muster at the Union camp no later than one-thirty."

"Or what," Jerry said, "they don't let you play? How we gonna work it?"

Hector had phoned this morning, so Robert was able to say, "Hector talked to Arlen. He says they'll go fists, knives, anything . . . rocks. Hector says even swords. There four of them counting Arlen, not counting Mr. Kirkbride. We might want to use him, and this other one, Bob Hoon, runs the meth lab. I drove out and spoke to him a few days ago, gave him some what-ifs, told him he ought to stay loose. So it's their four against us four, us being me and you, Hector and Tonto."

"And the two spades," Jerry said.

"You mean," Robert said, "Groove and Cedric? I told you where they gonna be."

"Yeah, I forgot," Jerry said, getting up from the table with the paper. "That's what I have you for, the details."

Robert watched him go into the bedroom and heard the bathroom door close. Now he saw Anne drilling him with her look and knew he was about to get yelled at through clenched teeth.

"I told you he'd come back. I walk in the room—what am I supposed to tell him?"

"Baby, I'm sorry. He was awake?"

"He was asleep."

"Then you had time to make something up."

"How do I know when he got back? I had to find that out first."

Robert moved toward her now saying, "Baby, what'd you tell him? It must've been good." He would have to take her in his arms now while her husband was in there taking a dump, give her some comfort, ready to, but then saw the ladder out there past her against the sky, and saw a figure standing on the top perch.

Now Anne turned to follow his gaze and said, "Is that Dennis?"

"It's Billy Darwin," Robert said. "He climbed up there once before. And climbed down," Robert's voice drifting with a thoughtful sound to it. "The cool hotel manager gonna find out if he's all the way cool. See Carla down there? By the tank with Charlie Hoke in his uniform. But the man is not doing it for them or anybody watching. I see Billy Darwin up there for his own knowledge of himself. He wants to know can he do it from the height of cool, eighty feet up. He's gonna do it, too. See him on the edge? The man's gonna do it."

Robert watched Billy Darwin raise his arms, look down at the tank and then straight out at the sky, watched him jump into space and drop sixty miles an hour in two seconds to smack the water with a sound Robert could hear.

Robert said, "Uh-oh."

His eyes holding on the tank, waiting for Billy Darwin to surface, as Anne told him she would never, ever, let him talk her into that kind of situation again, taking a chance that could get them killed, for Christ sake, for what? She said, "Hey, I'm talking to you. Where're you going?" raising her voice to Robert crossing the room and going out the door.

Two figures stood on the slope not far from the barn, a Yankee and a Confederate with a sword, Dennis halfway across the field before he recognized them, Robert and Charlie, and trudged up the slope with his rifle.

Charlie said, "We saw you coming—"

Robert got right to it, telling Dennis, "Billy Darwin went off the ladder. He might've injured himself."

"Bad?"

"Did something to his back. Carla went in and fished him out."

"With her clothes on," Charlie said. "He manages to take a few steps at a time, but stooped over. The Emergency people came, he didn't want to go with 'em. They strapped him down and took him anyway. Said they thought he ought to be x-rayed."

Dennis was shaking his head now. "Carla said he wanted to do it. He jumped?"

"Looked good, too," Robert said, "till he's almost to the tank and you see his legs go out in front of him like he's sitting down. Made a way bigger splash than any of yours. I believe his timing was off a speck, but he was cool to try it. Have to give him that."

Dennis said to Robert, "You're not gonna try it, are you?"

"Why would you ask me that?"

"Don't, okay?"

"No, man, I can admire it without feeling the need to do it. Listen, I told Jerry to look for you at the Federal camp. Where you going now?"

"Get my corporal stripes cut off," Dennis said. "Or Colonel Rau won't let me play war."

"What you do," Robert said, "stay close as you can to Hector and Tonto, you'll be okay. I told them to get up close to the woods on the north side, straight out there, and I'll give 'em the sign when to duck in."

"I'm not getting into anything over my head."

"That's what I'm saying to you. They'll see you don't get in trouble."

Charlie said, "The hell are you talking about?"

"I have to go," Robert said, and went off to join his Confederates.

Charlie watched him walk off and then turned to Dennis. "What's going on?"

"If I knew," Dennis said, "I'd tell you."

"Well, I gotta go study my script," Charlie said, and headed for the barn.

And now Dennis was on his way to visit the Naughty Child woman. See if she had a pair of scissors. It was strange, he could tell Loretta was younger than he was by a few years, and yet he thought of her as a woman and not a girl. Or as Arlen's wife.

23

SHE WASN'T OUTSIDE. SHE COULD be in the tent. And Arlen could be in there with her, but he doubted it. Dennis stepped under the awning.

"Loretta?"

"Who is it?" Her voice close.

He said, "Dennis," not sure if that was enough.

The flap opened and there was her face, no makeup, her features clean-scrubbed, shiny. She didn't give him much of a smile, but her eyes were calm and didn't leave his face.

"I need to get my stripes cut off."

"For leaving your post last night, huh? And you didn't even get any pie."

"I wasn't thinking of pie. But listen, all I need is a pair of scissors." He heard his voice taking on a soft accent to match hers.

"Well, come on in, take your jacket off."

Dennis laid his rifle on the table and stood by the tent flap unbuttoning the shell, got it open and took off his kepi to place it next to the rifle.

"You coming?"

He said, "What're you doing?" opening the tent and stepping into light that had lost its brightness, filtered through the canvas. She was wearing nothing above her long skirt but a thin, flimsy bra he could see through and holding a washcloth in her hand. Loretta didn't act surprised or self-conscious; or seductive, for that matter. She made it seem natural for him to see her this way, soaping her arm.

"Going to fight the battle?"

"I could get shot right here," Dennis said.

It didn't make her smile. She said, "I'll cut off your stripes," and held the washcloth toward him, "if you'll wash my back." Still natural making the offer.

Dennis took the washcloth. He thought she would turn. When she didn't he stepped around her and she lowered her head and reached back with both hands to lift her hair out of the way. He wiped the cloth across her back, trying not to touch the bra straps, smelling the soap, moving the cloth lower now and under her raised arm, the tips of his fingers coming to the slight swell of her breast.

"You have a nice touch," Loretta said.

Dennis worked his way over to the hollow beneath her other arm.

"I can see why those girls look at you as a possible. You always this tender?"

He thought to say, Well, I'm not washing a car. And scrapped it because he did feel tender moving his hand over her small bones, her white skin—though not as white as Vernice's, Vernice a lot rounder than Loretta, Loretta skin and bones by comparison, more athletic, that wiry type, sometimes a tiger in bed, though Vernice was active for her size.

"I said, are you always this tender?"

"I touched you," Dennis said, "and the tender feeling came with it. I'm having trouble, though, working around these straps."

"Why don't you unhook me?"

He did and she pulled the bra off in front of her. By the time he came around to her breasts, not near the size of Vernice's but a woman's breasts all the same, he could look over her shoulder and see them, Loretta pressing herself against him. They'd be on the cot anytime now and he had to think of what he'd take off. She lifted her skirt, gathering it above her hips, and turned to him bare underneath saying, "Don't take your clothes off. Let's do it right now."

Dennis said, "Just once?"

And Loretta said, "Oh, honey . . ."

They made love in the hot tent, Dennis in his wool uniform, pants around his knees, and it was like finding his match in a woman they were so natural with each other, playing, having fun, their eyes holding until first her eyes and then his squeezed closed. This time he did not think of Vernice.

She said, after, "You have a car?"

"Where do you want to go?"

She said, "Anywhere," and said, "I could announce your dives, do that cute patter about getting splashed."

It stopped him. "You saw my show?"

She said, "Honey, I watched you every night you dove."

The bivouac seemed more military than it did when he left: no clothes hanging from stacked rifles, not as much gear lying around, the Yankee reenactors taking down their tents, getting ready for battle. Dennis had slept in the open last night and shared the First Iowa soldier's breakfast this morning, fried salt pork and biscuits he'd brought from home soaked in the grease. With the coffee it went through Dennis like a fire hose.

The First Iowan said, "You missed the drill. We marched out there and showed our stuff. The colonel said we didn't look too bad."

Dennis, now a private, said, "I was getting my stripes cut off," and saw her face again close in that hot tent.

The First Iowan said, "General Grant showed up and the colonel wasn't too pleased to see him. The first sergeant says he was sore anyways 'cause of the truck still sitting in the bivouac. No keys and nobody'd come to pick it up. The colonel asked General Grant what kind of credentials he had. Who said it was okay for him to be commander in chief of the Union Army? The first sergeant said the general told him, 'Abraham Lincoln, who the fuck do you think.' "

Jerry was sitting on the tailgate of the pickup smoking a cigar, Hector and Tonto with him, Hector holding Jerry's sword. Dennis, approaching them, had already made up his mind he wasn't going to salute or call him general. He saw them waiting for him, Jerry saying to him as he walked up, "Where you been?"

Dennis said, "Getting my stripes cut off," and again saw Loretta's face. Then saw her another time, somewhere else, Loretta saying, *Feel like getting your stripes cut off?*

"These guys were about to go find you," Jerry said. "Drag you here if they had to. You understand? You got nothing to say about it."

"He means we need you," Hector said, "as the bait."

"We get 'em where we want 'em," Jerry said, "you stay close. Try to run, one of us'll shoot you."

They were talking about setting up Arlen and his guys, but it didn't make sense. Dennis said, "You don't have bullets in your guns. Nobody does."

Hector said, "Robert didn't tell you, uh? We trade them in, man, for loaded pistols."

"How do we do that?"

"You see it happen."

"You're gonna shoot those guys," Dennis said, "and then what, take off?"

"Man, Robert didn't tell you shit," Hector said.

"All you got to know," Jerry said, "you run, you're dead. By any chance you get picked up 'cause you're stupid and the cops offer you a deal to give us up? You're fuckin dead. You're in it. You understand? You told Robert you're in all the way, right?"

"He means the business part," Hector said.

"Not yet."

Jerry said, "There something wrong with you?"

"I'm thinking about it."

"You didn't jump on it right away you're not the guy. We don't need you." He said to Hector and Tonto, "You guys do all the work, you need him?"

"If Robert say he wants him," Hector said, and Tonto agreed, nodding.

"That's why I don't ask your fuckin advice," Jerry said, and looked at Dennis again. "You got till after we do this. But you fuck with me you know what happens."

"You're dead," Hector said.

"What kind of thing would I do," Dennis said to Jerry, "you'd think of as fuckin with you?"

"I just told you."

"Outside of if I run or cop to a deal."

"You're fuckin with me right now."

It was in his voice, the irritation.

"He means don't piss him off," Hector said, "that's all," and said to him, "Let me ask you something. You know how to fire a Colt pistol?"

"I know you have to cock it first," Dennis said, "each time you fire. Thumb the hammer back. Or you can squeeze the trigger and fan the hammer, the way Alan Ladd did in *Shane,* he's showing the kid how he shoots."

"That was a good part," Hector said, "before he faced Wilson, the hired gun."

"And blew him away," Dennis said.

"See?" Hector said to Jerry. "I told you Dennis would know how."

Jerry was shaking his head. "You guys kill me. You're fuckin morons, you know it?"

They stood in ranks while John Rau took them one by one through the safety drill. Each man's rifle, with only a cap in the breech, would be aimed at the ground and fired at a leaf. The rush of air moving the leaf meant the barrel was clear.

Dennis waited his turn, the clean smell of Loretta's soap on him.

He had said to her, "If you saw me dive, why didn't you know who I was?" Last night, when she was guessing what he did for a living. She said because she was never close enough to the tank when he came out, and because he didn't dive in a Yankee uniform with corporal stripes on it. She said, "Let me have your jacket," and snipped off in twenty seconds what had taken Vernice something like twenty minutes, talking the whole time, to sew on.

Yesterday, when he asked her why they called the pie Naughty Child, and she said, "You find out, let me know," he took his first step toward her, getting the feeling they were alike and could talk, not take things too seriously. Then in the evening, thinking of her as a country girl with theme parks in her dreams, he had stepped back for a moment, the daredevil king of amusement parks passing judgment. There was nothing wrong with theme parks. Some even put on high-dive shows.

Standing in ranks at attention he said to himself, You'll dive another three years, if that. What do you and your dive-caller do then?

He didn't know her but he kept thinking about her, seeing her, liking the way she moved and the sound of her voice, and her eyes, the way she looked at him. What was the problem?

Outside of her being married.

For the time being. That could change in an hour.

He saw himself in a dueling pose, in the trees, aiming a Colt revolver at Arlen running toward him.

With a sword, a big cavalry saber.

Could that happen?

John Rau said, "Private, tell me what you're waiting for?"

24

ROBERT WENT DOWN TO THE Confederate encampment in the orchard, his sword hanging at his side, his hand on the hilt to keep it from hitting his leg and tripping him up, swords not being as cool as they looked. Man, all the serious Southron types down here getting ready, Robert estimating their number at a hundred and a half easy, living in dirt and eating bad food and loving it.

He saw squads of them marching through the tangle of trees to drumbeats, some already taking their positions on the line. He saw a half-dozen cavalrymen sitting their horses, and three cannon Robert believed were six-pounders rolled out to aim across the field. There were hardcores who looked like they'd been doing this since Fort Sumter was fired on, along with farbs in half-assed outfits here to have some fun.

Robert came through brush strung along a dry creek bed that

separated the main Confederate camp from a gathering of hillbilly-looking rednecks with beards and black hillbilly hats that put Robert in mind of a biker gang without their leathers. He believed he was getting close to Kirkbride's outfit and identified himself to a group passing around a jar of shine.

"How you doing? I'm Forrest's chief scout, looking to report to the general."

What they did was stare with dumb, serious faces, looking at him with the kind of stares Robert was used to. First the sizing up, then the remarks to put him in his place, have some fun with him. Robert didn't let them get to that part. He said, "You fuck with me, I'll bring Arlen over to get on your ass. I laid in the thicket all night spying on the Federal camp and the general's waiting for my report."

Sounding official to confuse them, remind them of what they were doing here. It got him pointed to Kirkbride's tent, over there in that cottonwood shade: Walter Kirkbride with Arlen and his people and their fruit jar, Arlen looking this way and now all of them looking, Walter saying something, and now he was coming away from them, by himself.

Good. It told Robert Walter had been looking at his crossroads and was keeping Arlen out of it, the man cautious now, not wanting to get himself in the middle of any gangsta business. Still, Robert intended to hook him, show the man he wasn't home free.

Walter walked up looking like a general and Robert said, "How you doing? I understand you got little Traci in camp with you."

Stopped the man cold, whatever it was he might've had ready to say now gone.

"That cute girl has the trailer behind Junebug's? My man Tonto saw her walking around the camp. But was Wesley told me she's your sweetheart. Wesley, the bartender out there wears the undershirt?"

The man stood motionless in his officer's uniform, his hat on, his eyes sad, like a general tired of war and about to offer his sword. Bobby Lee at Appomattox.

Robert said, "Listen to me, Walter, I ain't holding Traci over your head, that ain't my business. You go on have your fun. What I'm saying to you, I realize the kind of mental defectives you have to associate with, and I know you're better than having to do that. I maybe even could use you in my business. You understand what I'm saying?"

Walter said, "I've got a pretty good idea," his voice showing some life.

"You don't deserve to go down with Arlen and his people. And they going down," Robert said, looking past Walter, "all of them watching us right now, wanting to know what I'm saying to you, they going down."

"Whatever happens—" Walter started to say.

Robert cut him off with, "Arlen's coming." Walter turned and they watched Arlen coming with his rifle, Arlen looking like a Confederate from out of the past in his uniform, his pistol, sword, pouches and canteen hanging from his belt, straps crisscrossing his chest, all the way hardcore except the cowboy boots.

"Arlen, you looking fierce," Robert said, "like you want to get you some Yankees."

Arlen didn't look at Walter, only Robert.

"Where they gonna be?"

"Up on the north side of the field. The idea is like you drive 'em into the woods and go in after 'em to finish the job."

"Like Tyree Bell's brigade," Walter said. "Though technically he flanked the other end of the Federal line."

"That's right," Robert said, glad to see Walter getting into it again.

Arlen said, "The one that thinks he's General Grant gonna be there, German-o?"

"Wouldn't miss it."

"And that diver?"

"He'll be there."

"Who else?"

"The two you saw last night."

"The greasers," Arlen said.

"Yeah, call 'em that we get out in the woods."

"How they gonna keep John Rau out of it?"

"You gonna do that," Robert said. "Take the man prisoner and tie him to a tree."

Arlen reset his hat thinking about it. "I never saw that done."

"It happened at Brice's," Walter said. "Old Bedford took hundreds of prisoners. Hell, most of the eighteen hundred the Yankees listed as missing."

Robert said, "You don't want him watching, do you? Those fellas over there look like hillbilly bikers—get them to do it. Bring him back here and tie him up, a sack over his head. Have some fun with him."

Arlen didn't say if he would or not. He said, "Where you gonna be?"

"Right around here. Take a stroll through the camp, look at those cannons. I'll be back."

"Ain't gonna stroll off, are you?"

"I had that in mind I wouldn't have strolled over here, would I?"

———

They watched Robert walk off through the orchard, Walter waiting for whatever Arlen would have to say now, get Arlen's take on the uppity colored fella.

What he said, his gaze still following Robert, "That smoke's got some kind of scheme in mind. I can feel it."

"It's your business," Walter said, "not mine. I don't want to know anything about it, whatever happens."

"I think he's trying to set me up."

"Arlen, it was your idea to get him in the woods. I can hear you saying it, in my office. Shoot 'em and after dark bury 'em. That still your plan?"

"We was talking about the nigger and the diver. Now they's four five of 'em."

"Well, just shoot the ones you want," Walter said.

It got Arlen to turn and put his dirty look on him.

"You think you're out of it? You're gonna be there with me, partner, loads in your pistol. I tell you to shoot, you better start shootin'."

Robert roamed through the camps getting looks, inspected the cannons, went up to the edge of the woods, came back thinking the battle was about to begin—uh-unh. What they said about being in the army all hurry up and wait? It was even true pre*tend*ing to be in the army. He hung around the edge of Arlen's people now, not wanting to push any more of their buttons. They were all juiced and seeing how ugly they could act.

Two of them, Fish and the one they called Eugene, kept yelling at each other about what happened to Rose, whoever Rose was, sounding like it was somebody the Fish had shot and killed. Man, these people. Eugene having a fit, getting into a high-blood-pressure kind of rage over it, the Fish raging back at him to defend himself, saying he had to do it. Next thing they were shoving each other and throwing punches—the one called Newton egging them on—till pretty soon they were both sitting on the ground trying to catch their breath in the heat, close on to a hundred degrees.

Robert asked Walter who Rose was and Walter said Eugene's dog. Robert said, "They trying to kill each other over a *dog*?"

Walter had his own problems, telling Robert that Arlen was making him go with them, saying they would have loaded guns when they went in the woods.

Robert said, "You didn't know that?" He said, "Don't shoot me, Walter, and I won't shoot you."

It didn't help. Walter's stunned expression remained set, the man appearing lost.

Robert kept a close eye on Newton, the dedicated racist with tobacco stains in his beard. His brother, Bob Hoon, was the one ran the methamphetamine lab Robert had spoken to about future business and seemed to have a larger-size brain than these other peckerwoods. They'd wonder out loud where Bob Hoon was today and ask Newton and Newton would shake his head and say he was suppose to be here. Robert took Bob Hoon's absence to mean he was interested in a future deal, didn't care who he sold his meth to or what happened to Newton, maybe even glad to be rid of him, Newton the kind of person should have a bounty on him.

Right before they finally went up on the line and the show got started, Arlen brought Newton over to where Robert was waiting.

"Newton don't understand," Arlen said, "what you're doing here on our side."

"Tell him I'm a freed slave, can do what I want."

"Newton says shit, you're the nigger we're after and you're standing right there. Why don't we hit you over the head and string you up?"

"Tell him he ought to be ashamed of himself."

"No, I said there'd be a time for it," Arlen said. "See, there's a bridge right over here on the Coldwater? The river's a mud puddle this time a year, but the bridge has a good height to it." Arlen said, "You ever thought you'd be hanging from one like your old grampa?"

"My great-grampa," Robert said.

"And I'll be standing on the bridge in the pitcher. I imagine, though," Arlen said, "one of us'll shoot you first." He nodded toward Robert's holster. "That gun loaded?"

Robert shook his head. "Not yet."

"It better not be. Weapons are checked before we go out there and put on the show. You know how to load it, you get in the woods?"

"I practiced," Robert said, "how you do it."

It got Arlen staring at him, Arlen rigged for war, that salty hat curling toward his eyes.

"You practiced. Have you fired it?"

"Couple of times."

Arlen squinted at him. "You lying to me?"

"No, I'm fuckin with you," Robert said. "You want to know can I shoot, come on out to the woods."

Arlen turned his head to look at Newton standing by, Newton's eyes glazed from the shine. Arlen turned to Robert again and for a moment looked like he might smile, wanting to. But he didn't, he stared and finally said, "You're pulling some kind of scheme on me, aren't you? Acting dumb like that."

Robert said, "You coming or not?"

All he wanted to know.

"You take off," Arlen said, "we gonna be after you."

"AND THE FIRST PRIZE," CHARLIE announced over the
PA system, "goes to Miz Mary Jane Ivory for her Yankee Doodle
double-crust Concord grape pie. Nice going, Mary Jane. Save me a
piece if you can and I'll be around later to have a taste."

Charlie sat at a table with his papers in the barn's upstairs loading
bay. Most of the spectators were spread over the slope directly below him, facing the battlefield. He tried to think of a segue from
Yankee Doodle to the New York Yankees, but nothing came to mind
that wasn't awkward. He settled on telling the folks there were
plenty of Yankees here today, not in pinstripes—the kind he was
used to facing during his eighteen years of organized baseball—but
wearing Federal blue.

"They've come to what we're calling Brice's Cross Roads,"
Charlie's voice announced to the spectators, "to put Nathan Bedford Forrest out of action and keep open the Federal supply lines to

their army in the east. Hear the drums? . . . Those are Federal troops moving up. And across the field comes General Forrest's cavalry, scouting ahead of his army."

The six Confederate cavalrymen had come out of the orchard to the right and were starting across the field.

Now Union soldiers were appearing out of the thicket to the left, firing puffs of white smoke at the cavalrymen, forcing them to wheel their mounts and head for cover.

"The Yankees' advance guard stops them. But now you're gonna hear the famous Rebel yell as the main body of Forrest's brigades charge the Federal line. You see the Yankees bringing up their cannon to meet the charge. Get ready. And here they come."

Charlie took the mike off its stand and walked around the desk to stand in the loading bay. He watched the reenactors out there in the hot sun giving it their all.

The Federal line along the thicket were now firing at will, the sound of their rifles coming in hard *pop*s, and the powder shooting out to become a wispy white cloud in front of them.

The advancing line of yelling Rebels stopped now to return fire, covering themselves in the smoke. And now cannon were firing from both sides of the field.

Charlie raised the mike. "Those are six-pounders out there making that serious racket and raising all kind of smoke. Imagine you're down there in a real battle, you see the cannon fire and you know this big goddamn iron ball's coming at you. Excuse my language, but it's a frightening situation to think about."

Charlie looked out at the field. All the shooting and not one on either side had taken a hit.

He looked for Dennis along the blue line, but he could be any one of those guys firing and loading. The one with the sword, out in front a few yards, looked like John Rau, a little more than halfway up the line. He was looking across at the Rebs falling back, leaving only a few skirmishers out in the field, all of them down on one knee to fire and staying down to reload.

And now Rau, yeah, it was John, with the sword, looked like he was yelling encouragement to his troopers.

Charlie raised the mike. "Well, the Rebels got turned back. But if you know what happened at Brice's, you know Old Bedford kept coming back—you wait and see—till he broke the Federal line. But listen, lemme tell you an interesting fact while both sides are regrouping. There was a Union soldier fought at Second Bull Run, Antietam and Gettysburg. And you know what he did some twenty years before the war started? His name was Abner Doubleday and he invented the game of baseball—a sport I gave eighteen years of my life to, in my prime able to throw a fastball ninety-nine miles an hour. Any you young boys out there think you can throw that hard, come on over to the Tishomingo Lodge and let's see your arm. We'll measure your throw with a radar gun. If you can trun a ball a hundred miles an hour we'll give you ten thousand dollars on the spot. Well, now I see General Forrest himself out there on his horse, riding up and down the line encouraging his boys to give those Yankees hell. That's Walter Kirkbride of Southern Living Village doing his impression of Old Bedford. . . . And now here they come again charging headlong into those Yankee guns, the Yankees coming out to meet them."

It was too late now to go from Yankee guns to Yankee bats, damn it, the battle was on, a bunch of Rebels in black hats getting more than halfway across the field when the Yankee cannon blew out a cloud of smoke and every one of those black hats went down, staggering, clutching themselves, making a show of dying. Some of Arlen's boys, the ones that practiced taking hits. Now they'd lie there sipping shine from their canteens till it was over.

Hey, but they were crawling forward on their bellies toward the Union line, getting to their feet now and rushing the officer out in front, John Rau, four of them taking him by surprise, grabbing John by his arms and legs between them, lifting him off the ground and rushing him headfirst like a battering ram through the Confederate line, the boys in gray stopping midfield to return fire. Charlie raised his mike.

"You see that, folks. The Rebs made a daring raid there and have taken a prisoner."

They saw it, all right, the whole crowd cheering, loving it, watching the black hats running with John Rau all the way across the field and into the orchard. Now the Confederate line was falling back.

Dennis turned to Hector next to him. "You see that? They got the cop."

"That fucking Robert," Hector said, "he must have thought of that."

Dennis let it go. Tonto stepped over to him saying, "How you doing? You got a load?" Dennis told him yeah, he'd only fired twice. After the first one he'd started to reload and Tonto exchanged rifles with him saying, "You shoot, I load. I don't get nothing out of shooting black powder."

Hector turned to Jerry staying in the thicket behind them. "The next time they come we go in the woods. You can sneak over there now, get a head start."

Jerry's voice came out of the thicket. "You saying I can't keep up with you?"

Hector turned away, not answering, and said to Tonto, "I insulted him."

"It's easy to do," Tonto said. "We carry him if we have to. Robert wants him there."

"I don't see Robert," Dennis said, looking across the field at the Confederates getting ready, loading their rifles.

"He took a hit," Hector said. "See the sword stuck in the ground? That's Robert." He said to Dennis, "They come this time we take off. Be sure you bring the rifle."

Dennis heard Charlie's voice over the PA system telling the crowd about Union soldiers playing baseball between campaigns to occupy their time. "They even played ball in Confederate prison camps," Charlie said, "and that's how us Southerners picked up the game. Pretty soon there was games between the prisoners and the guards. Well, I see casualties out there now in the hot sun, in their wool uniforms. I hope none of 'em have come down with heat-stroke, and are real casualties. You want to be sure and drink plenty of water. And here we go again, Old Bedford's boys mounting their charge. From Brice's, they run those Yankees all the way back to Memphis."

Dennis brought up his Enfield and looked down the barrel at the wall of gray uniforms advancing, Dennis thinking, Pick one. He wondered if that's what you did, or you fired into them coming three deep and were pretty sure of hitting one, or if you fired as soon as they came out of the orchard and would have time to reload, pour in the powder, the ball, ram it down the barrel, set the cap on the nipple . . .

He heard Hector say, "Let's go," and he fired and saw Hector and Tonto ducking into the trees, Dennis realizing there wouldn't be time to reload. Man, it would be bayonets then, close enough to see the faces of guys trying to kill you. He followed Hector and Tonto into the gloom of the trees, holding the Enfield in front of him straight up to brush through the branches, his running steps kicking up dead leaves. He saw Jerry ahead of them with his sword hacking his way through vines hanging from the trees, Hector and Tonto darting and weaving past him, and Dennis slowed up to stay behind Jerry—but why?—and ran past him without a word and saw Hector and Tonto break out of the gloom into a clearing, a glade, a scattering of tall trees in sunlight. Now Dennis was out and running, gaining on Hector and Tonto as they reached the other side of the glade and disappeared into a dense wall of trees. Dennis followed, made his way through to come out at a ditch and a bank of coarse grass that sloped up to a road of red dirt and a truck standing there: a commercial delivery van painted white over the original white, a thin coat covering an emblem that looked like red, blue and yellow balloons and words faintly readable that said WONDER BREAD.

Groove and Cedric, both stripped to the waist and wearing shades, stood in the road at the back of the truck.

Now Groove was giving high-fives to Hector and Tonto, and Cedric was raising the truck's loading door, running it up on its tracks, Hector saying, "Man, give us the iron, we got to move." He said to Dennis coming up the bank, "Leave your rifle there to pick up when we come back. Cedric's passing out the six-guns, tell him you want one or two and if you think you gonna need an extra loaded cylinder to snap in when the Colt's empty—you think you gonna do all that much shooting. Pick up the one you snap out. Any people you shoot, pick up their guns and bring 'em back here. Except the general."

Hector, looking at Jerry approaching the bank worn-out, trying to breathe, said, "We pick up after the general," and said to him,

"How you doing, you all right? You have cramps? You feeling dizzy, kinda sick?"

Dennis was up by the truck. He watched Jerry seem to cave in and sit down on the slope, watched him take off his coat and ease back to lie flat in the coarse grass, his shirt soaking wet. He didn't answer Hector.

"You sweating," Hector said, "that's good. You have a heatstroke you don't sweat none. Drink some water, it will pick you up."

Dennis took off his shell jacket and dropped it on the slope. He believed he could hear the popping sound of rifle fire coming from the battlefield, but it was so faint he had to stop and listen before he heard it again.

Tonto said, "They still playing." He took a Colt from Cedric and handed it to Dennis, Tonto in his headscarf and sunglasses looking into Dennis' face but not saying anything.

Dennis held the Colt in two hands and turned the cylinder to hear it click to each load and heard Jerry's voice, his growl:

"Gimme a Colt. I'm leaving this fuckin sword."

And Hector saying, "It's too heavy, uh?"

Insulting him again. Dennis thinking, He does it on purpose. And heard Jerry saying he could swing the fucker all day but he wasn't stupid, use a sword against a guy with a gun.

Close to Dennis turning the cylinder, listening to the *click*s, Tonto said, "It has beauty, uh, you think?"

Dennis nodded, feeling the shape of the grip that had always fascinated him. He said, "This is the gun they used in *Lonesome Dove*. They're in the bar, somebody throws up shot glasses and Robert Duvall and the other one pull these big irons and shoot the glasses right out of the air."

"Tommy Lee Jones," Tonto said. "You want two?"

Dennis said, "You're expecting me to get into this with you?"

"What else can you do, Jerry watching?"

"I don't know. Hide behind a tree."

"What did he tell you, he sees you not shooting?"

Dennis watched Hector go down the bank to hand Jerry a Colt and an extra cylinder. He said, "It'll happen fast, won't it, when they come?"

"They all come the same time it will."

"You shoot them, then what?"

"They go in the truck, also the pistols we brought, and nobody ever finds those guys. They disappear."

"How do you explain it to the cops?"

"Explain what? We weren't here."

Dennis said, "I know I shouldn't be."

"But you are."

"You actually think," Dennis said, "I'd shoot one of those guys?"

"I don't know," Tonto said. "You don't either."

"Well, I don't in*tend* to shoot anybody."

"Yeah, but you still don't know."

Robert Taylor in his youth was a down-the-block-and-around-the-corner kind of runner, not ever an oval-track runner or a cow-pasture runner, the ground all uneven and waiting to wrench your ankle, put you out of action at the wrong time. He saw the danger of it on the first charge, running with his sword pointing at the Yankees, yelling the famous Rebel yell, shit, and tripping on the rocks and ruts and clods of earth hiding in the weeds. On the second charge he took a hit and said, "I'm hit, boys, get the motherfucker shot me," and stuck his sword in the ground as he went down, first picking his spot, not a hundred feet from the trees on the north side. He crawled over that way as the Rebs fell back and lay there till the next charge came out of the orchard. Robert pulled the sword free, waved it in the air, and saw Hector and Tonto and Dennis break from the line and run into the trees. He waited, giving them time, wondering if Jerry would keep up. The Rebel charge came to a halt so they could fire their guns, have some fun, and Robert looked back toward the orchard to see Walter off his horse, with Arlen and his retards, Arlen careful, looking this way to watch him. "Well, watch this," Robert said and took off—forgot the sword, fuck it—got into the trees and remembered where he was going: through these woods and across the clearing and through some more trees to the truck waiting on the road. He asked Groove if he'd jacked it. Groove said no, man, he bought it off the bread people, the Wonder Bread bakery in Detroit being a casino now, dealing in the other kind of bread. Hey, shit, and there they all were, coming out of the trees on the other side of the clearing Robert thought looked like a park that hadn't been kept up. This was where he believed the shootout would happen.

Let's see, he'd put Hector and Tonto over on one side, down a ways in cover, Groove and Cedric on the other. Arlen tries to edge around the clearing either side, he'd run into somebody. Robert would stay back here with Jerry and Dennis—Dennis not looking too happy to be along.

Arlen started out loosey-goosey, sure he could get 'er done. Hell yeah, catch Robert in the woods loading his gun, the smoke not use to doing it, dropping bullets in the leaves. Step up to him and *bam*, one less smoke. Arlen believed he had the advantage knowing the woods, pretty sure General Grant and the two greasers would set up to hit him coming out of the trees into those glades. Get the smoke quick and don't even worry about the diver.

But now he didn't know where his boys were, slow coming into the woods and not paying attention or following him like he'd told them, Fish and Eugene still fighting over Rose. He'd hear them thrashing around in the trees, yelling at each other, both with a load on from the shine. He'd stop to listen and then wouldn't hear nothing. They sounded like they were somewhere off to the right. They couldn't be far. Newton could be with them but was drunker'n either one and wouldn't be any help. They might've stopped to load their weapons. He'd told them to do it before they left the orchard, but then was busy getting Walter off his horse and hadn't checked to see if they had. Arlen would bet that was it. He thought of sending Walter to find them, but knew Walter would run off he had the chance. All Walter did was piss and moan about this not being his business and he shouldn't ought to be here, till Arlen said, "I'll shoot you you don't shut up and do what I tell you. Stay close to me. We come to that open part, I got an idea how to play it."

Walter said, "You think they're gonna be standing out in the open waiting for you?"

Arlen the campaigner, gear hanging from him, a loaded Colt in his hand, said, "If they ain't, I believe I can bring 'em out."

Newton was the one remembered. He said, "Shit, we doodlin' around in the woods with empty weapons. Didn't Arlen tell us?— Yes sir, he did. But you two're barkin' at each other—shit, I forgot." Newton carried a 12-gauge double-barreled shotgun that was dark and scarred and looked almost old enough to be authentic. He brought shells from his pocket and slipped them into the side-by-side barrels.

Once they'd loaded their pistols, Newton pulled the cork on his canteen, still some corn whiskey in it, to pass it around. He said to Eugene, "Fish gonna pay you anything for his killing Rose?"

That started them again. Eugene saying Rose was worth more to him than any amount of money. Fish saying, "Then I don't have to pay you nothing. Which I wasn't gonna anyway."

Newton believed it was Fish's sissy tone of voice that hooked into Eugene—prissy, what it was, irksome—and got Eugene to slash the barrel of his Colt at Fish and cut him across the forehead. Fish was stopped and fell back. Eugene, the hook still in him, went at Fish to cut him again. Fish saw him coming and thumbed the hammer of his Colt and shot Eugene in the belly. It doubled him over, Eugene going "Unnnh," like he'd been punched, but was able to straighten enough to put his Colt on Fish and shoot him in the face almost the exact same time Fish fired his second one and shot Eugene through the heart.

In the quiet that settled, Newton said, "Jesus Christ."

They heard the shot and then two more that sounded almost like one and they listened until Robert said, "That's not us."

They were in the trees on the north side of Robert's park. Jerry came over and he told him the same thing he told Dennis, and said, "Let's wait and see what's going on."

A couple of minutes passed and Jerry said, "We're taking too fuckin long. I'm going home."

Tonto appeared as he was saying it.

"Two dead. The Fish and I don't know the other one."

"Not Arlen?" Robert said. "Or Kirkbride?"

"I don't know him."

"The one on the horse."

"No, it wasn't him."

There was a silence.

"Eugene," Robert said. "It was Eugene." He waited a moment, thinking about them in the camp, and said, "Jesus, Christ."

When Arlen looked up hearing the shots he turned toward the sound—from the same direction he'd heard his boys yelling at each other. Walter wanted to know who was that, as Arlen thought about it and said, "Shit, those're ours. Pistol shots, so it wasn't Newton, else I'd have voted for him." Arlen said, "I don't want to believe what I suspect happened." And said, "Jesus Christ."

Walter stood there crouching his shoulders. Arlen looked at him, studied him, and then nodded, giving approval to what he was thinking of doing, and said, "Come on." He brought Walter through the woods, a hand on his belt, to where they got close enough they could look out at the glades—at sunlight slanting through green ash and sweet gum standing out there—but not be seen from across the way.

"Go on," Arlen said, "show yourself and let's see what happens."

"You crazy?" Walter said. "I *know* what'll happen."

"Go on, or I'll shoot you myself."

"What am I supposed to do?"

"I don't care. Stand there and look around."

"What if they shoot?"

"I doubt they will. They do, I'll see their smoke and know where they're at. Go on, goddamn it, or I'll tell Traci not to fuck you no more."

Arlen came behind him to the edge of the woods, gave him a shove, and Walter walked out to the glade, the pistol held low at his side, took five strides across shafts of sunlight and stopped. He stared at the dark wall of trees no more than thirty yards away. If they wanted to shoot him he was dead.

Arlen's voice behind him said, "Go on out'n the middle there."

Walter didn't move.

Now another voice called to him from the wall of trees. "Walter, come on over here or get out of the way. We won't shoot you." Robert's voice, the voice calling again, "Come on, Walter."

But he still didn't move, afraid if he ran Arlen would shoot him. But now he saw Robert—there he was, like one of Old Bedford's colored fellas in his kepi, Robert stepping out in the open and waving his arm to come on.

Arlen yelled, "Shoot him," and fired past Walter. It got Robert to strike a sideways pose and return fire, squeezing off shots, Arlen firing back, Walter in the middle:

Walter aware of himself in his Confederate officer's uniform, standing there like the statue of some general nobody ever heard of, a stone figure in a park, of no more use than a place for birds to land and take a shit.

It was how he felt as the two-bit ex-convict yelled at him again, "Shoot, goddamn it!"

And this time he did. Walter half-turned raising his Colt and shot Arlen in the chest. *Bam.* It felt so good Walter thumbed the hammer back and shot Arlen again and watched him fall to the ground dead.

They came out of the trees from three sides: Hector and Tonto walking up to Walter; Groove and Cedric coming this way toward Robert, Dennis and Jerry with him, Jerry growling.

"This is how it's suppose to happen, these clowns shoot each other? This was some fuckin idea."

"I don't see nothing wrong with how it's turned out," Robert said, "except there should be one more, Newton. 'Less he passed out along the way. He might've been with Fish and Eugene and took off seeing the odds change."

Robert didn't sound worried about him.

Dennis watched Tonto down there taking Walter's gun from him. Now the two walked over to where Hector was looking at Arlen.

"Checking him out," Robert said. "How about old Walter? Surprised the hell out of me."

Jerry said, "Let's get outta here."

It sounded good to Dennis. But now he saw Hector down there saying something to Walter and saw Walter reach into his pants pocket and bring out something—a coin, yeah, because now he was going to flip it with his thumb, Hector and Tonto watching.

Dennis, Robert and Jerry were spread out and watching from about sixty feet away. Jerry still growling.

"The fuck're they doing?"

"It looks like," Robert said, "they gonna see who wins the coin toss."

"For what?"

"Have to wait and see."

They watched Walter toss the coin. He let it land on the ground and all three looked down, Hector and Tonto nodding their heads. Now Tonto handed Walter's Colt to Hector and Hector handed him Arlen's.

"The fuck're they doing?"

Robert didn't answer him this time.

They watched Tonto step away from Hector and Walter. They watched him pull a Navy Colt from his belt and stand looking this way, a gun in each hand.

He said, "Jerry?"

Jerry raised his voice. "The fuck're you morons doing?"

Tonto said, "Take your shot, man. Is in your hand when you feel like it. You go, I go."

Jerry looked at Robert. "He's serious?"

"He's calling you," Robert said.

"You fuck. You set this whole thing up for this?"

"That's your big ego talking. No, man, this part's an after-thought."

"You're making a mistake. You know I'm connected."

"Jerry, come on. You never had a friend in your life."

"I raise the piece I'm going for you."

"Don't matter who you raise it at," Robert said, "long as you raise it. Go on tend your business, Tonto's waiting."

Dennis, listening to all this, was thinking, Jesus Christ. He couldn't believe what he was seeing and couldn't help thinking, *Shane*.

It happened within the next few seconds. Dennis wasn't even sure if Jerry raised his gun or if it would've mattered. He saw Tonto bring up both of his—at his legs and the next second straight out in front of him firing, emptying both guns, and Jerry was blown off his feet.

Dennis didn't move. He watched Robert walk over to look down at Jerry.

"One in the chest. One in the neck it looks like, and one in both arms. Arlen, before—what'd he fire, three times?"

Groove, standing over to the side with Cedric, said, "He got off four at you, you come out waving your arm."

Robert said, "So Tonto hit him four times out of I guess eight, huh? Man, that's shooting. See how they grouped? Where's Jerry's coat at?"

Groove said, "I'll get it," but didn't move. "You never told me this was in the plan."

"Man, I didn't know it myself," Robert said, "till I saw the coin toss. You know, we'd talk about it. Anybody had a good idea . . . I saw the possibility soon as Walter shot Arlen, but didn't know Tonto and Hector did too. Man, we doing fine here."

Dennis still hadn't moved. He listened, not saying a word. Heard Groove say, "We put them in the truck?"

Robert said, "No, don't have to now. See, here's Hector coming with Walter's gun, the one shot Arlen. He's gonna put it in Jerry's hand. Look down there. Tonto's put his in Arlen's hands. Now he's telling Walter no, he didn't shoot Arlen, the general did. It might be a stretch, two-gun Arlen Novis hitting the general four times. I hope he was known as a deadeye 'cause that's how the police, the CIB, all those people are gonna see him." He looked over. "Dennis, you understand what happened?"

Dennis said, "I was standing right here, wasn't I?" an edge to his tone, though not because he resented the question or Robert's cool. It was being here, seeing two men shot to death and not knowing what to do because he was part of it and didn't want to be.

Robert was staring at him.

Robert said, "You weren't here."

"Like I wasn't there," Dennis said, "when Floyd was shot. I see three different guys killed in front of me and I'm nowhere around."

Robert stared another moment and turned to Groove and Cedric. "Get Jerry's coat and Dennis', the rifles, anything we brought from the reenactment. Put what you brought back in the bread truck and call me tonight. I want to know you got home."

Groove and Cedric moved off and now Dennis saw Tonto coming toward them, Walter still back there standing over Arlen. Now Robert was giving Tonto a high five, calling him "my man Tonto Rey" and saying nice things to him, that he saw it coming, but still was caught by surprise, loved how they set it up, loved the gunplay,

Dennis seeing how natural violence was to them, no big deal. Tonto looked at Jerry on the ground and said, "Today we had enough of him." He walked over to Hector, and Robert turned to Dennis again.

He said, "Listen to me," his voice quiet, serious. "I don't care how many people you saw get killed and you didn't do nothing. You understand? Nobody saw what happened here. These two hard-cores must've got so worked up, so intense reenacting, they came out here with live ammo to do it right."

"And happened to kill each other," Dennis said.

"Why's that hard to believe? Same as Fish and Eugene, but for a higher cause than a dead dog. That's the point to make. They met a few times and never got along, having opposite views of the war. They'd trade insults, put down each other's heroes, Arlen saying General Grant was a drunk and a speed freak, Jerry saying Stonewall Jackson sucked dick, and they come to face each other as a matter of honor. That's it, deciding the honorable thing was fight a duel, same as they would back in those days. What I'm leading up to, what we have to get ready for tomorrow or the next day, is all the press and TV's gonna be here from all over for the story. First Annual Tunica Civil War Muster turns into shootout. The first and I bet the last. You understand what I'm saying? They gonna ask us questions once the CIB's done asking, looking for the motive. I could say, well, I wasn't close to Germano Mularoni but I know he hated Southerners, along with all other races. Southerners, 'cause he watched videotapes over and over of that Civil War show was on TV and came to hate what the Confederacy stood for. He hated them still flying the flag and all that shit about heritage. Now take Arlen Novis, you have a diehard Rebel-type former convict who used to be a sheriff's deputy and packed a gun. They look Germano up and find there was a time he also packed and set off high explosives, too. They gonna say, but wasn't this Germano's first reenactment? Yes, it was, and you know why he never did one before? He thought reenactments were pussy, they didn't use loaded guns." He said to Dennis, "And that's right off the top of my head. We get into it I'll work all the motive shit into a routine."

He paused, frowning a little.

"But if nobody finds these two? I mean in the next couple of days. I don't want them turning to bones."

Dennis, caught up in it, said, "What's wrong with that?"

Robert said to Hector, "Listen to my man Dennis."

It encouraged him and he said, "You were gonna put them in the bread truck and they disappear." He wasn't trying to help, he was getting it clear in his mind. "What's the difference?"

"Jerry," Robert said, "changes the situation. No, I need to have them found soon, by tomorrow. And for a good reason."

"The missus," Hector said.

"You got it," Robert said. "Anne won't stand for Jerry being missing, have to wait. How long? She don't have the patience for that, she'd blow it, start talking." He looked at Dennis and said, "You understand?"

No, he didn't, and shook his head.

"The man has to be seen dead so she can collect on him, the house, the bank accounts, the insurance . . ." He looked at Hector again. "Somebody's gonna have to make the anonymous phone call to the Tunica sheriff. You and Tonto Rey go on with Groove in the bread truck. Make the call in Memphis and hang around there, Beale Street, man, and let me know where you are. I'll tell you when you can come back here. Hey shit, we're in business. It just hit me. Go on, before Groove leaves on you."

Dennis was watching Walter, down there at the edge of the trees. He said, "What about Walter?" nodding toward him as Robert turned.

"What? You think the man wants to look at a homicide conviction? Walter knows how to put on a face better than I do even."

"What's he doing?"

"Waiting to be called."

Dennis said, "You gonna tell Anne?"

"A widow lady, and she doesn't even know it."

It was the word, as Robert said it, that made Dennis think of Loretta. She didn't know either. He heard Robert talking about Anne, heard the words as he saw Loretta in the tent, saw her holding up her skirt and saw her outside in the chair and stayed with that one, Loretta's face composed. He saw her look up as he walked toward her and heard:

"You listening to me?"

"You said you have to keep Anne from celebrating too soon, like throwing a party."

"And I said I only have one worry."

"Yeah . . . ?"

"And it ain't Annabanana."

Dennis said, "Me?"

"You're here, you're in it same as I am. We not just witnesses, we conspired, we aided, we abetted. If that's true we could be facing prison. In Mississippi. I know you don't want that."

Dennis shook his head, no.

"Then why am I worried about you?"

26

NEWTON HOON SAT IN HIS trailer with a jelly glass of bourbon watching the news: that little TV girl with the two last names in the woods showing where James Rein and Eugene Dean had shot each other, saying both men were from Tunica but nothing about Rose.

There she was now in the glade saying this was where Arlen Novis, former Tunica County sheriff's deputy, and Detroit realtor Germano Mularoni staged their duel, calling them reenactors in a senseless confrontation of views that resulted in each man's death. Oh, is that right? No mention of Walter. No mention of the smoke or the two greasers—Newton thinking of the one he'd asked that time where the nigger was and the one said he'd gone to fuck your wife. It had set him off, sure, even knowing it wasn't true. One, Myrna wasn't ever home, she played bingo every night of her life.

And two, not even a smoke'd want to fuck her, Myrna going four hundred pounds on the hoof. Try and find the wet spot on her.

Now he was watching a helicopter view of the glades, the woods, the levee road and over to the reenactment site, the tents struck and gone, nothing to see but the barn with the muster sign still on it and empty land.

So much for believing what they tell you on the news. Hell, he'd seen the whole thing.

Phoned Walter yesterday and today and got his answering voice both times, Walter saying he was away from his desk but to leave a message. Both times Newton couldn't think of how to say what he wanted. Let Walter know he saw him shoot Arlen and it was gonna cost him. He didn't think he should leave that as a message, he needed to tell Walter to his face. He called Walter's office in Corinth and was told he was at Southern Living in Tunica. Newton said no he wasn't. They said yes he was, if he'd gone someplace else he'd have let them know.

Last night Newton had gone over to the Tishomingo, see if the smoke was still around, and there was the diver putting on his show. He had a good crowd, too, since he'd been on TV and people wanted to see him dive. Newton had nothing personal against the diver—else he'd set up in the trees with a deer rifle and pick him off the ladder. What Arlen should've done. He went inside the hotel to the reception desk and asked, the way Walter would say it, what room the colored fella was in. The girl desk clerk asked him who he was referring to. Newton said, "The jigaboo." He said, "Jesus, how many you got staying here?" The girl asked him what was the guest's name, so she could see was he registered. That was the trouble, shit, he couldn't think of it. Newton went out to the parking lot and roamed up and down the aisles for twenty minutes looking for the black car, came back to the front of the hotel and there it was. He might've known. The big-shot coon had it in valet parking.

Newton saw what he'd have to do: sit in his pickup with sweet rolls and Pepsis and watch the car. Mr. Negro leaves to drive back north, pull up next to him on the highway and give him a load of double-ought buckshot. After that he'd have time to find Walter and make his deal.

Annabanana wasn't buying the news accounts of what happened, but wouldn't ask Robert directly how he'd made it look the way it did. She'd say things like "Four different guys shoot each other at the same time, almost in the same place, and the cops don't have a problem with that?"

"You know why?" Robert said. " 'Cause they all bad guys got shot. Sheriff's people and the CIB won't have to deal with 'em no more. And what looks like happened is all they have. No witnesses, no kind of clues lying around out there to go on. Anybody look suspicious? Uh-unh, 'cause we all look alike in the uniforms, become part of the crowd. You know what I'm saying?"

Robert stood at the opening to the balcony watching the diving show, Dennis performing on the springboard at the moment, showing his stuff, Charlie making the announcements.

Anne was packing. She'd come out of the bedroom when she had something to say and Robert would catch her.

"What did John Rau ask you?"

"If I saw it developing," Anne said. "If I thought it had anything to do with Jerry's background, his Detroit connections. I said, 'In the real estate business?' "

"Same kind of things they asked me, for three hours."

"John was nice. I cried a little, sniffled, blew my cute nose. I could've had him on the floor."

"You think of any other strange places?"

"The shower?"

"Girl, your next husband, get yourself a straight-up business executive thinks doing it in the shower would be a trip." Robert put on his white voice. " 'In the shower? Really?' " And said, "They gonna let you have the body tomorrow for sure?"

"John doesn't see a problem. I'm not looking forward to the flight."

"Baby, they won't prop him up next to you, they'll put him in with the luggage."

"I don't know why," Anne said, "but I had a feeling he was gonna get popped."

Robert left that one alone. She asked if he was coming to the funeral. He said he'd most likely fly up for a day or two. Anne went in the bedroom and he looked out at the show, nothing happening, Dennis getting ready for the next one, taking time, maybe getting ready for the one Charlie told him Dennis was doing for the first time here, his fire dive.

He heard Anne say, "Are you worried about me?"

Robert turned to see her in the bedroom doorway in her little bra and panties. He said, "Not with all you have at stake. There ain't any way you'll blow it. But you know John Rau could come at you again, pull that Columbo shit. You think you're off the hook, he comes back and says, 'Oh, by the way, you not sleeping with that colored fella, are you?' "

She came toward Robert in her undies. "I'll tell him oh, once in a while, to change my luck. Shall we?"

"Baby, just another few minutes. Dennis is out there finishing his act."

"I thought you two broke up."

"I haven't seen him except on TV, but we talked on the phone. Gonna get together tomorrow. Baby, come on watch this with me, Dennis gonna light himself on fire and dive off the ladder." He looked out at the show again and said, "He's doing it, climbing up the ladder with his cape on." Anne came to him and he put his arm around her shoulders and felt her skin. He said, "You gonna miss me, you know it? Gonna miss the fun." He said, "Look, see him up there? The cape's been soaked in high-test gasoline. He wears two pair of black cotton warm-ups underneath, a hood on the sweatshirt he pulls closed with the string. He went in the pool a minute ago to get the warm-ups soppin', wet as they can get. I think it's his only protection."

"He lights himself?"

"Charlie lights him. They run a line from a battery up there to a squib, a baggie with black powder in it. Charlie pushes the switch and Dennis lights up, becomes a human torch. I said to Charlie, 'Is this symbolic? He's the fiery cross of the Klan, he hits the water and puts it out, extinguishes racism?' Charlie says, 'He just calls it the fire dive.' " Robert smiled with his white teeth.

They watched Dennis, at the forty-foot level, become a ball of fire and he stood there on the perch not moving, not even seen but he was there, inside the flames, and Robert yelled from the balcony, "Jump!" And Dennis did a straight dive into the pool.

Robert said, "Man."

Anne said, "Big fucking deal."

Dennis walked around the rim of the tank in sixty pounds of wet clothes looking for Loretta in the crowd, the young girls screaming, but didn't see her. Loretta hadn't been here last night, either.

Billy Darwin, bent over and walking with a cane, Carla helping him, came around behind the tank where Dennis was getting out of the wet warm-ups and the wet suit he wore underneath. Darwin didn't mention his injury. He told Dennis that fire dive was a show-stopper and asked if he could do it from the top perch. Dennis said he wouldn't want to go in headfirst from eighty feet with all that weight on him, it was too steep. He said he'd jump lit up, "But how would you announce it, as the death-defying fire *jump?*" Billy Darwin said, "Going off the top's tricky, but you sure get a rush, don't you?" Carla didn't say anything about the fire dive. She said, "You looked cute on TV, in your uniform." Meaning when Diane and her crew caught him in the Union camp Sunday.

It was right after the shooting and he had come back through the woods with Robert, Dennis trying to decide if he should go tell Loretta what happened or wait till she heard about it, and there was the video camera in his face. All Diane asked him about was the reen-actment: if he had fun, if he took it seriously, if he thought he'd ever do it again. Robert stood watching and John Rau, coming into the camp, had looked over at them. Dennis answered yes to all the ques-tions, not having time to think with all he had on his mind. After the interview Diane said, "Are you ready to talk to me yet?" Meaning the Floyd Showers business. "Remember you said you would." He remembered it wishing he'd never told her he was on the ladder that night—Diane using her soft eyes on him, asking if he wanted to go to Memphis. Once she found out Arlen was dead . . . Robert saved him, Robert saying, "Come on, man, we gotta go," and Dennis told her he'd be in touch. In the car Robert said, "You notice John Rau was let out of their prison? He saw us, too, knows we weren't some-place else." That was Sunday, the business with Diane.

Billy Darwin and Carla left and Charlie said the TV lady was here tonight, without her crew. "I imagine you'd like to see her. She said to tell you she's in the bar. But let me mention, Vernice's fixing a late supper for you. She's hoping you come right home after this. You don't, you'll miss a fine spread and Vernice'll be hurt, but what do you care?"

Dennis was dressed now in his jeans and a work shirt. He said, "Wait for me. I have to go up and unhook the squib wire." Charlie said he'd be in the bar and Dennis said, "But Diane's in there."

"You're a big boy," Charlie said. "You don't want to talk to her, you say you have to go home and eat."

Dennis went up the ladder to the forty-foot perch, unhooked the wire and dropped it. He stepped around to the other side of the ladder to go down, and saw the figure standing out on the lawn watching him. No one else around. He knew without seeing her face it was Loretta.

In a short black skirt and some kind of light-colored blouse. She said, "I couldn't come yesterday, I was at the funeral parlor."

"I looked for you."

"I wanted to but—you know, there things have to be done."

He said, "Do you have a car?" and saw her smile because she had asked him that.

"I do now. I have two, but don't know where one of 'em is."

"Can we go somewhere?"

"I won't take you home. There's still too much of Arlen in the house." She said, "Did you want to get something to eat," her voice slowing down, "or go to a bar, or a motel?"

"I know where we can go," Dennis said, took Loretta into the hotel where they got a suite for one night and had a wonderful time.

They did. They turned on music and took their clothes off and just let loose being a man and a woman who couldn't keep their hands off each other. They made love and had vodka drinks and calamari. Loretta said, "Sunday was the best day of my life. I don't mean—you know, Arlen dying. I mean from the time you came in the tent to wash my back. I'm amazed I asked you to do it, but I'm so glad I did. I can live offa that one the rest of my life. Even with it being so hot in there. Now I have another one—whatever this day is, Wednesday? I'm gonna think of them both together."

Dennis said, "We're just getting started."

She said, "Oh, God, I hope so. Did you burn yourself out there?"

"I never do."

"God, you're a daredevil and you're fun. You aren't the least bit stuck on yourself."

He said, "I saw you standing in that black skirt and I knew it was you."

She said, "It's old."

"I love your legs. I love your body."

"How about my head?"

"I love your head. Are you hungry?"

They had room-service crawfish étouffée Dennis said was as good as you got in New Orleans. He told her about a guy named Tonto Rey who said the best he ever had was in Tucson, Arizona. How about that. Loretta said she'd never had it before but it was good. They watched each other as they ate and would touch each other's hands. They didn't talk about Sunday. She didn't mention Arlen. She didn't ask Dennis what he did after he left the tent. He asked if she watched the battle reenactment. She said no, "I sat outside in that dumb skirt and thought of you, and smelled you, and could feel my hands in your hair. You have nice hair." She said, "Are we spending the night?"

"I was planning on it."

"Tomorrow's the funeral. I have to leave here early." She said, "I hate to come right out and ask, but am I gonna see you again?"

She fascinated him. He said, "Of course."

"You're not running off right away?"

"This is my last week, but I'm pretty sure I'll be here the rest of the summer. My boss has come to respect what I do."

"You know what brought us together?"

"Yeah, Naughty Child Pie."

She said, "You care for me, don't you?"

"I really do."

"You know why?"

"It's something that, I don't know, just happens. I meet girls and I think, Yeah . . . ? I meet you and I think, *Yeah*, 'cause you're on my mind every minute after."

"That's how I feel," Loretta said. "I can't wait to put my dear husband in the ground and get on with my life."

Dennis said, "Will you hurry?"

He got home at eight-thirty the next morning: Charlie still in bed, Vernice in the kitchen, her magazine open on the table. She said, "Well." She said, "You must've had quite a time. Did you fall in love?"

He could say yes, he believed he did, but told her he fell asleep.

"That's what you do, after. You go to Memphis?"

"Why would I?"

"Charlie said you were meeting that TV girl with the two names."

"I wasn't meeting her."

"Well, according to Charlie, she was meeting you. He said a fan bought him a drink, he turned back around and she was gone. He thought you two must've got together."

"I never even saw her. Listen, I'm sorry I missed supper. What was it?"

"It don't matter now, does it?"

"I stayed at the hotel. I took a room, see what it was like. You know that desk clerk Patti, blond, semi-big hair?"

"Yeah, Patti."

"She comped me."

"You dog. You seeing her?"

"She's way too young."

"And she's got that overbite," Vernice said, "we use to call buck-teeth."

"She's nice though."

"She better be. You want some breakfast?"

"I've had my coffee."

"Sit down, I'll fix you some eggs. You diving this afternoon?"

"I'm not sure yet. Robert's picking me up."

"You haven't mentioned him since his friend got killed. The one Charlie went to Memphis for, remember? I saw his wife in the lobby, sunglasses, a cute black suit. She can wear clothes. But there's something—I don't know what it is. Like I wouldn't be surprised to turn the page of this magazine and there she'd be, in the sunglasses."

"How're Nicole and Tom doing?"

"They've learned the identity of her secret lover."

"Who is it?"

"Some Eyetalian guy. You want a couple fried eggs or not?"

Newton watched the valet boy get in the Jaguar and pull out to circle around to the hotel entrance where Mr. Negro was there wait-ing, his sunglasses on. Newton had slept in his truck all night and had a cup of coffee to go earlier. He wedged a hunk of Copenhagen behind his lower lip, sucked on it and turned the key. He was surprised when Robert Taylor—that was the boy's name, same as a movie star's the way to remember it—drove south to Tunica and stopped at a house on School Street, up from those bail-bond offices. He was surprised again when the diver came out of the house and got in the car. Now where? It turned out they went south again on Old 61. Newton didn't care where they were going. This stretch of road was the place to pull alongside and give 'em the double-ought buck.

Except, goddamn it, he could keep the black car in sight, but not catch up to it to do the job.

Robert didn't put his music on this time, in the car. He'd asked Dennis to drive with him to see Walter Kirkbride. There was something he wanted to tell Dennis and they could talk on the way.

Riding along now Robert said, "The fire dive—man, I saw that, I knew more than ever you're the man I want."

Dennis said, "Thanks anyway."

"Your conscience," Robert said, "won't let you do it. That's the trouble having a conscience, why I control mine, only listen to it when I want."

"You have your own way of reasoning things," Dennis said.

"Bend it when I see the need. I told you everybody believed Robert Johnson must've sold his soul to play the way he did? But Robert Johnson never said he did or didn't?"

"I remember."

"Well, who would know better than the man himself? What he did was leave the Delta, went down to Hazlehurst where his mama lived, and went to the woodshed. You know what's meant by woodsheddin'? It's getting off by yourself and finding your sound, your chops, what makes you special. Robert Johnson went off for a couple of years and learned his style. He went back to the Delta . . . Sam House says, 'He finished playing and all our mouths were standing open.' You understand what I'm saying?"

"You want something," Dennis said, "work for it. If I want to run a diving show, get off my ass and make it happen."

"What I want to tell you," Robert said, "I could help you. I won't make a promise till I see how this deal goes, get Walter Kirkbride in line. It works, I could maybe back you."

"Why?"

" 'Cause you my man. 'Cause you got the nerve to douse yourself in high-test and go off the ladder."

"You mean if Walter goes in with you?"

"If Walter works for me. That's part of what I need to know. See, I been looking for him, but Walter's hiding out, shaky after killing a man. But I believe I know where to find him."

No more than a minute later they turned left at the Dubbs intersection and Dennis said, "We're going to Junebug's?"

Yes, they were, through the lot and around back to where the two trailers stood, and a car. Robert said, "You recognize it?"

"Arlen's Dodge."

"The one Walter drives," Robert said, "when he comes to see his sweetheart, Walter keeping his romance a secret."

Dennis said, "Unless Arlen left it."

Robert turned the car around to drive out. "That's what we gonna find out."

Newton came along expecting to see the black car parked in front of Junebug's. It wasn't. It wasn't up the road, either, even though it was heading that way and couldn't be out of sight this quick. Newton coasted past the roadhouse, got ready to give her the gun and glanced at his rearview mirror. Hell, there it was, coming around from behind Junebug's, and stopping to park.

They went in, Robert carrying his attaché case, and crossed the dance floor to the bar, both of them glancing around to see the place empty, Robert saying now, "My man Wesley. I brought you a present, man, you gonna love. Gonna not want to take off." He laid the case on the bar, snapped it open and brought out a LET'S SEE YOUR ARM T-shirt. Robert held it up for Wesley to read and then tossed it to him. "Take off that redneck tank top, Wes, and slip into something stylish."

Wesley said, "Why can't I put it on over?"

"Do it, man, be trendy. But tell me something. How long's my buddy Walter been back there with his honey, a few days now?"

Wesley said something with his head inside the T-shirt.

"What was that, Wes?"

He said, "Yeah, I guess," pulling the shirt down his narrow trunk. "The girl took food out there to him. I wondered, you know who's gonna be running this place now?"

"My man Dennis'll fill you in," Robert said. "Fix him a cocktail while I go look in on the lovers."

Newton parked next to the black car. He took his shotgun from the rack across the window behind him and slid out of the pickup. He was anxious now and it made him want to take a piss. He was thinking he could step inside, shoot both of 'em and then go to the men's. No, he better take his leak first, right here. Piss on Mr. Negro's car.

Dennis had a longneck beer he took sips from telling Wesley he wasn't exactly sure if the ownership would pass to somebody, or if there were other partners. Dennis said, "But they could be dead, too, couldn't they?" Thinking of Jim Rein and Eugene Dean. And that other one, with the beard, the one they didn't know what happened to. Or would it go to Arlen's wife?

How about that? Loretta could end up owning this place. And if Robert wanted to use it as a dope store he'd have to buy it from her. It could speed up getting Loretta out of that life she was in.

Robert walked around the Dodge Stratus to the trailer, went up to the door that had Traci lettered on it in that old-fashioned script and knocked. He waited and knocked again.

"Traci?"

Her voice came from in there. "I'm not seeing anyone today."

Robert said, "Girl, I don't want you. I need to see my business partner, Mr. Kirkbride. Would you open the door, please?"

It opened a few inches and he saw her face, showing concern, looking out at him.

"What is it you want?"

Robert raised his voice. "Walter, step out here, will you? While I'm still exercising my patience?"

Wesley laid his forearms on the bar and leaned on them, his white skin blue with old tattoos Dennis couldn't make out. He moved Robert's attaché case aside and brought the lid down without snapping it closed. He had asked Wesley how long he'd been working here. Wesley said since Arlen bought into Junebug's.

"I'm Arlen's uncle on his daddy's side."

Dennis said, "You aren't that much older."

Wesley said, "You don't need to be."

He looked past Dennis and pushed up from the bar to stand straight. Dennis half-turned and saw Newton inside the door with his double-barreled shotgun, pointing it this way as he came toward the bar and then stopped about twenty feet away to look around.

"Where's everybody?"

Wesley said, "Nobody's come in yet."

"Where's the nigger?"

Wesley motioned toward the back. Dennis looked that way, in time to see the door next to the bandstand come open. There was Robert, there was Walter coming behind him with Traci. Dennis watched Newton put the shotgun on them.

Newton saying, "My Lord, I couldn't prayed and expected this. Both of you at once?"

"Newton," Robert said, "you come by for a cold beverage?" Like he didn't see the shotgun pointed at him. "Lemme buy you a beer." Robert started toward the bar.

Newton yelled at him, "Stay where you're at!"

Robert stopped and looked puzzled, frowning at Newton.

"What's wrong?"

Newton motioned with the shotgun for Walter and Traci to move away from Robert, saying, "Walter, I don't want you hurt. We gonna talk after."

Dennis, his eyes on Newton, slipped his left hand inside the attaché case, his fingers working through papers and folders to feel the grip of Robert's pistol, the Walther PPK that James Bond carried.

Walter was saying, "After what?"

"After I shoot the nigger," Newton said. "We're gonna go to your office for my paycheck."

Walter said, "I don't know what you mean."

Dennis had the gun in his hand now. He was sure Robert kept it loaded, but didn't know if it was ready to fire. Or if he'd have to pull back that top part first, the slide. If there wasn't a bullet in the chamber there'd be a click when he pulled the trigger and then, he was pretty sure, there'd be one in there.

Robert, still frowning, was saying to Newton, "Come on, man, tell me what's on your mind."

Newton had already said it, he was going to shoot him, and had the shotgun at his shoulder aimed right at Robert. Dennis didn't see he had a choice now, he pulled the trigger and the gun fired inside the case, through it and took out a bottle of Jim Beam behind the bar. He had the gun out now, saw Newton swinging the twin barrels at him and Dennis shot him, knew he'd shot the man even as the shotgun went off and he heard glass shattering and heard Robert yelling to shoot him again, but saw the blood on Newton's shirt, high on his chest, Newton's face blank as he dropped the shotgun and went to his knees, something brown coming out of his mouth, and fell to the floor on his face. Dennis laid the gun on the bar and tried not to look at Newton.

Dennis watched Robert in action now, taking over, Robert the first one to speak, Robert looking at Dennis to say, "You my hero. You got nothing to worry about." Looking at Traci then. "Honey, you saw what happened, didn't you?"

She said, "Yeah, he shot Newton."

" 'Cause Newton shot at him."

She said, "Yeah, I guess."

"We have the broken bottles," Robert said, "to prove it," and looked at Walter. "Walter, you didn't see nothing, 'cause you aren't here. You understand? You don't frequent this kind of place." He said, "See how good I am to you?" and turned to Wesley. "What happened, Wes?"

"What she said. Newton tried to shoot us."

"Trying for you as well as Dennis."

"I was standing right here."

"And the gun was on the bar, huh?"

Dennis watched Robert getting into it.

"The one you keep back there, Arlen's gun. You were showing it to Dennis. Newton shot at you. You picked up Arlen's gun and plugged him."

Dennis stopped him at that point. He said, "Robert, if you want it to be Arlen's gun, that's okay with me. But I shot him."

"You want the credit for it."

"No, I want to keep it simple."

Robert looked at Wesley again. "You know it was Arlen's gun, 'cause he put it there. The sheriff's people, whoever, they'll look at it good and give it back to you and then it's yours, Wesley. You can keep it behind the bar where you had it." Robert said, "Hey, and I can give you some more T-shirts. 'Let's see your arm' means you'll arm-wrestle anybody wants to try you. They win they get a free T-shirt."

Dennis watched him looking at Wesley's stringy, tattooed arms, Robert saying then, "You don't have to—it's something we can talk about. I'm getting ahead of myself here." He said to Dennis, "There's always something, isn't there?" and kept looking at him

and said, "Man, you saved my life," sounding surprised now to realize it. "You know that?"

Dennis said, "Yeah, I know it."

Robert said, "Man, I owe you, don't I?"

Dennis said, "Yes, you do."

Robert said, "Tell me what you want."

Dennis said, "Let me think about it," and paused and asked
Robert, "You know anybody in Orlando?"